A Feast of Poisons

A Feast of Poisons

C. L. Grace

St. Martin's Minotaur ❧ New York

www.minotaurbooks.com

Library of Congress Cataloging-in-Publication Data

Grace, C. L.
    A feast of poisons : a Kathryn Swinbrooke mystery / by C. L. Grace.
    p. cm.
    ISBN 0-312-31014-5
    EAN 978-0312-31014-1
    1. Swinbrooke, Kathryn (Fictitious character)—Fiction. 2. Great
Britain—History—Lancaster and York, 1399–1485—Fiction.
3. Louis XI, King of France, 1423–1483—Influence—Fiction.
4. French—England—Fiction. 5. Walmer (England)—Fiction.
6. Women physicians—Fiction. 7. Poisoning—Fiction. I. Title.

PR6054.O37F43 2004
823'.914—dc22
                                                        2003066816
First Edition: June 2004

10 9 8 7 6 5 4 3 2 1

Dedicated to the memory of
Tatiana Faye Micallef
"returned untainted to God's bosom"

List of Historical Characters

THE HOUSE OF LANCASTER

Henry VI: Henry of Lancaster, son of the great Henry V, regarded by some as a fool, by others as a saint, by a few as both. His weak, ineffectual rule led to vicious civil war between the Houses of York and Lancaster.

Margaret of Anjou: French Queen of Henry VI and the real power behind the throne; her hopes of victory were finally quashed by two outstanding defeats at the hands of Yorkist forces at Barnet and Tewkesbury in the early months of 1471.

Beaufort of Somerset: Leading Lancastrian general and politician; reputed lover of Margaret of Anjou, killed at Tewkesbury.

Henry Tudor: Last remaining Lancastrian claimant. By 1473, in exile at the Courts of France and Brittany.

THE HOUSE OF YORK

Richard of York: Father of Edward IV. Richard's overweening ambition to become King led to the outbreak of hostilities between York and Lancaster. He was trapped and killed at the Battle of Wakefield in 1460.

Cecily of York (née Neville): "The Rose of Raby"; widow of Richard of York; mother of Edward, Richard, and George of Clarence.

Edward IV: Successful Yorkist general and later King.

Edmund of Rutland: Edward's brother, killed with the Duke of York at Wakefield.

George of Clarence: The beautiful but treacherous brother of Edward IV; a Prince who changed sides during the Civil War.

Richard of Gloucester: Youngest brother of Edward IV; he played a leading part in the Yorkist victory of 1471.

ENGLISH POLITICIANS

Thomas Bourchier: Aged Archbishop of Canterbury.

William Hastings: Henchman to Edward IV.

FRANCE

Louis XI: King of France, the "Spider."

Charles: Duke of Burgundy, Louis's foe.

And when a beest is deed he hath no peyne;
But man after his deeth moot wepe and pleyne. . . .
—Chaucer, "The Knight's Tale,"
The Canterbury Tales

In the Middle Ages women doctors continued to practise
in the midst of wars and epidemics as they always had,
for the simple reason that they were needed.
—Kate Campbell Hurd-Mead,
A History of Women in Medicine

A Feast of
Poisons

Chapter 1

The Carl spak oo thing, but he thoghte another.
—Chaucer, "The Friar's Tale,"
The Canterbury Tales

*L*ouis XI, by the wrath of God, King of France, was busy fishing. Louis was content. He'd journeyed up and down the Loire Valley stopping at his royal residences to check his menagerie, in particular, his elephant and a rather clumsy camel, not to mention the leopards, ostriches, and other beasts. Louis himself was a spider in human flesh. Paris was the centre of his web but he'd spun it so the web now covered every city and province in France. Louis was content. He had outfoxed and out-manoeuvred his enemies but, although he loved his country, he did not trust it. Its narrow, winding forest trackways had flour-ished long before the time of Caesar. Rebels could lurk there, plan ambushes, plot treason, and carry out regicide. So Louis, who could never keep still, continued his restless journeys more by water than horse or carriage. He sailed the great rivers of France on boats of his own design. Splendid affairs, great barges on which he built wooden houses furnished with chimneys, glass windows, and all the comforts of a palace.

Louis loved hunting, be it the quarry of the forest or some great noble or merchant who would not accept his rule. He had recently crushed a rebellion on the borders of Burgundy. A barge farther down the river carried cages in which he'd placed his principal prisoners. He would use them as he would the animals in his menagerie, show the people that he was King. No force of man or nature could escape his grasp. On the prison barge he'd erected poles to carry the severed heads of other traitors; one of them he'd hooded and lined with fur so as to distinguish it from the rest. Now Louis was resting. He stared up at the blue sky and gripped his fishing rod. The previous night a firebreak, a burning comet, a ball of flame, had cracked through the heavens. Was that a warning, he wondered? But did it matter? "*Alea iacta*, the die is cast!" he murmured. Whatever dangers threatened, he must confront them. He'd sent money to the nearest shrines and churches, ordering hundreds of special masses to be said to ward off any danger. He'd also promised St. Martin of Tours, the patron saint of France, to buy a shiny metal trellis to enclose his tomb. A veritable work of art, the trellis would be made of eleven thousand pounds of the finest silver. He'd also sent messages to Amboise, where his infant son, the Dauphin Charles, was kept in strict seclusion, far away from would-be kidnappers as well as the grisly effect of any of the legion of diseases that prowled the roads and haunted the cities of his kingdom.

Louis was glad to be away from such places, especially Paris; the clanging of its bells was a constant source of irritation, its crowded, narrow streets an ever-living threat to his own power, a place where ideas and new fears teemed like weeds on a dung heap.

"Your Majesty?"

Louis turned his head.

"Your Majesty?" the young squire repeated. "They say a church spire was attacked by Satan last night, burnt to a cinder. The demon's claw marks can still be seen up and down the walls."

"Is that correct?" Louis muttered. He turned back as the rod jerked. Was it a demon, he wondered, or just lightning? That was what a scholar had once told him, how buildings, which pointed to the sky, always attracted heaven's fire. Nevertheless, he had to be sure. Louis always took precautions. He'd told the envoys dispatched to check on his son that an iron knife must always be hung over the child's cradle and pots of salt placed in every corner. Iron and salt, not to mention the many saintly relics hanging from the beams of the nursery, would keep away demons. Louis grimaced with annoyance. He thought he'd lured a fish but the rod was now slack, like so many things in life. The King moved restlessly, spurs jingling on his boots. He stared across the river. The mist was lifting. The day would prove fine even if the seasons were changing. Already he could glimpse the gold through the green. The morning breeze was cold but this would fall as the sun rose. Nevertheless, the King was warm enough. On either side of him glowed capped braziers, their fiery charcoal red and crackling, now and again hissing as drops of river water splashed through the grille.

Louis flexed his fingers. He was booted and spurred, ever ready to leave his barge and ride to face any danger or confront some rebel. He was dressed in his usual grey gown, furred with white lambskin, over his head a monk's cowl. On top of this Louis wore a large broad-rimmed hat, which weighed heavily due to the many silver medallions, all depicting his favourite saints, closely stitched there. Louis picked up a piece of cheese and munched noisily. He'd spent the previous day plotting, before travelling to a nearby castle where envoys from Spain had brought red-skinned pigs for him to look at, not to mention a host of goldfinches, magpies, turtle doves, as well as two greyhounds wearing collars of Lombardy leather and leashes of dried wolfskins. Louis breathed out, the steam hanging in the morning air. In the mist farther down the river were barges packed with his bodyguard and, on either bank, troops of Norman cavalry kept pace with the royal barge, *The Glory of the Lilies*. Louis heard shouts, a slight thump as a boat came alongside the barge. He smiled. His visitors had arrived. He passed the rod to a valet. "Hold it firm," he ordered. "If the fish bite, draw in quickly."

Louis, spurs jingling, the mother-of-pearl rosary beads around his neck clicking and glittering, walked up the leather-rimmed steps into the royal cabin. The chamber boasted a window high on each wall, the walls themselves covered in thick draperies woven in a series of eye-catching colours—fiery reds, deep blues, glittering golds—all depicting the life of the King's saintly ances-

3

tors. The floor was of polished wood and covered against the cold with the skins of bears and wolves. A royal scribe was seated on a high stool copying out the letter Louis had dictated just after he had attended his third Mass. The King took off his gloves and spread his fingers over a dish of smouldering charcoal. It was still cold in here.

"Take a letter," he ordered, "to the Treasurer—tell him to bring me an animal skin, like that the Bishop of Valence gave me. It covered my back completely, and could spread out over my horse's rump." Louis's finger tapped the end of his pointed nose. "When it rained," he continued, "I had no need of a cloak, while in the hot weather it was as good as a cooling breeze. You understand that?"

The scribe nodded.

"Good!" The King clapped his hands. "Then get out and bring my visitors in." Louis crossed to the throne on the small dais, set against the far wall under a blue awning, displaying the golden fleur-de-lys. He made himself comfortable, pulling across the lambskin coverlet. He'd spent too much time fishing, he was freezing! The door opened and three men entered. They gathered in the shadows before coming forward. All were booted and spurred, heavy woollen military cloaks across their shoulders. They approached the dais, pulled back their cowls, and sank to one knee. Louis let them remain so while he studied them. The rather short, redheaded man in the middle, the Vicomte Sanglier, was Louis's personal envoy to England.

"My Lord Vicomte!" Louis leaned forward. "You had a good journey?" The envoy lifted his pale face, the green eyes red-rimmed, russet moustache and beard neatly clipped. Louis noticed how the Vicomte used his beard to hide his pitted cheeks, the ravages left by the pox.

"Your Majesty." Sanglier wetted his lips. "We have travelled like dogs and slept like dogs. The food was either burnt or undercooked, whilst the wine tasted like vinegar."

"Would you agree with that, monsieur?" Louis turned to François Cavignac, keeper of the Outer Chamber, a young man with neatly cropped black hair and a rounded face. He always reminded Louis of a choirboy, with his innocent eyes, smooth cheeks, and rather affected ways. Nevertheless, Cavignac had proved himself to be a most able spy, responsibly controlling Louis's agents abroad. A scholar of the Sorbonne, Cavignac was sly, cunning, and ruthless in dealing with Louis's enemies. A commoner promoted by Louis, his loyalty to the Crown was second only to his ambition for himself. Despite Louis's best efforts, Vicomte Sanglier had discovered little that was extraordinary about Cavignac's personal habits except that he was a most dedicated man of letters. Cavignac was a scholar who had studied for the priesthood, and he loved to send secret messages in cipher based on quotations from the Bible. Yet Cavignac's private life was of no real interest to Louis, who was only concerned about one thing: was Cavignac loyal? There was no doubt of that! Cavignac knew the rules of the French House of Secrets. Any betrayal, even the slightest, meant sudden, violent death.

"Monsieur." Louis leaned forward. "I asked you a question."

"Your Majesty, I apologise." Cavignac stirred. "My knees are sore. The Vicomte is correct. My only solace on our journey was the companionship of my colleagues and the prospect of entering your presence."

Louis smiled. At least half the statement was true. It also reflected how the intense rivalry for his affections dominated the lives of these three men.

"And you are well?" Louis turned to the man on his right. Beneath the military cloak Claude Delacroix, keeper of the Inner Chamber, was dressed in the black-and-white garb of a Dominican, yet he was not a friar, let alone a priest. Delacroix dressed like this because of a vow he had taken to his parents that he would become a Dominican friar. However, as soon as his parents had died, Delacroix had left his priestly training to study medicine at Montpellier. A lean, gaunt-faced man with furrowed cheeks, jutting mouth, and hollow, deep-set eyes, Delacroix reminded Louis of a favourite whippet he'd once owned, sinewy, swift, and vicious. Delacroix had a skill in tongues, not only English and Norman French but also classical Latin, German, and even the lingua franca of the Italian cities. Delacroix was responsible for Louis's agents in France, as well as hunting down and destroying those of other powers. Delacroix was as determined as his master to keep Edward of England and his warlike brothers, Richard of Gloucester and George of Clarence, out of France. One day they would recover the only French town held by the English, Calais, and drive a wedge between England and France's mortal enemy—the one great lord who threatened the unity of the kingdom, Charles of Burgundy.

"The journey must have been especially hard for you, monsieur," Louis declared. Delacroix lifted his head, eyes wrinkling in amusement. Louis prided himself on knowing the little secrets of all who served in the inner household. Thanks to Sanglier he certainly knew Delacroix's, who had left the Dominicans because of his hungry passion for soft, perfumed flesh. Delacroix was a constant visitor to the courtesans in the House of Joy, which stood in its own orchards and gardens not far from the Gate of St. Denis.

"Your Majesty." Delacroix's voice was as soft and melodious as a gentle priest's.

"We have journeyed, now we are here to listen to your will."

"Aye." Louis straightened. "So stop kneeling there as if you're statues."

For a while there was some confusion as they brought forward leather stools to sit before their King. Louis made them wait for a while, plucking at the lambskin rug that covered his knees.

"Later today," he began, "you leave for England. You are my envoys to the Court of Edward of York. You have your instructions?"

"To journey to London?" Cavignac asked.

"No, to Walmer on the Kentish coast," Louis answered as if speaking to himself.

"Lord Henry Beauchamp, your old adversary, keeper of the Secret Seal, waits to welcome you to his manor. He will be joined by an Irishman, one of Edward's own company, Colum Murtagh."

"Ah!" Sanglier unclasped his cloak and let it drop to the floor.

"You have met Murtagh before?" Louis smiled.

"I have," Sanglier replied. "Murtagh is a warrior, a merce-
nary, keeper of the King's stables, at Kingsmead, outside Canterbury. I have spoken about him before, Your Majesty."

"He is dangerous?"

"He can be."

"Do you fear him?"

"I fear the woman he is betrothed to, Kathryn Swinbrooke.
She is a physician hired by the Court as well as by the Archbishop
and City Council of Canterbury to investigate certain matters."

"I have heard of her." Louis waved a hand. "As I have heard
that she and Murtagh are to be married, yet I can't see how they
might interfere in what you have planned. You must travel to England; Lord Henry will be your host. You are to use what you
know to ensure that they will stay out of France and give no help
or sustenance to Burgundy."

Louis abruptly rose and his henchmen did likewise. The King
crossed to a small ornamentally carved coffer with three locks.
He took the small key ring that was hanging on a hook on his
belt, undid the three locks, pulled back the lid, and brought out a
similar coffer, much smaller, no more than a polished square.
Sanglier noticed the three miniature keys inserted in their locks.
Louis first ensured that each of these would turn before drawing
out the keys, and gave one to each of his envoys. He then handed
the polished coffer to Sanglier.

"Keep it safe. Let the English know that you could have it. Edward of England would give all the jewels of his chamber to own
it." Louis laughed at Sanglier's puzzlement.

"Do you know what this coffer contains?"

Sanglier shook his head.

"It's the English Book of Ciphers," Louis whispered, fearful
his voice would carry any farther than it should. "This book will
allow us to understand any secret messages sent by Edward of
England to his agents in France, as well as the true names and
whereabouts of the same agents."

"Where?" Sanglier stammered. "Your Majesty, how did you
obtain this? We have been searching for it. . . ."

"It does not matter." Louis stroked the top of the coffer as he would some hunting bird. "Just let Edward of England know you have it. Indeed, I have already dropped hints."

Louis sucked on his teeth, his tongue feeling out the sore points in his gums. He studied his three envoys. He'd caught the confusion of Delacroix, the darting glance between Sanglier and Cavignac. There was some mystery here but Louis could not grasp it. After all, Sanglier was the one who had reported how the real Book of Ciphers, together with its keeper, the Englishman Marshall, had disappeared along the Seine. The King sighed and gestured at the tray of wine cups on the table near the dais.

"Refresh yourselves, taste the wine, it's the best Burgundy can offer. I must go back to my fishing."

The three men hastily bowed as Louis, humming a hymn beneath his breath, left the chamber, shouting at the squire to ask if he had been able to catch anything. Once the door closed the three men relaxed. Delacroix splashed the wine into three goblets and served it. They toasted each other, warmed their fingers over the dish of charcoal and, like children eager to unwrap a present, inserted their keys into the coffer. Sanglier turned them and pulled back the lid. Inside was a small book, it looked like a psalter with its shiny cover studded with precious stones. He undid the clasps and gasped. The pages within were blank, page after page of cream-coloured vellum, all neatly stitched together but devoid of any mark, symbol, or picture. Sanglier sifted through the pages, the parchment crackling, then he pulled off the leather cover and carefully studied the pieces of hardboard beneath.

"There's nothing." He handed it to his two companions, who likewise searched. Cavignac took it over to a candle to scrutinize it more carefully. Delacroix then snatched it from his hands. Sanglier began to laugh. Cradling his goblet of wine, the Vicomte sat back on his stool. He tried to drink, only to splutter, coughing the wine onto the floor. Delacroix stared crossly at him. Had Sanglier been aware of their King's little riddle? Had he shared it already with his good friend, Cavignac? Delacroix hid his fury.

There was, as he'd whispered to Louis, some mystery here. There had been ever since Marshall's disappearance. Was this precious pair trying to exclude him? Sanglier the fox, with his secret knowledge about the Lord Henry Beauchamp? Sanglier, who quietly boasted about having a spy even in Walmer Village? Delacroix glanced quickly at Cavignac but he'd stepped back into the shadows as if to hide his face.

"Go on." Sanglier waved a hand. "Pull that book to pieces. Smell its every page. There's nothing. No Book of Ciphers!"

Delacroix stared at him; he had no choice but to join in the laughter. Sanglier turned and bolted the door through which his master had left.

"Let us toast the Spider!" He grinned. "Six months ago"— Sanglier wiped his mouth on the back of his hand—"Sir Henry was in Paris. We know he met Edward of England's principal spies there. Now Lord Henry's clerk, William Marshall, allegedly carried a Book of Ciphers. Well, to bring my story to an abrupt end, Marshall disappeared, and so did the Book of Ciphers."

"Of course," Cavignac stated. "I remember this. He went boating on the River Seine? An accident, they say, he drowned."

"His corpse was never discovered," Sanglier continued. "According to all reports, Marshall was carrying the Book of Ciphers, and that too disappeared. Now our master wants to threaten Edward of England. . . ."

"That we have the Book of Ciphers," Cavignac answered.

Sanglier nodded and raised his goblet. "Just think of the confusion that will cause."

Old Mother Croul was not born in Walmer but many miles to the north. She'd come to the village as the bride of Crispin the carpenter. When he died of the sweating sickness, Mother Croul had married Ambrose, her husband's apprentice, but he'd been steeped in wickedness and was hanged. Mother Croul had grown old alone in her two-room thatched cottage with its packed-mud floor and bed loft, near Blacklow Copse, a small wood on the edge of Walmer Village. The cottage possessed a derelict workshop and a makeshift stable, though both were now empty. Mother Croul depended more on her stick than some expensive palfrey. On that day, the eve of Michaelmas, when the first horrid poisonings took place, Mother Croul was already uneasy. The sun had begun to set. She'd wandered out into her herb garden to be amongst the maleficia, those deadly herbs, nightshade, foxglove, and water hemlock, plants that could stop a man's heart in a few breaths. Mother Croul did not grow them for that reason but because, in small doses, such herbs could be beneficial to the stomach and the heart. Mother Croul was truly wary of such plants. She fully believed in the Christ Jesus yet she was very conscious of those demons, evil sprites and goblins who haunted muddy wastes and woodlands. Mother Croul was particularly careful when she dug up the mandrake. She only pulled that herb out of the ground with a piece of string tied to her stick.

Mother Croul's two cats came with her into the garden, Gog and Magog, two furry tabbies, hunters in the dark, the terror of local birds, not to mention the vermin swarming in from the fields. The old woman was glad of their company as the unease seethed within her. She'd had dreams and nightmares. She'd glimpsed fiery devils on the road and, at night, she'd heard the ghosts gibbering from darkened corners. Mother Croul was not frightened easily. She could read and write. Many years ago she'd possessed a hornbook, she'd even been along the road to Canterbury and gone to wonder at London Bridge with its many arches that supported houses and shops, not to mention those long poles bearing the skulls of executed traitors. Nor was Mother Croul fanciful. She was careful of what she ate. She'd talked to enough leeches, apothecaries, and cunning travelling men to recognise that certain herbs could turn the heart to strange imaginings. So, what was the source of her deep anxiety? She walked down the garden path and opened the shabby wooden gate. Mother Croul turned round and stared back at her cottage and the few scrawny hens bathing in the dust before the door. The cottage didn't look like much; she'd saved a few pennies and often thought of hiring a mason or thatcher to make it look more homely but what was the use? "Corrupt and mouldy" was the way she described her cottage.

"Corrupt and mouldy," she spoke out loud. "And riddled with wormholes, just like me." The old woman smiled. Yet, many years ago on a balmy night, with the birds singing and the air soft with rose scent, she'd lain there with her only true love, Crispin, the finest carpenter in the shire! Crispin, with his sinewy body and hot passionate kisses . . .

"So long ago," Mother Croul murmured, and started as a weasel darted across her path, so swift even her cats didn't stir. But, there again, they'd leave the weasel alone; wasn't it a sign of ill luck and wasn't the breath of the weasel stale and corrupting? Mother Croul stared up at the blue rain-washed sky. The sunset was now hidden by clouds. The autumn day was dying and Blacklow Copse was coming alive with the sounds of the night. A cold breeze blew and the crows, circling above the trees, cawed noisily. Mother Croul crinkled her rheumy eyes and stared into the distance. She could make out the lights of the village, the glow of candles, the fire from the smithy, and the glitter of lantern horns outside the taverns. Here and there pricks of torchlight as the labourers returned from the fields. They'd gather in the taproom of the Blue Boar Tavern or the more spacious Silver Swan before making their way home. They'd sit and drink blackjacks of fresh Kentish ale, brewed from hops, and swap stories with the fishing folk who were preparing for a night's work out at sea.

"Harvesting the earth, harvesting the sea," Mother Croul whispered. She followed the line of the land, watching it rise. She could make out the fields, clumps of trees and, on the clifftops, the glowing lights of the great manor house, the home of Sir Henry Beauchamp, a Lord of the Soil, friend of the King, who'd drunk deep on the wine of life. Lord Henry, with his blond hair, gentle face, and strange blue eyes, a man of Kent, a Squire, who'd been sent to the halls of Cambridge to study to be a clerk. Lord Henry had also proved himself to be a soldier. He'd followed the banner of York, fighting alongside Edward the King at one bloody battle after another, so the Crown had been generous. Oh yes, very generous! Edward the King had sent Lord Henry into Walmer like an avenging angel, God's judgement and bloody vengeance on the gang of wreckers who'd sunk many a ship off the coast and sent the murdered souls of their crews before God's throne. One victim had been Lord Henry's beloved brother. After that, the King had turned Walmer over to him for vengeance! What retribution he had wrought, building the great gallows on the clifftop and hanging the miscreants as a farmer did the corpses of marauding crows. Once this was over, the Crown had favoured Lord Henry even further. Mother Croul had stood under the lych gate at the parish church of St. Swithun's and heard the gossip. How Sir Henry had been given lands, meadows, pastures, woods, fishing rights, the length and breadth of Kent. He'd come back to this village, he'd pulled down the rotting castle and built a new manor house, ringed by a great wall. People said it was like paradise, a great house of honey-coloured stone specially brought in from the Cotswolds. It contained a chapel, outer buildings, stables, and storerooms all of the same glowing stone with red and black slate roofs and tiled floors. The servants who worked there described the chambers, their walls covered with dark, rich oaken wainscoting over which glowing tapestries and gilt-framed pictures had been hung.

Oh yes, Lord Henry was a great man in both Court and the shire, Mother Croul mused. A member of the Privy Council, he was also keeper of the Secret Seal and had the ear of the King and all the great ones of the land. Yet, Lord Henry had paid an exacting price for such glory: wasn't it just over a year ago, his wife, the Lady Mary, she of the beautiful auburn hair, had fallen from the cliffs near Gallows Point? Nobody knew what she was doing out there all by herself. A servant said she left the manor house in an anxious state, refusing to take any maids or retainers with her. A travelling tinker found her horse whilst her sea-washed corpse was discovered on the rocks below. Some claimed Lady Mary had slipped. Others, more malicious, claimed her wits had turned and that she had jumped. Elias, the blacksmith, full of ale, had even claimed she might have been pushed. But, there again, Elias did have a wicked tongue and was very jealous of Lord Henry. That was the problem with Walmer, a peaceful village, yet like the nearby sea its tranquillity hid dark swirling secrets that could suddenly erupt, whipped up by too much ale and a storm of passion.

Mother Croul decided to walk farther along the path, still staring up at the manor house. She'd heard that great ones had arrived, members of the French Court, not to mention others, including a woman physician—what was her name? Mother Croul closed her eyes, for the life of her she couldn't remember. She leaned on her stick, staring into the darkness, ignoring the cats brushing her ankles. She knew all the gossip of Walmer. Who hated whom, who lusted after this maid or that, who bestowed her favours here and there. How Daniel, the baker, often put his finger on the scale or mixed chalk with his flour. How Roger the Physician charged fees even to the poor. How Elias the Blacksmith was only too willing to sell a horse that wasn't his. How Isabella, the Blacksmith's wife, was often seen on the edge of the woods talking to this man or that! The rankling petty disputes and vicious jealousies, the greed and avarice that, like demons, could raise their ugly heads and set neighbour against neighbour, friend against friend.

Mother Croul was shrewd and never missed much. She had that gift of sitting amongst others listening intently to what they said, a keen observer of the sly glance or sharp look. She didn't fear the villagers of Walmer—they might go to Adam the Apothecary or Roger the Physician, but Mother Croul was also called to help with birthing, to treat a bruise, a sprained wrist, or broken ankle. Of course, a few whispered she was a witch. Mother Croul laughed softly to herself. Any woman would be called a witch who lived by herself, had reached the age of three score and ten, possessed knowledge of the world, a skill with herbs, and lodged with two cats. In her writing chest, back in her cottage, she had protection against such diatribes. Mother Croul held a letter from the Archdeacon's Court at Canterbury, praising her skill and bestowing upon her the benediction of the Archbishop for her work in that city when she journeyed there as a pilgrim, during the time of the plague.

Mother Croul stared up at the darkening sky. So why should she be concerned? She glanced at the jutting gables of St. Swithun's Tower. Ah, that was it! Yesterday was Sunday and the parishioners attending morning Mass had been astonished to find, scrawled on the floor, just near the baptismal font, the words "*Mene, Mene, Tekel Parsin.*" Everybody knew what they meant. The words were copied from one of the wall paintings in the church transept, an eye-catching picture of the Prophet Daniel in the Lion's Den. Above this, written on a scroll were those words from the Book of Daniel, Chapter Five: "*Mene, Mene, Tekel Parsin.* I have weighed the balance, I have numbered, I have found wanting." All the parishioners, even those who couldn't read or write, had been taught about that painting and the strange words written above. How God's own finger had inscribed such a warning on the wall of a pagan King just before he brought the power of that King to nothing. Father Clement, their parish priest, usually a kindly man who lodged in the priest house with his sister Amabilia, had truly lost his temper. After Mass, still garbed in his green-and-gold vestments, he'd climbed into the pulpit.

"This is the house of God!" Father Clement's eyes were bright in his lean, pale face. "This is the house of God and the gate of heaven! A terrible place which houses God's own Son and a host of angels. How dare anyone inscribe such words on the floor of our church?" The priest had then passed on to other things as if the blasphemy had unlocked the gates of his heart. He had thundered to his parishioners about their selfish ways, their lack of care, their jealousies and spiteful moods. He had hinted at even more sinful secrets but then restrained himself. All the parishioners had been deeply aggrieved. Father Clement was usually as gentle as a dove. On that morning, however, he had appeared more like that itinerant preacher who'd recently arrived in Walmer with his sun-scorched skin and straggling hair and beard. A fearsome figure at the village cross who warned how the Day of Wrath was close at hand, how God's anger would soon make itself felt.

Mother Croul wetted her lips and sniffed at the breeze: the

seasons were changing, she could smell the decay of autumn. All things were decaying—she'd thought that only an hour ago when she had sat with the rest of the Parish Council in the priest's house. They'd been talking about that strange preacher who'd appeared out of nowhere to walk the village and preach at the market cross. Mother Croul had stared round at their faces. Father Clement and Amabilia seemed tired. Benedict the Notary and his wife Ursula, sharp featured as usual but rather withdrawn; Roger the Physician was his usual arrogant self, whilst Simon the Sexton and Walter the Constable had both drunk too much. Elias and Isabella, strangely enough, had excused themselves; perhaps that was it. The blacksmith was always loud-mouthed, ready to liven things up in a quarrel with Adam the Apothecary, yet even that merchant of potions and powders was subdued. The atmosphere had grown so uneasy, Mother Croul had excused herself and left. Nonetheless, she was still troubled. Walmer was like any village, yet life had never been the same since the end of the war when those Lancastrians, three refugees from the great battle in the West Country, had arrived at Walmer seeking passage abroad. A squire and two archers, the Lancastrians were journeying in disguise. Of course, they were soon recognised for what they were. By then the news of Edward of York's victories had swept the length and breadth of the kingdom. Woe betide anyone who helped Lancastrians fleeing for their lives. The three had tried to seek sanctuary in the church but the villagers, led by the Parish Council, had caught up with them in the cemetery, God's Acre, and cut them down. They'd stripped the bodies and threw their naked corpses on the steps of the market cross as proof of their loyalty to the House of York.

Mother Croul glanced up. Someone was running up the path. Her cats started back. Birds burst out of a tree alarmed at the evening silence being shattered. The old woman strained her eyes and ears. A dark form was stumbling towards her. A child . . .

"What's the matter?" she called.

"Mother Croul." A young boy stumbled to her feet out of breath. "Mother Croul, you must come."

"Must come, why must I come?" She peered down at the

blacksmith's boy. "Has your master been drunk again, has he burnt himself?"

"Mother Croul." The boy wiped the sweat from his face.

Mother Croul stooped down. "You look like an imp out of hell with all that ash on your face and hands."

"Master Elias is having a fit! He is dying!"

Mother Croul hobbled down the path as fast as she could. The boy ran beside her, describing in great detail how Elias had been at his forge, a busy furnace glowing. The blacksmith had taken a stoup of water, drinking great gulps, spluttering it out when, suddenly, he'd given a hideous cry and fallen like a stone to the ground.

"Shaking and jittering, like a fly on a hot plate! Eyes rolled back in his head, white froth from his lips!" The boy imitated the blacksmith, flapping his arms and shaking his head from side to side. They reached the High Street, a broad track hardened with cobbles, houses on either side. People clustered halfway up the street on the corner of Carters Lane, which led down to Elias's forge, only two arrows' length from the church. Mother Croul, stick banging on the cobbles, forced her way through, down the lane and into the blacksmith's yard behind his stone house. The air was hot, reeking of sweat, urine, charcoal, and burnt hair. Elias, however, was beyond her help. He lay stretched out on the ground, his wife, Isabella, beside him. She was kneeling, body moving backwards and forwards as if in prayer. In the light of the dying forge fire, the muscles of Elias's face seemed hardened; his eyes were rolled back so that the whites of his eyes glistened like those of a blind man, a creamy froth stained his moustache and beard, his tongue was wedged tightly between his teeth. Mother Croul felt the muscles of his face and arms; they were rigidly stiff.

"Is it a fit?" The boy asked.

Mother Croul pressed her hand against the blacksmith's neck, she could feel no beat of life. She asked the boy to bring the water stoup, and he did so. She sniffed and gagged at its acrid smell.

"Where did this water come from?" she asked. The boy pointed to the water butt across the yard. Mother Croul looked around, picked up an axe, and turned to the men who'd followed her into the yard. "Shatter the water butt," she shouted.

"Why? the blacksmith's wife screamed. "What is happening?"

"Shatter it!" Mother Croul repeated.

"Mistress." She patted Isabella gently on the shoulder. "God forgive me, but I believe your husband has been poisoned." Her words were greeted by cries of disbelief.

"Poisoned?"

Adam the Apothecary stepped into the pool of light, a tankard in his hands.

"What makes you say that?" There was no love lost between Adam and this wise woman.

"I know the effects of deadly nightshade," Mother Croul replied. "And if you don't believe me, why not drink the water yourself?"

"But who put it there?" the boy asked.

Mother Croul got to her feet and walked across to the water butt. The light was poor so she leaned down. She couldn't detect anything through the covering grille, but there again, so many smells rose from the pools of urine and midden heaps of the yard.

"Boy," she called out. The blacksmith's apprentice ran across. "Who filled the stoup?"

"I did, mistress," the boy answered.

"And you took it across?"

"Yes, my master was waiting for it."

"In which case"—Mother Croul handed him the axe to break the barrel—"if anyone drinks from that, they will follow the same path as your master."

A hideous scream echoed across the yard, now lit by men carrying pitch torches. Mother Croul hobbled across the cobbles as fast as she could, past the blacksmith's corpse and into the kitchen. Isabella, the blacksmith's wife, now lay writhing on the floor, the cup of wine splattered all around her as she jerked, kicking her legs out at the pain in her stomach. Mother Croul could only stare in horror. The wooden table had been laid for supper with platters, knives, a water jug, and a pewter wine holder with a large handle, its beak carved in a shape of a duck's bill. A pale-faced maid, fingers to her face, stared at her mistress screaming and spluttering on the floor. Others came in. Mother Croul knelt down as she tried to restrain the blacksmith's wife. It seemed as if the woman was choking. Mother Croul tried to put her finger into Isabella's mouth but withdrew quickly, gasping at the sharp bite. The woman was now losing consciousness, eyelids fluttering, she tried to pull herself up to vomit, only to fall back on the floor. She was beyond all help. Mother Croul picked up the wine cup, sniffed, and recoiled at the pungent smell of almonds.

Kathryn Swinbrooke, Physician of Canterbury, newlywed wife of Colum Murtagh, keeper of the King's stables at Kingsmead in the same city, stared down at the two naked corpses. They lay on wooden pallets in the death house, just behind the Chapel of St. Fiacre, the patron of gardeners, in Walmer Manor. Kathryn sighed once again and held the pomander against her nose. Although the corpses looked fresh they already had the awful smell of death and corruption. She walked away and peered out of the small window. The heavy cloak about her shoulders and the scented braziers in the far corner of the roof softened the effect of the cold breeze. The night was dying, Kathryn reflected, the sun would rise later. She closed her eyes. Here she was, only a bride of a few days, with the love of her life; she was supposed to be enjoying the richness of her marriage-first days, not examining the hapless victims of some assassin.

"I don't accept this," she murmured. Kathryn turned in surprise as she realised she had spoken aloud.

"It is, I admit," Father Clement declared, misunderstanding her, "hard to believe. A poor man, murdered in his workshop, and his wife poisoned in her own kitchen? How could such dreadful deeds happen?"

Kathryn studied this simple priest in his brown robe and sturdy sandals. He stood between the wooden pallets, a black woollen cloak over his shoulders from which jutted a long, scrawny neck. Kathryn considered his face to be that of an angel: Father Clement was gentle eyed and soft mouthed, white wisps of hair framed his hollow-cheeked face.

"I gave them the Last Rites, didn't I, Amabilia?" Father Clement turned to his sister-cum-housekeeper. A small plump woman, Amabilia was dressed in a tawny gown of fustian, a wimple circling her pudgy, calm face; her eyes were black and large as damsons, with a snub nose above a merry mouth. Amabilia was red cheeked with the cold; she kept pulling at her black mittens and blowing on the tips of her fingers. She dropped her hands and smiled at Kathryn.

"Father and I were absent at the time. We went to visit a farmer on the other side of the bay and didn't return until after dark." She blinked and shook her head. "We couldn't believe what had happened. By then the corpses were brought into the porch of St. Swithun's Church. I lit the candles. Father blessed and anointed them." Her voice trailed away. "And then," she added as an afterthought, "we sent a message to Lord Henry."

Kathryn glanced at the lord of the manor standing guard near the door. Despite the early hour, Lord Henry was dressed as if ready for Court, his blond hair, moustache, and beard neatly clipped and combed. He'd donned a cotehardie of green velvet decorated with golden lozenges above leggings of blue murrey thrust into brown leather boots, around his slim waist an embroidered belt with a silver buckle from which a gold-edged scabbard hung. The perfect courtier, Kathryn reflected. Lord Henry stood so elegantly, one hand playing with the buckle of his belt, the other beating a slight rhythm against the dagger sheath.

"My lord?"

Lord Henry broke from his anxious reverie. He had the strangest blue eyes, they made Kathryn feel he was staring right through her.

"I asked that the corpses be brought here." Lord Henry shrugged. "I thought you might help."

"They are dead, they have been poisoned." Adam the Apothecary, who'd decided to join the cortege to the manor, stepped forward as if he were the lawyer for these cold, disfigured corpses. Adam had taken an instant dislike to Kathryn and didn't bother to conceal it. His sullen face, framed by long black hair, was tight with anger; he kept patting his paunch as if to curb the agitation he felt.

"They'd been poisoned, so why bring them here? The only question we must ask is who is responsible?"

"More importantly," Mother Croul declared, sitting on a stool in the corner. She smiled as everyone looked at her, "is why?"

Kathryn warmed to this old woman with her winsome face, her grey hair, parted down the middle, falling to her shoulders. Mother Croul was dressed in a patched green gown over a white shift, which was tied high beneath her chin. A soiled woollen cloak was draped across her shoulders, battered sandals on her feet and a brown broad-brimmed hat rested on her lap. Nevertheless, despite the shabby clothes, Mother Croul sat like a Queen, her sharp, black cat eyes bright with life.

"Why," the old woman repeated, "should two lives be taken, two souls sent into the dark?"

"An accident?" Amabilia spoke up.

Mother Croul threw her head back and laughed.

"Tell me," Kathryn asked, "what happened?"

"A normal Monday at the forge." Adam replied. "Elias was busy, shoeing horses, mending kettles, fashioning a new scythe; his wife, Isabella, had been down to the marketplace. She came back to prepare the evening meal, a piece of beef specially preserved." Adam glanced at the priest. "Father, you have spoken to everybody."

"Nothing suspicious happened," the priest murmured, sitting down on the stool between the two corpses, his hands going out to touch both.

"Nothing at all?" Kathryn answered. "No unexpected visitors, no strange occurrences?" The priest shook his head.

"Ask for yourself, Mistress Swinbrooke, a normal Monday, the usual routine."

"Did they have children?"

20

"None who survived."

"Did they have enemies?"

The apothecary looked away.

"Well, did they?" Kathryn insisted.

"Everyone has enemies," the priest replied, "just as we have friends. In a village like Walmer passions run high but not hot enough to cause murder."

"Tell me about their enemies." Kathryn insisted.

"They had their enemies," Father Clement admitted. "Elias was a good blacksmith, a true disciple of St. Dunstan's." Kathryn stared down at the corpses. Elias was a thickset man, the hair on his chest and legs long and curling. The skin was now sallow and rather dry, the stomach stained above the navel by a dark mulberry patch. Despite the best efforts of those who'd tended to him, the blacksmith's face was contorted in the rictus of death, eyes half closed. Only the whites could be seen, the body muscles were hard, his stubby fingers curled as if claws. His wife's corpse was equally grotesque, head slightly to one side, the hideous grimace on her face hidden by her corn blond hair, still sweat soaked, eyes glaring, mouth gaping, teeth clenched tightly on the tip of her tongue. She too bore the marks of poison, dark red stains on her chest and stomach, her skin dry to the touch. Yet, in life, she must have been comely enough with her graceful long legs, her breasts still full and ripe.

"You were saying?" Kathryn glanced at Father Clement.

"He liked his ale, did Elias, he'd always be holding forth in the taproom of the Blue Boar about this and that. He was a wealthy man, and could buy goods from London and Canterbury, even luxuries from across the seas. He bought his wife a fine gown from Bruges, edged with miniver. I suppose"—the priest shrugged—"he could excite both anger and envy."

"And his wife?" Kathryn asked.

"Bosom merry," Old Mother Croul spoke up, "but they were always at each other, daggers drawn!"

Kathryn turned.

"Daggers drawn!" the old woman repeated.

"He didn't just hold forth in the taproom, Elias was a great one at tumbling wenches."

"And Isabella?" Kathryn asked.

Old Mother Croul stared silently down at her feet. Father Clement rubbed his face.

"Mistress Swinbrooke, I hear the confessions of my parishioners, but what they confess must be kept secret under the seal of the sacrament. All I will say is that Elias suspected that Isabella bestowed her favours on others."

Mother Croul laughed softly to herself.

Kathryn stared sharply at the old woman, who probably knew more than she'd confessed, reluctant to say more in the presence of the likes of Adam the Apothecary. Kathryn walked back to the oriel window. The manor was now stirring. A cock crew harsh and shrill. The laughter and chatter of servants, as they gathered round the well, carried on the breeze. Kathryn decided not to ask any further questions. She had no doubt that both husband and wife had been murdered. She'd first considered suicide but quickly dismissed it. Elias and Isabella had not planned to meet their Maker yesterday evening. An accident? Impossible! A coincidence? Kathryn pulled at her cloak. It was too incredible to believe that Elias had planned to murder Isabella, and she him at the same time, in the same place and the same way. So it was murder, but by whom and why? She heard the others coughing and shuffling behind her so she returned to the two corpses.

Kathryn had listened very carefully to what had happened, how Elias had been drinking water from the butt, then fell to the ground in a fit. His wife, distraught, had gone back into the kitchen for a goblet of wine. She'd drunk half of this when she too had suffered convulsions. The source of the poisoning had been the water butt just inside the yard and a small tun of wine from which the maid had filled the jug. Kathryn first examined Elias's corpse. Turning his head, trying to prise open his jaw, she sniffed carefully, a sharp acrid smell like that of fruit turned sour. She then moved to Isabella, the stains on her skin, the hardness of her muscles. Kathryn pressed her nose against the woman's clenched teeth and smelt the sickly sweet odour of almonds. She sat down on the stool vacated by the priest.

"Could you bring them in?" she asked.

Sir Henry himself opened the door and ushered in the blacksmith's apprentice and maid. The boy was dressed in old hose and a tattered leather jacket over a small worsted jerkin. The girl was in a dark yellow gown, a black shawl over her shoulders. Both looked frightened and cold, eyes watering, noses pink. Kathryn let them warm themselves at the brazier, then asked them to sit before her.

"Your master and mistress are dead. They've both been murdered." She smiled at their brown-eyed stare. "Did anything happen yesterday to account for these deaths?"

The young boy shook his head.

"Then tell me about the day?" Kathryn asked, aware of how quiet the death room had fallen. The young boy stared at the corpses on either side of him. The young maid began to shiver, eyes half-closed as she dared to look. Kathryn got to her feet and covered both corpses with sheets. She wished she could question these two elsewhere even as she recalled the old legend, how the corpse of a murdered victim could, in the presence of his or her murderer, rise up to tell the truth. Kathryn retook her seat.

"Don't worry." She patted them both on the hands. "These corpses are only empty houses now, soon to be committed to the soil. Their souls have gone to God. Father has said the prayers and I am sure Requiem Masses will be sung. Now God wants the truth. God, the King, and Lord Henry. Your master and mistress were murdered. I must know what happened yesterday." She paused. "Were Elias and your mistress happy?"

Both the boy and maid nodded in unison.

"They had not argued or quarrelled?"

"We knew nothing of their business," the maid replied. "We ate and slept alone, they were kind enough."

"Are you brother and sister?" Kathryn asked.

"Orphans," Father Clement declared. "Taken in by the blacksmith and his wife. I doubt if Master Elias discussed his business with them."

"They were happy enough." The young boy spoke up, frightened. "On that day, yesterday, they seemed contented. They were looking forward to an evening meal, a special meal."

"Why special?" Kathryn asked.

Both brother and sister shook their heads.

"It was the eve of Michaelmas," Father Clement intervened. "Today is the Feast of St. Michael the Archangel, a time for celebration." He looked wistfully at the hour candle burning on its black iron spigot beneath the large wooden crucifix on the far wall.

"I should be celebrating Mass, we need all the help of the Heavenly Host."

"So." Kathryn ignored the priest. "Your master and mistress were preparing to celebrate Michaelmas?"

"Yes," the two chorused.

"Master Elias worked in the smith all day?"

Again, both agreed.

"And Mistress Isabella went to the market?"

"She went to the flesher's stall and bought some beef, freshly slaughtered, not salted or pickled."

"Where else did she go?"

"She bought some spices and cloth. She talked to different people but then came home," the maid replied. "I spent most of the afternoon polishing pewter and brass before I laid the table. When I wasn't doing that, I was busy at the spit or helping my mistress bake bread. We took fresh milk from the buttery and a jug of wine from a small barrel of claret."

"When did your mistress buy that?"

"I don't know!" the girl wailed. "All I know is that she brought it up from the cellar and had it prepared. She drove in the spigot and said she would taste some before the evening meal."

"And Master Elias? Come on, boy!" Kathryn urged. "I know you are cold, but when I am finished with you, there's a cup of buttermilk and a hot oatcake laced with honey and nutmeg."

"Oh, it was a normal day," the boy replied. "People coming and going, people waiting. Master Elias was shoeing and, when he wasn't busy with a horse, he was fashioning a scythe. He boasted it would be the best Walmer had ever seen."

"Did he drink water during the day?"

"Oh no, Master Elias never did that. He drank light ale, he had a leather blackjack always by his side."

"So why did he drink the water?"

"That was his custom, mistress. He always drunk two tankards of fresh water at the end of the day."

"Ah, always from that water butt?"

"Oh yes. He claimed it was his water, the butt was always kept covered by a wire mesh."

"So where did Mistress Isabella take water?" Kathryn turned to the maid.

"There was another inside the house," the girl replied. "Master Elias always kept that water for himself. It stood just within the gateway, it took rain direct as it fell, not from the roof."

Kathryn smiled and nodded. Back in Canterbury her maid Thomasina did the same. Rain from the roof or eaves was never as pure as that which fell straight into a butt or bucket.

"So, Master Elias's water butt was special?"

"Oh yes," the boy replied. "Lined with copper it was, to keep out the dirt, that is why they found it hard to shatter it." He pointed at Mother Croul. "When you told them to do so."

"And your master always drank in the evening from that same butt?"

"I've said that," the boy replied. "Mistress, I know nothing else. I have talked to my sister, we do not know why anyone should do such a dreadful deed."

Kathryn gently patted each on their cold hands.

"Go outside," she whispered. "Down to the kitchen." She glanced at Sir Henry.

"Tell them Lord Henry sent you and ask for what I promised you."

Chapter 2

No deyntee morsel passed thrugh hir throte,
Hir diet was accordant to hir cote.
—Chaucer, "The Nun's Priest's Tale,"
The Canterbury Tales

T his is very strange," Kathryn declared. "Here is a man and wife, they may have had their troubles but they were preparing to celebrate a feast day. She had prepared beef and a casket of the best claret. He was working in his smithy. They followed their usual routine. At the end of the day Elias always asked for a stoup of fresh rainwater from his special butt. The boy lifts the cover, fills the stoup, and brings it across. Elias drinks that and asks for another. He is then discomforted by violent pains; he falls to the floor and dies shortly afterwards. His wife comes rushing out, she kneels by the corpse, and becomes hysterical. Mother Croul arrives. Elias the Blacksmith is dead, his soul gone to God. Mistress Isabella returns to the kitchen. She feels sick, weak, and dazed. The table is laid for supper as they'd planned. Shocked, she broaches the wine, drinks a cup, and she too is poisoned." Kathryn stood in the centre of the room and surveyed them all.

"Two great mysteries here. First, the poisons are definitely potions. I suspect Elias was killed by a very potent infusion of belladonna—all its parts, especially the roots, leaves, and berries are highly poisonous. No one knows how it works but the purple-black berries taste sweet and have the most fatal consequences. The victim's vision becomes blurred, his heartbeat increases, he feels very hot and dry mouthed, blotches of red appear on his skin."

"I know the power of belladonna," Adam the Apothecary interrupted. "But usually it takes hours to kill its victim."

"Not so, not so." Kathryn shook her head. "If given in its most potent form and drunk quickly, belladonna can kill within a few heartbeats."

"And Mistress Isabella?" Father Clement asked.

"Ah!" Kathryn replied. "What the leeches call the juice of almond. This can be distilled from seeds and pips of fruits such as peach, apricot, apple, wild cherry, or plum. Its effect is immediate: loss of consciousness and hideous convulsions. The victim struggles to breathe but death can occur within minutes. I believe both Elias and Mistress Isabella were given strong infusions of these two different, but very potent, poisons."

"And the second mystery?" Lord Henry interrupted.

"How did the poisons get there in the first place? We know that the water butt in the yard was Elias's special preserve. No one was allowed to go near it. What I suspect, and suggest to you, is that someone during the day entered the yard. This assassin put the purest belladonna powder into that water butt. It may have been early in the day, midafternoon, or later on. Remember, the boy drew the water when darkness was falling. He wouldn't have noticed anything. By then the powder would be fragmented by the water yet, in all its dire richness, floating on the surface, which the boy scooped up. Elias, breathing in the fumes of his own forge, the burning charcoal, the charred hair, the stale urine and fiery iron, would not detect the taste until it was too late. He was thirsty, eager to cleanse his stomach before his evening meal. One stoup of water, followed by another, and death ensues. How Mistress Isabella died is even more mysterious. Here we have a woman who goes down to her cellar and brings out a sealed cask or tun of claret. According to custom, that cask had been sealed in Bordeaux, put upon a ship, brought to England, and sold to a wine merchant from whom Elias or Isabella possibly bought it. It would take a year and a day to find that merchant. I doubt if the cask was poisoned when Elias and

Isabella bought it, so that means somebody entered their house, went down to the cellar, chose a wine cask, broke the seals, opened it, put in this deadly poison, resealed the cask, and stole out of the house. What is even more mysterious is the assassin apparently knew that particular cask would be opened the same evening that Elias drank the poisoned water."

"So both poisonings were planned?" Lord Henry asked.

"That's what the evidence suggests," Kathryn replied. "Lord Henry, what other explanation can there be? Here we have a very skilful, subtle assassin who has chosen his two victims, God knows the reason why, Elias and Isabella, and plans to murder them together. Indeed, if Elias hadn't drunk from the water, both he and his wife would have drunk that poisoned wine. Whatever happened, the assassin plotted that both husband and wife should die at the same time, in the same place."

"But why?" Lord Henry demanded.

Kathryn shrugged. "That, Lord Henry, I cannot explain!"

*   *   *

And the Great Angel Michael appeared in the Heavens,
With fiery sword he demanded, "Who shall be like unto God?"

Father Clement intoned the introit for the Mass of St. Michael, in the Chapel of St. Fiacre. Kathryn, standing beside Colum Murtagh, hurriedly crossed herself. She still felt uncomfortable, rather bad tempered after being hustled from her marriage bed. She'd left the death house and returned to her own chambers to find Colum sleeping, sprawled out on the bed like a babe. She'd hurriedly undressed, washed herself, put on a dark purple gown and a white shawl with a gauze veil over her raven black hair. She hadn't painted her face. She thought that was inappropriate, as she'd muttered to herself, "The festivities are over and this day will prove to be a hard one!" She'd put on woollen stockings, slipped her feet into soft leather boots, and left the chamber, going out for a short walk across the fountain courtyard, which divided the chapel from the great hall of Walmer Manor. The Mass bell had begun to toll but she'd waited for Colum, still sleepy eyed, to join her. She stared round, her bad temper receding; the sight of Colum still swaying half-asleep on his feet made her smile. The chapel was a beautiful gem of a building, built of the same lustrous honey-coloured brick as the rest of the manor, with black beam rafters and wooden sills beneath oriel windows on either side. There was no rood screen before the altar but Lord Henry had already hired painters to cover the white plastered walls with vivid paintings to depict St. Agatha before her Roman torturers, and Sebastian, lashed to a pole, being shot to death by arrows.

Above the altar was a small rose window. Its coloured glass caught the early sun and bathed the white stone sanctuary in rays of flashing light. The altar was a simple wooden table on a raised dais, approached by three steps. Behind the altar were more steps leading up to a tabernacle where the pyx was kept. Before it a red lamp glowed, a sign that this chapel housed Christ's body.

Father Clement, in the golden gorgeous robes of the liturgy of the day, was intent on saying Mass. He stood before the lectern carved in the shape of a soaring eagle and recited the first reading. Kathryn watched the flames of the candles on either end of the altar dance and flicker in the breeze. The air smelt sweetly of incense, beeswax, wine, and the fragrance of the flower baskets placed around the church. Elias's young apprentice had volunteered to serve as altar boy, and now he hovered behind Father Clement looking around in wonder, searching for the cruets of wine and water so as to be ready for the Offertory. His gaze caught Kathryn, who indicated with her hand the small recess in the wall, just beside the lavarium, where the wine and water were stored in small glass jugs. The boy nodded and scampered across. Father Clement continued with the Mass. Kathryn, distracted, kept staring around. She found it such a contrast to come from the hideous scenes of the death house to such a place of worship, light, incense, and purity. Others were also gathering in the church, late risers, including three newly-arrived French visitors. Vicomte Sanglier caught her eye and bowed, but in a mocking gesture, eyes narrowed with sardonic amusement. He stood beside his two colleagues to whom Kathryn had already been introduced, Cavignac and Delacroix. She disliked both.

They looked at her as if she had no place at Walmer and dismissed her title as physician, preferring to call her a leech. Lord Henry, standing on her left, coughed and muttered under his breath about the bad manners of his guests. Colum started and stared down at Kathryn, who glared back.

"Sleepyhead," she muttered. He leaned down and kissed her gently on the cheek, his lips brushing her skin.

"And whose fault is that?" he murmured.

Kathryn poked her elbow into his side and, joining her hands, composed herself, and listened intently to the Mass.

*   *   *

> *"Three parts make up the Fountain flow, the stream, the spout, the bowl.*
> *Although these are three, these three are one essence of the same.*
> *Even so the waters of salvation run."*

Kathryn quoted the famous poem about the Trinity as she studied the small fountain splashing water into the dark blue bowl before it. The fountain was topped with a bronze image, the water pouring through lion-headed masks. The grass around the fountain was neatly cut, a few daisies still sprouted there. The entire miniature garden was ringed by trees, a pleasance specially created by Lord Henry's gardeners.

"The apples look good." Colum followed her gaze. "They'll be ripe within a month, juicy and soft." He smiled down at her. "Just like you."

Kathryn poked him in the stomach. "Sleepyhead! I was aroused from my marriage bed by Lord Henry's servants and brought down to inspect two corpses in the death house while you slept like a child, not a care in the world!"

"I have already explained myself." Colum's dark face creased in a smile, blue eyes crinkling. He clawed the black hair tumbling about his face, trying to straighten it out with his fingers. Kathryn gazed passionately at him. Colum hadn't shaved, he still looked as if he could go back to sleep and, of course, he hadn't dressed properly. The white shirt beneath the leather jerkin was the same as he wore yesterday; the jerkin was wrongly buttoned up while the green leggings were pushed into different boots. Colum found it very hard to distinguish one pair from the other, especially first thing in the morning.

"Colum"—she gripped his hands—"we've only been a few days married yet it seems like a year ago since we exchanged vows on the porch of St. Mildred's Church. Do you remember the feasting which followed? In the Chequer of Hope, the bagpipes wailing, the drums, the flutes, Thomasina singing and dancing?"

Colum laughed. "I shall never forget that, or Father Cuthbert from the Poor Priest's Hospital dancing with her."

Kathryn closed her eyes. Their marriage had taken place on the most beautiful of September days. They'd exchanged vows during the morning Mass, then gathered with their friends in the church-yard. Afterwards they'd returned to their house to receive the congratulations of Wulf, Agnes, as well as the rest of her neighbours, many of whom were her patients. Early in the afternoon Kathryn had dressed in a cream-coloured gown, a veil covering her head and face, a pair of dark green slippers on her feet. She'd been mounted on a palfrey and led by Colum through the streets of Canterbury to the Chequer of Hope Inn. Guests followed, throwing flowers, singing songs, and pressing small presents into baskets on either side of the palfrey she rode. The feasting that followed had been regarded by everyone as a great success. Wines brought from the royal cellars of Windsor, a personal gift from the King, the best Bordeaux, the coolest Rhenish, beer and ale. One dish had followed another; swan, peacock, pheasant, beef, lamb— all served up in different sauces; followed by sweets, blancmanges, jellies, and fruit tarts covered in cream. Speeches had been made, toasts exchanged followed by poems from the minstrels Colum had hired. As darkness fell, the real revelry, the music and dancing, had begun on the green outside. Afterwards she and Colum had retired to the special chamber they'd hired in the inn. . . .

Kathryn opened her eyes and grinned at Colum.

"You may be sleepy headed now, my fierce Irishman, but that night you certainly weren't."

Colum drew her close, put his arms around her waist and kissed her passionately on the lips. Kathryn clung to him, holding him tight. Even now, she thought, though they were well away from Canterbury, Colum still smelt of horses, sweat, and straw. She laughed quietly to herself.

"What's the matter, light of my heart?" he whispered.

"The other matter," she murmured, "is that you move from one extreme to another, either sleepy eyed or burning with passion."

"We should eat." He stepped away but still held her hands. "We should go to the hall and mingle with the others. Lord Henry expects us."

" 'Lord Henry expects!' " Kathryn mimicked. "Has anyone told Lord Henry, not to mention His Grace the King, that I am a bride of a few days, how you are the love of my life, and that we should be somewhere all by ourselves in a love nest of our own creation? Why, Colum, why are we here? We could have stayed in Canterbury or gone elsewhere."

He pulled her close and went to put his arms round her but she pushed him away.

"Nights of passion," she whispered with tears in her eyes. "Colum, I have never been so happy, yet now we're at Walmer, the French envoys are waiting to treat with us whilst the corpses of murder victims have been brought up from the village. Is that our lives, Colum? Always pursuing the sons and daughters of Cain?"

Colum went down on one knee, took her hand and pressed it against his face.

"I swear, Kathryn, by land, sea, and air, by fire and water and by the Holy Rood and the glories of St. Patrick, that, when we have finished at Walmer, we will go to a place where no one knows us. We shall be alone."

He stood up, took her over to a turf garden seat, and sat down. Kathryn, at peace now, revelled in the sunlight even as a strengthening breeze stirred the dried leaves.

"A beautiful plesaunce," she remarked. "Yet soon the flowers will die, the leaves will fall. Summer is ending, Colum."

"But spring will come soon enough," he replied defiantly. "Now, listen, Kathryn, this is why we are here. Louis XI, the Spider of France, has sent three envoys. The Vicomte Sanglier, we have met him before, twisting like a snake in the grass. He has brought two other vipers with him, Delacroix and Cavignac. All three are close to the French King. They know the secrets of his heart. They whisper to him in his Inner Chamber. Three men, Kathryn, who have been responsible for the deaths of some of my friends, agents who worked in France. We are locked in a deadly game with them, like Hooded Man, when someone binds your eyes and you have to search them out and catch them. Only this time, you're armed and they're armed. They're blind and you're blind. You lash out, perhaps you can hurt your opponent, even kill them. This game is *à l'outrance*, to the death."

"But they're not here to do murder?"

"No, Kathryn, but they're here to plan it." Colum drew a deep breath.

"Ostensibly, Louis of France the Spider King, wants to seal an eternal treaty of peace with Edward of England." He laughed abruptly. "Such peace treaties have been signed before and last no longer than a year. Louis's real concern is to keep the English out of France, to have them locked up in Calais and not provide help to his great opponent, Charles Duke of Burgundy. If Louis is allowed a free hand in France, he will bring all the great lords to heel. The power of France will grow. Our King understands that. Edward has no desire to interfere in Louis's fish pond. However, what our King wants is to receive an annual pension from Louis in return for his goodwill and peaceful ways. In particular, Edward wants Louis of France to expel, or hand over, the last Lancastrian claimant, Henry Tudor. He and his uncle Jasper are a thorn in York's side. If Tudor was assassinated, or reduced to a penniless exile, Edward of England would sleep most sweetly. Now, about six months ago, Lord Henry Beauchamp was in Paris with his clerk, William Marshall. You'd like William Marshall, Kathryn, a merry dancer with nimble wits. He had the soft face of a girl, black curly hair, a lion for the ladies. He was sharp witted and skilled, able to translate the most complex cipher. According to reports, Marshall went fishing along the Seine but never came back."

"Murdered?"

Colum pulled a face. "We do not know, his body was never found. According to Lord Henry, Marshall carried at the time a Book of Ciphers, like a priest's psalter, bound in leather. This contained, in cipher form, the names of all English agents in Paris and elsewhere, merchants, tinkers, noblemen, scholars, students, and priests. People who collect information and pass it on to England for either favours or gold. It also contained the key to translate all letters the English Chancery sent in cipher to France."

"And did the French find that?"

"They may have done. Marshall's body was never discovered but the French Court has begun to hint that they may have found this book."

"So why don't they use it?"

"Ostensibly because a truce exists between England and France."

"Ah! I see." Kathryn smiled. "So, if England breaks the truce, and goes to war with France?"

"Louis and his ministers," Colum replied, "would have every right to arrest all those listed as helping the Crown of England. Now this unholy Trinity—Sanglier, Delacroix, and Cavignac—have come to England. They may want the truce converted into a lasting peace. If Edward of England agrees to that, without receiving a pension from the French Court or demanding that the Tudor be expelled, Louis is hinting the Book of Ciphers will be handed back."

"If not?"

Colum shrugged.

"Can't Edward warn his agents?" Kathryn asked. "Can't the Chancery change the cipher?"

"Easier said than done. Oh, the cipher has already been changed. However, if Louis discovered our secrets and unmasked England's hidden agents, what's the use of sending messages to France if there's no one there to receive them?"

"So, the cipher could already be translated, the French poised to act?"

"We doubt it," Colum replied. "It's complex and might take years. Louis knows that and so do—"

"So you know nothing," Kathryn asked, "of the truth?"

"A marsh of mysteries," Colum mused. "A tangled morass. Is Marshall dead, or alive, kept hidden in some French prison? Is he being tortured to break, to confess, to translate the Book of Ciphers for his French captors? Or is Louis just looking for an excuse to break the truce and go to war? Will he have his troops sweep through the towns and cities of France arresting all those in the pay of Edward of England?"

"So, who asked for these negotiations?" Kathryn asked. "Edward or Louis?"

"Actually, it's more Lord Henry's idea. He sent messages to France, asking if Louis wished to discuss the truce in the more informal setting of Walmer Manor. He specifically asked for our treacherous three to be despatched here. Louis believes Lord Henry is deeply worried, he wishes to exploit that so the envoys were sent."

"What does Sir Henry want to find out? If Louis will sign a new peace treaty, the whereabouts of Marshall or the truth about the Book of Ciphers?"

"Perhaps all three?" Colum replied.

"Could Louis or his agents have murdered Marshall?"

"It's possible, but, there again." The Irishman spread his hands. "Marshall was an accredited envoy. Kings take sacred oaths that such people are sacrosanct. If we can prove that Louis was behind Marshall's death, or privy to it, he'd be castigated the length and breadth of Europe. He could even be excommunicated by the Pope. No one would trust him. Who would dare to send him envoys? No, it would seem that Marshall and his Book of Ciphers simply disappeared: that's one fact Lord Henry wishes to establish with our French visitors."

"And Lord Henry himself?" Kathryn asked. "He seems gracious enough but very withdrawn."

"I wondered when you would raise the matter." Colum put

his arm round her shoulders. "Sharp-eyed Kathryn, you know there's a mystery here." He paused, collecting his thoughts.

"Lord Henry was the son of a local squire. His father sent him to Cambridge, where he proved to be a brilliant scholar and the most able of clerks. He was given a post in the Exchequer and, a year later, moved to the Chancery, the Great Writing Office at the Palace of Westminster. He also proved to be a fighting man. Now, Lord Henry's older brother, Maurice, was a merchant. He owned a cog, the *Holy Angel*, which did business out of Gravesend sailing to northern waters. Some years ago, wreckers along this part of the coast used beacons and false lights to bring ships in and wreck them on the nearby rocks so as to plunder the cargoes. The *Holy Angel* was one of those wrecked, its crew either drowned or murdered, its cargo stolen. Lord Henry was beside himself with rage. By then, he'd brought himself to the attention of Edward of York through his bravery at the Battle of Mortimer's Cross. He became our young King's bosom friend. Henry wanted vengeance. Edward agreed. Warrants were sworn out, allowing Lord Henry to hunt down the wreckers of Walmer. Lord Henry was ruthless. He set up a six-branched gibbet on the clifftops, now known as Gallows Point, and pursued the wreckers, his brothers' assassins. Eventually he caught them, a gang of about twenty-four, men and women. Some of them are related to the present-day villagers. Lord Henry had all the power of Oyer and Terminer, his justice was swift and brutal. All twenty-four were convicted, all declared guilty and all sentenced to hang. Lord Henry himself supervised the executions, four batches of six. He then erected makeshift gibbets around the great scaffold. The corpses of the malefactors were tarred, chained, and allowed to hang until they rotted, a warning to all would-be wreckers. After that, no ships sailing along those coasts were ever troubled. Lord Henry became Edward of York's man, both body and soul. He fought beside him in one battle after another, protecting his back, on one occasion even saving his life. When Edward of York's fortunes dipped, so did Lord Henry's. When Edward of York went into exile, Lord Henry followed. About two years ago, Edward of York decided to settle matters once and for all with the House of Lancaster. You know that. Your first husband, Alexander Wyville, joined the Lancastrian troops which left Canterbury. . . ."

Kathryn repressed a shiver. Even though she was ecstatically happy sitting next to the man she loved beyond all measure, the ghost of Wyville, her drunken, violent first husband, still haunted her memory.

Colum sensed Kathryn's change in mood and continued, eager to distract her. "Lord Henry fought at the great battles of Barnet and Tewkesbury. For his reward he was given extensive estates in Kent. Now, Lord Henry had been given Walmer Castle a few years before. He's spent his treasure pulling the old castle down and building this new manor house. He calls it his private residence, his Plesaunce of Pleasure."

"I would agree with that."

Kathryn rose to her feet. This miniature garden lay at the centre of a larger one with apple, pear, and cherry orchards, and green lawns with little multicoloured pavilions where visitors could sit during inclement weather. Trellises covered with climbing roses circled rich flower beds. Lord Henry had dug wells, built fountains, paved courtyards, and stocked deep carp ponds. Kathryn had counted at least three dovecotes, two kennel yards for hunting dogs, and stable housing for a troop of horses. Such opulent wealth and luxury was also to be found within the manor house itself. She'd walked its galleries and corridors admiring its chambers, writing office, and solar, all of them built in that eye-catching, honey-coloured stone, their walls half covered with oak linenfold wainscoting. Windows filled with glass poured light onto tiled floors, tapestries and gilt-edged paintings. A broad sweeping staircase covered in Turkey carpets swept up from the main hallway and everywhere candleholders and candelabra made out of pewter and bronze flared merrily so even at night the darkness was held back.

Kathryn walked across to a small herb plot.

"Look, Colum." She pointed out the different herbs, basil, fennel, and peppermint.

"Lord Henry is skilled in gardening," Colum declared.

"And poisons?" Kathryn asked.

Colum grasped her arm. "I heard from a servant what happened. Two villagers foully poisoned?"

Kathryn told Colum what she'd seen in the death house. "Looking at this herb plot," she continued, "I do wonder where the poisoner obtained such potions but, there again, the fields and meadows are full of dangerous plants."

"You don't suspect Lord Henry?" Colum joked.

"He was very quiet," Kathryn replied, "and stayed near the door. He"—Kathryn chose her words carefully—"he looked subdued."

Colum drew her close and put his arms around her. "Kathryn, I'm going to tell you something. I understand Isabella, the wife of Elias the Blacksmith, was murdered."

Kathryn nodded.

"Lord Henry is a courtier, a scholar," Colum continued. "Before he married the Lady Mary he was, in every way, a lady's man."

"Did he have a relationship with the blacksmith's wife?"

"Perhaps," Colum whispered, kissing Kathryn gently on the brow. "They say ladies in the village were much taken by Lord Henry. On his arrival in Walmer he was not lacking in a host of admirers."

"And the Lady Mary?"

Colum stepped back squinting at the sky. "I would call Lady Mary a mouse of a woman. She was pleasant and comely, auburn haired, sweet faced, with a rather plump figure. Her father was also a friend of the King so Edward himself arranged the match. It was a marriage of friendship rather than love. Lord Henry brought his wife to Walmer; she seemed happy enough, but then, about a year ago, she left the manor house just as the building work was being finished. She said she wished to ride, get away from the clutter, confusion, and dust. She rode to Gallows Point. Darkness fell but she never returned. A search was organised the next morning, a local wench found her body on the rocks below the point." Colum glanced away.

"What's the matter, Colum? Did she commit suicide? Was it an accident?"

Colum breathed out noisily.

"Colum," Kathryn warned. "this is one of the reasons I'm here, isn't it? There's more to this than meets the eye."

"A coroner's jury was empanelled," Colum replied slowly. "A verdict delivered that the Lady Mary had slipped, the victim of an unfortunate accident. Everyone accepted that. Lord Henry grieved and his wife's body now lies buried in the crypt at St. Swithun's Church."

Colum sighed, undid his wallet and drew out a square piece of parchment. He handed this to Kathryn. She unfolded it slowly and read the neatly formed script. The letter was written in Norman French but she could translate it easily enough.

"To the Lord Chancellor," the letter began,

Health and Greetings.
It grieves me, my lord, to lay this information before you, but I swear by all that is holy, by the body of Christ and by His sweet Mother, that I, Mary, wife of Lord Henry Beauchamp, was brutally murdered, thrown from the cliff. The perpetrator of this foul act was no less the person than my husband, Lord Henry."

Kathryn gazed up in surprise.

"Read on," Colum urged.

Kathryn did so. The letter continued, giving details of how Lady Mary had saddled her horse the previous August and ridden out to Gallows Point. How her husband, lately returned from the wars, had followed her there. As evening fell, they quarrelled and he had pushed her over the cliff. Kathryn stared in astonishment. The letter was signed, "Lady Mary Walmer." It bore her seal, a blob of green wax displaying a falcon on a perch, though the date given was the Feast of the Annunciation, March of this year.

She handed it back. "Colum, what does this mean? It's a forgery, an evil joke, a silly jape, some malicious soul hates Lord Henry."

"I wish I could say that," Colum replied quietly. "But the writing is exactly that of Lady Mary. The seal is hers and the details she gives would seriously concern any jury empanelled to hear the case."

"But the letter is written some eight months after her death."

"That's the mystery Kathryn. Nevertheless, here's a letter written in Lady Mary's hand, approved with her seal, despatched to the Lord Chancellor of England, the very man to whom Lord Henry Walmer accounts."

"I see." Kathryn closed her eyes. "The Chancellor of England is no less a person than Thomas Bourchier, Archbishop of Canterbury, who also hires me as physician for both the Crown and the city of Canterbury." She opened her eyes. "So that's why we're here?"

Colum nodded. "The King has a great respect for you, Kathryn. He knows you have crossed swords with the Vicomte Sanglier before, so does the Archbishop. They appreciate your quick wit, your sharp observation, and your tart comments. They are also deeply troubled by this letter. Yes, it could be some malicious jest, some nasty soul turning, but nevertheless, the Archbishop of Canterbury, the Lord Chancellor of England, has received a letter alleging that Lady Mary Walmer was murdered by her husband. Now, of course, this begs other questions. Was the corpse found at the foot of the cliffs Lady Mary's, or someone else? Our Lord Chancellor has made his own careful enquiries. According to the village leech, Lady Mary's face was almost unrecognisable due to the fall and the way the body had been washed up constantly against the rocks. At the end of the day"—Colum sighed—"the King wishes this letter to be investigated. He demands that justice be done and seen to be done."

"But not only for justice? The King is a wily soul."

"The King is very fearful and so is the Archbishop. If this writer were to send such a letter to them, then why not to Lady Mary's kinsmen? If such a letter became public, a blood feud might occur which would divide the court. More importantly, the King has promised that none of his subjects are above the law, and that includes Lord Henry Beauchamp. I am asking you, Kathryn, whatever way you can, to investigate this matter, but discreetly."

"Does Lord Henry know?"

Colum opened his mouth to reply, then paused, listening to the sound of swordplay from the tiltyard on the other side of the manor.

"I met him last night after you'd withdrawn from the table. Lord Henry remarked on a certain coolness on the part of the King, and asked if I knew the source. Of course, I just shrugged and laughed it off."

"But if I investigate," Kathryn declared, "sooner or later he will wonder why."

"Then sooner or later," Colum replied, "he will have to know, won't he?"

"Is Lord Henry liked in the area?" Kathryn asked. "If he came here years ago to hang the parents, the older brothers and sisters of the villagers of Walmer, there must be a blood feud between him and certain of his tenants?" She leaned against Colum and eased off her boot. She counted the pebbles lodged there.

"The wreckers came from the village but also from the farms around," Colum answered. "Evil men and women responsible for the destruction of at least a dozen ships and the deaths of over a hundred souls. There was very little sympathy for such outlaws. The village of Walmer is now peaceful. There's been petty feuds, the occasional murder and outbursts of violence, but Lord Henry seems to be well liked and respected, especially by the ladies."

"Is there anything else? Why did Lord Henry ask for you, Colum?"

"Well, because if I came, you'd have to come." Colum grinned.

"But you are a comrade of Lord Henry?"

"We came here just after the war, before I moved to Canterbury to take over the royal stables and meet a certain physician."

Kathryn picked up a fallen cherry and threw it at him. Colum quickly ducked.

"After the Battle of Tewkesbury," Colum explained, "Lancastrian rebels fled to all corners of the kingdom, some north, some into Wales, others to Cornwall. A few decided to reach Kent and its many ports, to sail for the Low Countries or France. The King divided some of his best troops into posses, each led by one of his lieutenants. Lord Henry was given a warrant to search the Weald of Kent for any Lancastrian exiles; I was part of that posse. We hunted down Lancastrians. Some resisted and were slaughtered where they stood. Others surrendered and, unless they were on the attainder list, disarmed and allowed to go home. Now, we heard of a group which had fled to the coast near Walmer. Lord Henry set off in pursuit. They decided to stand and fight, a few archers and men-at-arms whom we easily dispersed. Eventually, we were hunting the leader and two archers. We received intelligence that they'd reached Walmer and were thinking of seeking sanctuary in the church if they were unable to take ship. We followed in pursuit. However, by the time we reached Walmer, the villagers, eager to show their loyalty to the King and Lord Henry, had killed all three men. Apparently, these refugees had reached the cemetery wall and been attacked by the villagers, who hacked them to death, stripped their corpses, and threw them onto the steps of the market cross. Lord Henry, of course, had no choice but to applaud the villagers, congratulate them on their loyalty, and order the swift burial of the three corpses in the Poor Man's Plot in St. Swithun's Cemetery. And that"—Colum threw up his hands—"is what I know."

Kathryn returned to her seat and sat, hands in her lap. Colum joined her.

"Your thoughts?"

"My thought, Irishman"—she leaned over and kissed him—"is that you should shave, wash, and change. For I'm sure soon Lord Henry will wish to meet the French envoys."

"Will you come with me to rest?"

Kathryn pushed Colum gently away and smiled impishly at him.

"I still feel tired after last night. Am I not allowed to rest?"

"These murders." Colum ignored her good humour. "Do you think it's just a feud between villagers?"

"I don't know, Colum, except that, once again, we are surrounded by mystery and, before we leave Walmer, the truth will have to emerge."

Colum gripped her by the shoulder and kissed her brow.

"I shall return," he murmured.

My swaggering Irishman, Kathryn thought, watching him go. Yet Colum, in many ways, was a man-boy, some part of him had not grown up. He loved horses, he had a passion for their care. He'd talk about them or his native country until people begged him to stop. Kathryn laughed to herself. Colum was a soldier. He could be violent. He had a warrior's soul, a skilled swordsman, yet he was also gentle, passionate, and loving. Kathryn recalled the previous night and blushed to herself.

She stood up, returned to the herb plot and stared down at different plants, so beautiful under the sun. She wondered what further mysteries were hidden beneath the serenity of this luxurious manor house and the wealthy village only a mile from its gates. She could make no sense of the poisonings. Perhaps someone had a blood feud against the blacksmith and his wife? If that was the case then, perhaps, sooner or later, the assassin would make a mistake. Kathryn stared at one of the apple trees. Or was this the beginning of more poisoning? And Lord Henry? Kathryn chewed on her lip. How on earth could a letter come from his supposedly dead wife, accusing him of murder, providing details of how it happened? The letter had been on good vellum and written in a clerkly hand, the Norman French precise and correct. So it wasn't one of the villagers but someone skilled in letters. Kathryn crouched down and trailed her finger around the plants, lost in the maze of mystery growing all about her.

Adam the Apothecary was a deeply agitated man. He'd been only too pleased to escape from Walmer Manor and make his way back to his own house on Winingate Lane, which led down to St. Swithun's Church. The two-story wooden-and-plaster house stood on a stone base bordered by a garden at both front and back. Its upper level could be approached by an outside staircase as well as one within. Adam was profoundly concerned by the previous night's hideous occurrences. Elias and Isabella gone, like two candles snuffed out, leaving nothing but faint smoke in the air, their corpses stretched out on those pallets! That snooping physician from Canterbury! Adam resented her. In truth he feared her. She was sharp, that one, quick-eyed and keen witted! Her serene face, black hair, and calm eyes were a comely exterior but Adam recognised a true physician when he met one. Swinbrooke was a *peritus*, truly skilled. She knew all about herbs and potions. So how long would it be before she came down to Walmer and started prying here?

Adam sat on a three-legged stool and stared round his chamber of powders. Here, on the counter, he would distil his own potions and philtres. He'd deliberately painted this chamber black, the walls and ceilings, whilst its one window was always shuttered. Adam preferred it that way. When he ushered his customers into the room, he wanted them to feel they were in a different place, a room of power, a chamber of dark secrets. Beneath the window stood his table, mortar, pestle, measuring cups, balls of string, and pieces of leather. On the shelves around the room, neatly arranged and carefully tagged, ranged the different pots and jugs, jars and sacks, each containing a certain herb. Adam was a tidy man. He liked everything orderly. On the left, herbs for childbirth and children's diseases. White horehound, which, if boiled in water, would ease women in labour pains. Creeping Jenny, very good for a child's cough. Garlic, horinga, and camomile for the agues. Stitchwort, what was stitchwort good for? Adam prided himself on his knowledge but he was now so agitated he'd forgotten.

The apothecary sat on his stool cradling his precious blackjack of ale and gazed at the other different herbs that this chamber of secrets held. Herbs for rheumatism, gout, and painful joints: herbs for the household, for animals, for insomnia, and for those whose dreams were plagued by demons. Beneath the table, with its stout lock, stood his casket of poisons, and that's what troubled Adam; that coffer contained juice of almond, arsenic, foxglove, henbane, belladonna, and a few lesser-known poisons. So how long would it be before Mistress Swinbrooke, or some other clacking tongue in Walmer, began to wonder how the blacksmith and his wife came to be poisoned at the same time, but by different potions? Adam closed his eyes. He thanked God that his bed ridden mother, Mathilda, must be fast asleep. Adam made sure she was. He'd grown tired of her ringing that bell, banging her stick on the floor or shouting his name so loud even the neighbours in the alleyway beyond could hear. He just wanted peace. Deep in his heart he wished his mother would die and, oh, he'd been so sorely tempted! Perhaps a powerful potion just before she fell asleep?

Adam shivered, opened his eyes, and stared at the crack of light coming through the shutters. He'd done that! Yes, he'd done the same three years ago with Margaret, his wife. Margaret, always shouting and having tantrums, a scold, a harridan, and a very untidy one to boot. The kitchen was never washed, the table never scrubbed, mouldy bread never thrown out, then she'd come in here and cause the same chaos. She'd help herself to this or that. She was constantly moaning, why should they stay in Walmer? Couldn't they move to one of the great towns like Canterbury, Maidstone, or even London? Yet Adam had been born in Walmer. He wished now he'd chosen a Walmer woman for his wife instead of Margaret, who was a daughter of a local farmer some ten miles to the west. He'd married her and soon realised what a mistake he'd made. He'd never forget that screeching voice, those bony fingers poking him in bed, church, or wherever Margaret wished to bring some matter to his attention, her mouth close up against his ear whispering this or that, always resentful, jealous of everyone. Indeed, Adam believed that if he'd taken much more he would have gone deaf, and been forced to treat himself with blessed thistle, or some other remedy. Eventually he found that Margaret couldn't sleep, so it was just a matter of increasing the powders and potions mixed with a little arsenic. No one had noticed, not even her bitter-faced sister, Ursula, married to that pompous notary.

Ursula was just as bad, no wonder Benedict, her husband, liked scampering off, carrying messages for Lord Henry. A strange one, Benedict! A little richer than he should be—and why had that strange preacher, who'd appeared out of nowhere, been so interested in Master Benedict? The preacher had drawn Adam into conversation asking him questions about the notary. Adam yawned, his mind going back to Margaret. It had taken three months in all. He's started round midsummer and yes, today was the anniversary, 29 September. Three years ago Margaret had been buried, silent forever under a headstone in St. Swithun's Cemetery. Adam thought her ghost would haunt him; in fact, he'd found her murder a blessed relief. He was free to manage his house, free to go wherever he wished, free to talk to whoever he'd wanted, and that's when he'd caught Isabella's eye. Adam had always secretly lusted after her slim waist and proud breasts, that cloud of blond hair, those full red lips.

Adam recalled Isabella's corpse, lying so pathetically on the pallet. He tried to whisper a prayer but, even though he went to church, Adam believed he had no soul; if he had, it was already with the devils. The apothecary took a deep breath. What should he do? Reason told him that any poison could be collected in the fields around Walmer. Yet he had his enemies! He was frightened lest someone may have known of his secret meetings with Isabella in the woodlands, in the copse, or out in the fields, where she had lain naked and allowed him to enter her. Now she was dead, would some keen-eyed villager, or gossip—an old one like Mother Croul—recall what they'd seen? Would they start the whispering in the village marketplace about Adam the Apothecary, who lusted after Isabella, the blacksmith's wife, and didn't he know all the secrets of herbs?

Adam stared at the ceiling. Usually he lit a candle but now he'd rather sit alone and ponder in this darkened chamber. Adam was fearful of the villagers. After all, he'd remembered what happened over a year ago when those three Lancastrian refugees had come seeking sanctuary. He, and other men and women, led by the council, had raised the hue and cry with shouts of "Harrow!" and seized their swords, clubs, spades and mattocks, anything they could lay their hands on. They'd pursued these rebels down to the church. Had they slaughtered them in the heat of battle or was it a massacre? Adam had felt like a true soldier that day. The three men had tried to defend themselves, but they were weak, tired, and hungry. They'd protested their rights of sanctuary, all of it ignored. Adam had led the attack, killing one of the archers while Elias and the others surrounded the other two and cut them down. Afterwards they'd boasted about it in the village, acting like Hector or the other great heroes, yes, the Knights of Arthur's Round Table. Elias had trumpeted that he'd killed all three, only to be cried down by the rest. Others had not been so sure. The calmer souls looked sad eyed and, after all, what was so glorious about three corpses stripped and hacked, lying on the steps of a market cross? Lord Henry had come with his posse. He'd dismounted, stared at the three corpses and, not looking so pleased, ordered their burial as quickly as possible. Father Clement and his merry-eyed sister, Amabilia, had not been there that day. They'd journeyed across the Weald of Kent. On their return they had simply been informed that their cemetery had three fresh graves in the Poor Man's Plot.

Adam returned to the problem of the poisons. The fields around Walmer held herbs and plants, poisonous and beneficial, but who knew their properties? The priest and his sister? Adam smirked to himself. Neither had shown such knowledge, yet others in the village could list the dangers of mandrake or tell which mushrooms were poisonous or not. He must prepare such a list just in case he was accused. He stared at this chamber door, now locked and bolted. No one could get in to him. He'd stay here, sipping his blackjack until his tremors settled. Perhaps he'd take some camomile to ease his humours and peppermint to soothe his stomach. Swinbrooke was frightening enough, but meeting her in the presence of Lord Henry! Adam was truly fearful of that great lord of the soil. He recalled stories about how Lord Henry had hunted down the wreckers. Adam smiled weakly. For that, he really should thank God as well as Sir Henry. One of the wreckers had been Adam's uncle, he'd been hanged on the great gibbet, and this house, and all within it, had passed to Adam's father and then on to him.

The apothecary glanced up at the ceiling again. His mother was very quiet, by now she must have realised that her son had returned. Any moment now she would be shaking that bell or banging on the ceiling. Ah well, perhaps she was still asleep. He could wait. He cradled the blackjack, his thoughts going back to Lord Henry. He always liked to sit here with this blackjack, feel the leather and know what it really contained. He always relished drinking from it. He lifted it to his lips and took a deep draught. The ale tasted good; he'd drawn it fresh from the barrel in the kitchen.

Adam felt a stomach pain and recalled Elias's corpse lying out in the smithy's yard. The pain returned, a tongue of fire in his belly. He sprang to his feet, the pain spreading round to his back and up his chest, stabbing his flesh. Adam fell to his knees, the tankard slipping from his fingers. He found it difficult to breathe. He wanted to be sick, his eyes stung. What was the matter? What poison was this? Was he now a victim of the very powders he'd sold? He stared in terror at the door. He wanted to move, to crawl across, to draw back the bolt, turn the keys, scream for help, but he felt his body lacked all energy. It was so difficult to breathe, his face felt flushed, his stomach churning whilst at the same time a clammy sweat broke out. He was slipping into a nightmare. He recalled Isabella, her corpse on that wooden pallet, legs stretched out, head to one side, that hideous look on her face. And those three men, the Lancastrians on the steps of St. Swithun's Church, begging for mercy, bereft of their swords and daggers. Elias closing in, lifting the great axe he'd taken from the garden outside. The pain was so intense! Adam tried to be sick but found he was unable to; he tried to crawl, only to roll onto his side. He wondered about his mother's silence. Was there someone upstairs? Had something happened? Adam became lost in his own pool of pain, his legs kicking, coughing and retching as he died on the floor of his own secret chamber.

The library at Walmer Manor was small yet a place of beauty. A narrow-beamed ceiling spanned the chamber. A small red brick fireplace with a mantel of shiny oak was built into the outside wall. Of course, being September, the grate was empty and the fireplace hidden by a coloured screen emblazoned with the Beauchamp arms. On either side of the fireplace, to allow in as much light as possible, were two oriel windows. Beneath these stood elegantly carved carrels where Sir Henry or any scholar could sit and use the full light of the day. On the wall to Kathryn's right were shelves of books and manuscripts; she'd already taken some down, copies of Froissart and Joinville, two works of Aristotle, and St. Augustine's *City of God*. A fine collection of books, some bound in dark brown leather, others in rich red burgundy. At the far end, the wall was wainscoted, above it, a beautiful triptych depicted the Holy Family in the center with an angel on either side. The floor was polished and smelt fragrantly of beeswax. Kathryn sat at a table of purest walnut. On her left, at the top, Lord Henry stared down at a schedule of documents he'd taken from a bag. To her right sat Colum Murtagh, who'd now washed, shaved, and changed, so as to meet the French envoys, who sat opposite.

Kathryn smiled across at them. Vicomte Sanglier, in the centre, acknowledged her and bowed. *He looks like a fox,* Kathryn thought; the Vicomte's hair was brushed back, his moustache and beard neatly cut. Sanglier was not wearing his usual red but the royal colours of France, a blue-and-white cotehardie edged with fur, its sleeves gathered up. Underneath this a padded creamy doublet, the collar held close at the neck by a golden fleur-de-lys. On his head an elegant chapeau with a liripipe, which fell down under his chin and across his right shoulder. Delacroix and Cavignac were dressed similarly and, like Sanglier, wore two rings: the first displayed the royal fleur-de-lys, the other, the oriflamme, the banner kept behind the Chapel of St. Denis in Paris, which the French displayed in battle when they intended to take no prisoners.

Sanglier was intent on making sure that Colum and Lord Henry realised that they were French envoys, here to negotiate, to dictate terms, not simply accept whatever Edward of England wished to hand out.

Kathryn herself had changed into a snow white smock, over it a sea green gown tied just above the breast, on her head a simple white veil kept in place by studded clips, on her wrist a gold bracelet, a gift from Colum. Cavignac, fascinated by this, kept staring across. Kathryn noticed the smudge of red on the corner of his mouth, possibly blood. Cavignac, aware of this, rubbed at it with his fingers, their nails polished bright, and returned to his close scrutiny of her, particularly the bracelet. Unable to bear such examination any longer, Kathryn took off the bracelet and handed it to him for inspection. Cavignac studied it carefully, rolling it in his fingers.

"A work of art," he murmured. "Mistress, this is truly beautiful."

"It's Celtic," Colum spoke up. "A morning gift to my wife."

Cavignac handed it back and bowed. Sanglier kept looking at a point above her head. Kathryn didn't know if he was smiling to himself or enjoying some private joke. They'd been in the chamber for some time. The hour candle in the centre of the table, flanked by small pots of flowers, had noticeably diminished. Lord Henry seemed ill at ease. He had begun the meeting only to refer to his documents about certain items Sanglier had raised, minor matters regarding shipping in the Narrow Seas and the safe conduct of envoys in London.

Kathryn watched the lord of the manor carefully. Was he a murderer? she wondered. Did he kill his wife? She was still puzzled by that letter. How could a woman write some eight months after she'd been killed? If it was some silly jape or malicious jest, how could someone copy her hand so closely, and where did the signet seal come from?

Lord Henry coughed again and cleared his throat. "I think"— he looked up, tapping the manuscript with his finger—"I think this is a good place to start, my lord."

"Which point, my lord?" Sanglier retorted. "Where shall we

begin? Why should we begin? We've been here a while. Lord Henry, you seem at a loss. We are here at your invitation, we wish to know the contents, the thoughts of your royal master. Once we know these we will reply with thoughts of our own."

Kathryn felt like shattering these diplomatic niceties by shouting across, "Do you have the Book of Ciphers? Do you know the whereabouts of William Marshall?" However, she was only here, as Lord Henry had made very clear, as an observer, someone who'd once crossed swords with Sanglier and come off the better.

"I mean"—Lord Henry rubbed his cheeks, then leaned back in his chair—"this question of envoys! Six months ago I was accompanied to Paris by my clerk, William Marshall."

Sanglier tuttered under his breath, shaking his head.

"You may tut and you may protest," Lord Henry declared heatedly, spots of anger high in his pale face, "but William Marshall was a friend and an accredited envoy, a high-ranking clerk in the Chancery of the Green Wax. He went boating on a Tuesday afternoon, he left just after noon saying he would be back before the bells tolled for Vespers."

"I know, I know," Sanglier broke in, "and the boat he'd hired was found drifting, it was brought back to the quayside." The Vicomte spread his hands. "But of William Marhsall, or his property, no sign."

"Has the river been searched?" Colum asked.

Delacroix laughed to himself but kept his head down.

"I am sorry, sir," Colum retorted. "Am I amusing you?"

"You might as well look, how do you put it?" Sanglier scoffed. "Yes, for your proverbial needle in your proverbial hay stack, Irishman. The Seine is a great river, it is deep, beneath its surface lies the rubbish of centuries. People are lost along that river every day, their corpses never discovered."

"Did you try?" Colum asked. "Was a search party sent out?"

"The King's own fishing fleet was deployed," Sanglier replied coolly, "and they found nothing. Don't forget, my Lord Henry"—he jabbed a hand in the direction of his host—"we only have your word that Marshall was on that boat intending to fish."

"Why should I lie," Lord Henry replied, "about my friend, a high-ranking clerk? I saw him to the boat myself."

"Was anyone else with you?"

"No!" Lord Henry grasped the edge of the table as if to steady himself. "But you have my word on oath. Why should I tell a lie regarding these matters? William Marshall was hale and hearty, looking forward to a good supper. He left. I returned to my own lodgings. He never returned."

"My lord, my lord," Sanglier said, trying to soothe Lord Henry's mounting temper while he smiled at Colum, still annoyed at Delacroix's mocking laughter, "please accept my apologies."

"It's your assurances we want," Lord Henry answered, "that you know nothing of Marshall's disappearance."

"Are we here," Delacroix's voice cut across the room like a whiplash, "to debate a peace treaty between our respective masters or the disappearance of an English clerk in Paris?" He spread his hands. "My Lord Henry, every day in your great cities people disappear. We are sorry that William Marshall suffered an accident on the Seine, but it's not our fault."

"Was he not close?" Cavignac spoke up, his pleasant, youthful face hiding the malice of his words.

"Was not William Marshall close to your late wife, my lord?"

Lord Henry's agitation was apparent. He stared at the triptych and then down at his manuscripts, hands trembling. He tried to distract himself by playing with an amethyst ring on his left hand.

"Is that correct?" Sanglier took up the hunt. "Was William Marshall close to your wife? We were so sorry, Lord Henry, to hear about her unfortunate death. However, we understand that Marshall was often your messenger between yourself and Lady Mary. Perhaps he was distracted when he went boating, perhaps he was thinking of the unfortunate accident your wife had suffered?" The baiting continued. Kathryn felt a shiver of cold. These three agents of Louis XI were well briefed. They'd come to bait Lord Henry, to twist and turn like the weasels they were. They clearly had Lord Henry at a disadvantage.

"Do you have the Book of Ciphers?" The words were out of Kathryn's mouth before she could think, and the effect was immediate. The French envoys fell silent. Cavignac, smiling to himself, leaned back in his chair and crossed his arms. Delacroix joined his hands as if in prayer. Sanglier looked at her one eyebrow raised.

"The Book of Ciphers, mistress?"

Kathryn ignored Colum's nudge beneath the table, and Lord Henry's embarrassment.

"Yes, the Book of Ciphers," Kathryn declared.

"I thought you were an observer to these proceedings." Cavignac spoke without lifting his head. "I didn't realise you are now a royal envoy."

"Master Murtagh's lady wife," Lord Henry stammered, "may speak when she wishes. She enjoys the full confidence of my master, as you do yours." The manor lord was clearly relieved to be no longer the object of their taunting.

"I asked a question," Kathryn repeated. "Do you have the Book of Ciphers?"

"Mistress, what is the Book of Ciphers?"

"It was a book carried by William Marshall." Kathryn leaned forward. "About the size of a book of hours, a psalter, or breviary. It contained key ciphers, which the English Crown and its ministers used when communicating with their agents abroad. It also contained a list of names of those agents England has in France. You, I am sure, have the same arrangement in this country. William Marshall's disappearance also masks the disappearance of that Book of Ciphers."

"Well." Sanglier laughed. "If we'd found Marshall we would have found the Book of Ciphers. True." He smirked. "We have heard something about this. Mere rumours . . ."

"If we'd found the Book of Ciphers," Cavignac drawled, "I assure you, our master's soldiers would have been busy arresting those traitors who dare sell information to other princes."

"My Lord Henry," Sanglier smacked his lips, "I am hungry. We came at your request. We hoped the truce would be converted into a peace treaty to establish lasting friendship between the Kings of England and France. Yet, here we are on a pleasant September morning, making enquiries about an English clerk and a mysterious Book of Ciphers." He pushed back his chair. "Perhaps"—he gazed slowly around the chamber taking Lord Henry, Kathryn, and Colum in his glance—"when things are more organised, we could return to these matters. Until then, my lord, we shall not exchange pleasantries until we dine later today." All three rose and left the chamber.

Kathryn sat back in her chair and stared at the painted glass in a windowpane. It depicted Satan, playing bagpipes, leading a legion of souls into the dark, cavernous mouth of hell. On either side of the trackway, flames leaped and demons danced. In another scene above it, the blessed, clothed in white and gold, were being marshalled by the angels to banquet tables glowing with food and drink. The tables stood in a broad green garden where Christ and his Mother sat in a bower of flowers.

"You shouldn't have done that." Lord Henry took his hand from his face. "Mistress Kathryn, you should not have done that."

"Shouldn't?" Kathryn replied without shifting her gaze. "My lord, we have come here for that very purpose. Do the French know the whereabouts, the fate, of William Marshall; secondly, do they have the Book of Ciphers? If they do, that poses great difficulties for you and your royal master. If they don't, you can negotiate as equals."

"But now you have alerted them!" Lord Henry seemed like a hunted man, distracted, his wits frayed. He glanced away but, as he did so, Kathryn caught, just for a moment, the pleasure in his eyes. Was he acting? she thought. Is this why he kept covering his face, rubbing his cheeks and eyes. Kathryn had seen one of her patients do the same to appear fraught, to drain the face of blood and make the eyes red-rimmed.

"Well?" Lord Henry blinked, discomforted by Kathryn's hard scrutiny.

"My lord, we have made no mistakes," she replied. "I welcome your hospitality here but, I know, as you do, how the Vicomte Sanglier can dance and twirl like any maypole dancer. We need to reach the truth. You must move these proceedings on."

Lord Henry put his face in his hands again. "I shall," he said, his voice sounding hollow, "reflect on what you say, Mistress Kathryn." He took his fingers away and smiled. "Perhaps you are right. This is a matter we must settle once and for all." He shook his head. "I admit, I'm tired. These poisonings in the village have disturbed me." And, gathering his documents, Lord Henry rose, bowed, and left the library.

"You're blunt, Kathryn." Colum turned and placed a finger on the tip of her nose. "Your words were sharp, you certainly brought that meeting to an abrupt end."

Kathryn stared round this beautiful chamber with its leather-covered books, the manuscript neatly stacked, some tied with red ribbon, others with blue or green: the carrels with their ink pots, pumice stones, quills, all waiting for the scholars, the sunlight pouring through the windows, the vivid images ready to catch the eye.

"We are not really here," she murmured. "Colum, it's as if we've gone down to the coast and taken out a boat. We have no sail and the oars are gone, so we're twisting and turning on a mist-shrouded sea. I can make no sense of what has happened. But come."

They left the library and entered the small courtyard, which separated the library and chapel from the long hall of Walmer Manor. They crossed this, went through a small wicker gate, and walked over to a stone bench, standing near a small garden laid out around a fountain pool. Every type of wildflower perfumed the air about them. The fountain itself was carved in a shape of a hideous gargoyle. Kathryn wondered why the sculptor had chosen such a theme for such a pleasant place. The gargoyle was horrific. He carried the top of the fountain on his scaled back, his face demonlike with a roaring mouth, popping eyes, the taloned hands curved, ready to spring.

"The sculptor wants to illustrate how every garden has a serpent, every plesaunce its demon." Kathryn remarked as they sat down on the bench. "Walmer certainly has."

"I had to ask about the Book of Ciphers," she continued, nestling close to Colum, leaning her head on his shoulder, "to distract Sanglier from baiting Lord Henry. Colum, the situation is very dangerous. Here we have William Marshall, a trusted clerk of the Crown, a friend of Lord Henry, as well as being a friend of his late wife, who died in suspicious circumstances. Marshall disappeared in equally mysterious fashion a few months later whilst carrying the invaluable Book of Ciphers—a document of vital importance to both England and France."

"I must admit," Colum said, unclasping his leather jacket and loosening the shirt beneath, "I have never seen Lord Henry so distracted. Usually he masters such situations, skilful and quick, but today he fumbled like a school boy before his masters."

"And there's this other business," Kathryn declared, "the village has its constable, hasn't it?"

Colum nodded.

"So why did Lord Henry have the corpses brought here for me to inspect? It was obvious they'd been poisoned, murdered by person or persons unknown. It's almost as if . . ." Kathryn straightened up. "It's almost as if Lord Henry is deliberately drawing me in, wanting me to discover something. Was it guilt? You claimed there might have been a relationship between the dead woman Isabella and Lord Henry?"

Colum just shrugged. "I merely repeated gossip."

"What hour is it?" Kathryn suddenly felt sleepy, heavy eyed.

"About midday!"

Kathryn jumped at the voice behind her and spun around. Lord Henry stood there. Kathryn, peering round him, glimpsed the young boy shifting from foot to foot outside the gate.

"My lord, we did not hear you."

Lord Henry, now more composed, stared coolly at her. "Mistress Kathryn, I must ask another favour, a message from the village. There's been another poisoning, the man you met this morning, Adam the Apothecary. He's been found dead in his chamber. I would ask you, as a favour. Would you act as my coroner and investigate?"

"Dead?" Kathryn stood up.

"Poisoned!" Lord Henry answered. "That's what Walter the Constable claims. According to the boy, and his story is garbled, Adam was drinking a blackjack of ale. His bedridden mother in the chamber above shook the handbell and beat her cane on the floor but couldn't summon her son. A short while ago, a visitor to the house heard the mother shouting, the bell clanging, and went up the outside stairs. Adam's mother explained what had happened so the visitor unlocked the inside door and went down into the house. The apothecary's chamber was locked and bolted. After a great deal of knocking, the visitor realised that something was wrong and sent for the constable. The door was forced, Adam found sprawled on the floor within."

Kathryn decided to confront Lord Henry. "Why should I go there? There's a constable, a physician."

"I know your reputation, Mistress Kathryn." Lord Henry smiled. "Sharp-eyed, and keen witted. Compared to your skill, the villagers know nothing. I would deeply appreciate your involvement."

"We shall go." Colum rose, tightening his belt.

"Do you need horses from the stable?"

"No." Colum shook his head. "We'll walk down. It will do us good."

"My lord, you are not coming?" Kathryn asked.

"No, I will not." Lord Henry had turned away but came back, close to Kathryn, those strange blue eyes studying her carefully. "No, Mistress Kathryn, I will not go. I have guests and I must compose myself to be more, how shall I put it, skilful before we meet again?"

A short while later Kathryn and Colum left by the main gateway of the manor, following the trackway that wound down the hillside into the village. They'd only gone a few yards when Kathryn paused and stared out at the view.

"It's beautiful, isn't it, Colum? Look, we can see the entire village from here. There's the houses, the marketplace, the winding lanes and alleyways, the High Street. On such a day like this everything is as open as it is to God."

"Except man's heart," Colum quipped.

Ah, yes, Kathryn thought, staring down at the peaceful village, true, except for the secret doings of the human mind. Nonetheless, Walmer was a pleasant scene: its houses, fields, and small garden plots, the square tower of the church with its red tile roof. She could make out the priest's house behind the church and the great cemetery that surrounded it. Between the village and the coastline, trees and shrubbery stretched to a strip of sand, then the sea, glittering serenely under the sun. On the other side of the village rolled the countryside with its fields and meadows. The autumn harvest had been brought in early and the land slept as if enjoying the last warmth of summer. Kathryn turned and walked back towards the manor. She raised her hand to the guard. She walked past the small postern gate and, ignoring Colum's questions, continued round the wall until she stood on the brow of the hill, which swept down to the countryside below. The green pasture dipped, then rose towards Gallows Point. Kathryn could clearly make out the stark, black, three-branched gibbet, the place from where Lady Mary had fallen to her death.

On a day like this, Kathryn reflected, Lady Mary left the manor and rode up that hill. She'd have dismounted, perhaps sat under the gallows, and then what? If Lord Henry was in the manor when she died, William Marshall would have been there as well. Was that what Sanglier was hinting at? That Marshall and Lady Mary may have been lovers? Such occurrences, she mused, are not uncommon in large households, where a young squire plays court to his mistress, and affairs can quickly get out of hand. Was it possible that Lord Henry, in a fit of jealousy, killed his wife and later plotted to slay her lover?

"You're thinking about Lady Mary, aren't you?" Colum put his arms around her waist, pressing his face into the side of her neck. "Kathryn," he muttered, "we have other business."

She stood for a while, just enjoying the beautiful sunlight, the cooling breeze, the different scents of the flowers and freshly cut hay. From the manor she heard a bell chime, the sound of raised voices as maids and scullions went about their business.

"We best go down," Colum declared, "we have to see what's happened in Walmer."

Kathryn agreed and, hand in hand, they went down the trackway. At first it was rather steep. Kathryn and Colum laughed as they missed their footing but, eventually, they reached the bottom of the hill, following the track into the village. They passed the houses of wealthy farmers with their white plaster and black wood walls built on a red stone base. The roofs were no longer thatched but tiled, a sign of the growing wealth of this village, surrounded by its fertile farmlands and drawing on the profits of the sea. The High Street itself was cobbled and, because of the fair weather, doorways were opened, women gathered either talking or busy on tasks such as brewing or spinning. They paused as Kathryn and Colum passed, whispering amongst themselves, now and again a hand raised in salutation or someone calling out a greeting.

The High Street brought them into the small marketplace, where the stalls and booths were doing a merry trade. A few sold pedlars' goods such as leather, cloths, pewter, or copper, but most stalls belonged to the villagers, farmers selling their produce, fishermen eager to get rid of their previous night's catch before the day grew any longer. The crowd was busy, people moving from stall to stall or stopping at the cookshops and alehouses that surrounded the marketplace and filled the air with savoury odours. Kathryn's mouth watered at the fresh smell of baked bread and spiced meats. She realised that, apart from breakfast early in the morning, she'd not eaten. She'd like to have stopped, gather the texture of this place, move among the stalls and even visit an alehouse, but Colum, more purposeful, hurried her on. They crossed the marketplace and went down an alleyway into Winingate Lane.

Adam the Apothecary's house stood in its own ground, and a small crowd had gathered at the wicket gate. The important notables of the village were already present. Father Clement, in a grey gown, the hood pulled up against the sun, introduced Kathryn and Colum to the rest: Walter the Constable, a burly man with a bloated face and the features of a fierce mastiff under a shock of black hair, Master Benedict, the village notary, and his wife, Urusula, well-fed, self-important people with plump, arrogant faces. They had been looking forward to a busy, prosperous day in the market. They both seemed angry that they had been pulled away, yet curious, slightly fearful. Next to them, Amabilia, deep in conversation with Simon the Sexton, a red-faced balding man dressed in Lincoln green, lean and sinewy like a hunting dog. Kathryn did not like him, with his sly eyes and twisted smirk. Roger the Physician, another member of the Parish Council, was eager to get into the house. He nodded quickly at Kathryn, his narrow, unshaven face slightly flushed, eyes watering as was his beaked nose above thin, bloodless lips. He was dressed in an expensive cotehardie with a silver chain round his neck and kept sniffing at a pomander as if unable to bear the smell of his colleagues. He dismissed Kathryn's title of physician with a blink of his colourless eyes and a twist of the mouth. The medallion on the silver chain proclaimed Roger to be a member of the Guild of Physicians of Farringdon Ward in London, and Kathryn wondered why such a man should be living in Walmer. Mother Croul was also there, standing slightly apart, resting on her cane.

The priest finished the introductions and the villagers gathered round Kathryn. Ursula, the notary's wife, sharp-eyed and vinegar mouthed, surveyed her from head to toe. She had what Kathryn considered a nasty face, made more so by the white coif she'd bound tightly to her head. Walter the Constable was all puffed up like a barnyard cock, ready to protest at Colum and Kathryn's interference, though he knew better: Lord Henry was not only lord of the manor, he also had the power of a coroner, and could decide who should investigate any mysterious death. Kathryn kept smiling, despite the near-open hostility of these village people. She turned to Father Clement. Behind him stood Amabilia, hands clasped as if in prayer, Ave beads wound between her fingers.

"Father, what has happened here?"

"I shall tell you what happened here." Ursula spoke up harshly. "I came, as I always do, to visit Adam's mother, Mistress Mathilda. I was only halfway up the stairs yet I could hear her shouting, the stick banging on the floor, bell jingling, so I continued. When I opened the door"—she pointed to the top of the outside stairs—"what a sight! Mistress Mathilda was sitting in bed, shaking her bell, screaming as if possessed. I calmed her down and she explained what had happened. So I undid the bolt—"

"Undid the bolt?" Kathryn intervened.

Ursula tilted her head back, like a hungry chicken. "No, I unlocked the door, that's it, I unlocked the inside door. I went down the stairs into the rest of the house. The small cellar was empty, as were the kitchen and scullery. I thought, ah, Adam must be in his, what he called his chamber of powders, sometimes his dark chamber. He liked to tease people, did Adam, even frighten them. Anyway, I knocked on the door, I heard no reply, so I came out here. I met Walter the Constable and asked if he'd seen Adam in the marketplace, he said no."

"I'm always there," Walter spoke hoarsely. "I am always in the market looking for those who steal. We have a legion of beggars, mistress! A veritable legion of beggars! I hadn't seen Adam," he added as an afterthought. "So I joined Mistress Ursula inside the house. We banged and we knocked so, eventually"—he sniffed up all the importance he could muster—"I gave the order for the door to be broken down. I went outside and commandeered certain men. We forced the door. Once we were inside it was terrible, Master Adam lying on the floor all contorted, his face well, you can see for—"

"On that day," a strong voice echoed from the market behind them. "On that day, the Lord God will come with his angels and, with all the fires of hell, the angels will sift the good from the bad, the sheep from the goats so, on that day, where will you be standing? Remember this—on the Day of the Wrath and the Day of Mourning, we shall see heaven and earth burning."

Kathryn whirled round and stared back across the marketplace. The market cross was now empty of the children who had been playing there, the women sitting and chatting. Instead, a sombre figure, dressed like a raven in black from head to toe, was holding forth. Kathryn couldn't make out his face but the voice was strong and as vibrant as a trumpet. She left the group and walked back across the cobbles.

"What shall we be pleading?" The preacher was now attracting a goodly crowd. "What shall we be pleading when the just are mercy needing? Oh, see what fear our hearts will rend when from heaven the judge descends." His melodious, chanting voice caught peoples' attention.

Kathryn forced her way through the crowd. The man was of medium height, black hair and beard straggling down, his face burnt dark by the sun, his powerful hands punching the air as he cried out his dire warnings. The very music of his sermon, the way he moved, made the crowd forget they were in the marketplace. Instead, in the twinkling of an eye, this man was making them think about what would happen when the world ended and the elements melted in fire.

"You people of Walmer." The preacher now decided to notice the crowd. "You people of Walmer are no different from any others." And he launched again into the horrors yet to come.

Kathryn stood for a while. She was always fascinated by such preachers, the way they moved, the power of their voices, the colour of their language, the way they could entrance a crowd: she often wished other priests who sermonised on Sunday had a little of the fire which inspired such men.

"Kathryn." Colum caught her arm. "He's just a wandering preacher. Father Clement says he arrived here some days ago. We mustn't give offence to the others, they are waiting . . ."

Kathryn walked back to the group and apologised for being distracted.

"I wish he'd go," Walter growled. "I wish he'd just pick up his staff and go elsewhere. Life can be difficult enough without being reminded of the four last things."

"Which are?" Kathryn teased.

"Why, mistress, heaven, hell, purgatory, and judgement." Walter screwed up his eyes. "I'm only a constable, sometimes a painter, not a theologian. I think you best ask Father Clement.

I've not put them in the proper order, have I, Father?"

"The preacher does no harm." The priest gestured across the marketplace. "And why should I object to those who wish to help my work in the Lord's vineyard? Mistress, you'd best come in and see what I have."

Chapter 3

They entered the house by the back door. Kathryn noticed how clean and tidy everything was: a small house, and yet everything had its place. In the whitewashed solar fresh rushes were strewn on the floor. The wooden tables and chairs, as well as the brass implements hanging near the fireplace, had all been polished so they gleamed in the poor light coming through the windows. The same was true of the passageway, which smelt richly of herbs. The kitchen and scullery were scrubbed clean, and crushed herbs had been sprinkled on the stone-flagged floor. The door of the chamber of powders still hung awry on its hinges. Inside Kathryn caught those smells so familiar to her from her own shop in Ottemelle Lane in Canterbury. Again, everything was orderly, the shelves around the room neatly labelled and divided into sections. Herbs for children, herbs for childbirth, for animal husbandry. Kathryn spent little time on these, but crouched beside the corpse lying on the paved floor. Someone had thrown a blanket over it. She pulled this back. Adam the Apothecary sprawled there, face slightly crooked as if trying to look up at her, eyes open, the irises rolled back, lips gaping. A white froth dripped from the corner of his mouth to stain the floor. His face had a ghastly colour, as if someone had smeared purple powder on either cheek. She felt his neck—his skin was clammy cold—

his shoulders and fingers already stiffening in the rigidity of death. She picked up the blackjack and examined it. The acrid odour convinced her. She'd smelt the same on Elias the Blacksmith.

"Deadly nightshade," she muttered. "Someone put deadly nightshade in his tankard of ale. She saw the three-legged stool also knocked over and, gingerly walking round the pool of poisoned ale, put this right and sat down cradling the blackjack in her hands.

"Adam came here this morning, probably after he returned from Walmer," she declared to those gathering around her. "He wanted to be by himself and sat here sipping the blackjack. He locked and bolted the door, and that sealed his fate. He would have had but little time to cry for help." She sniffed at the blackjack. "This was a powerful infusion. He'd feel suddenly ill, sickness would begin, and the effects would be wrenching. Adam would turn giddy and faint, his knees would buckle, he'd fall to the floor and find it difficult to move, that's why he never reached the door to raise the alarm. Where did he draw the ale from?"

"The kitchen." Walter spoke up. "Come, mistress." The constable seemed slightly more mollified. "I will show you."

They all went back along the passageway. Kathryn wished the constable had kept the others out but she didn't want to give offence so she allowed them to stand around the table while she examined the jug of ale, and the barrel it was drawn from.

"Neither are tainted," she declared, after examining both. "So how did this happen?" Immediately above, a voice shouted. Kathryn ignored it. She noticed a shelf high on the kitchen wall under which hooks had been placed. From each of these hung three blackjacks; the fourth hook was empty. Kathryn went outside, sprinkled what was left of the poisoned ale onto the soil, came back, and placed the blackjack on the empty hook.

"This is indeed a mystery. Adam came in here, took the blackjack down, and filled it with ale from the jug which he'd drawn from the barrel in the buttery. He then went down to his chamber of powders. Adam wanted to sit there alone. He locked and bolted the door. He must have been worried," Kathryn continued, "probably reflecting on the mysterious death of Elias and his wife yesterday evening. He drinks the ale, is poisoned, and dies without raising the alarm. Now, what is most mystifying is how the poison got into the ale."

"Perhaps he put it there himself." Mother Croul, standing behind the rest, spoke up. Walter the Constable turned and tutted under his breath.

"Someone must have put it in the tankard," Ursula said.

"Yes," Kathryn replied. "But how did they know that Adam would take that particular tankard down this morning. Moreover, there are only two entrances to this house. One is the back door—"

"And Adam kept that locked all the time," Walter interjected, "because of his precious powders; he always kept the key safe."

"And if someone had broke in here yesterday, or this morning, while Adam was up at the manor," Kathryn replied, "the apothecary, a very neat and careful person, would have noticed that."

"And the outside stairs to the other entrance," Father Clement declared, "are very steep. I used to visit Mistress Mathilda but now I can't." He leaned down and rubbed his knees. "Inflammation, needle pain! Adam used to give me some powders, but eventually I stopped coming, nothing really works."

"It's your poor knees," Amabilia intoned. "It's his knees, mistress, he finds it difficult even to climb into the pulpit."

"But someone," Walter spoke, "could have come up the outside staircase, visited Mistress Mathilda, unlocked her door, and come down the inside stairs."

"But that's impossible," Ursula snapped. "Mathilda would allow no one to go through that door, and, I tell you, she is a light sleeper. Moreover, even if they stole down here, they'd have to move silently. Mathilda's legs may be poor but her hearing and her eyesight are keen enough."

Kathryn, mystified, returned to the chamber of powders. She had no doubt that Adam was a victim of the same assassin who, the previous evening, had killed both Elias and his wife, but again, the real mystery was how and why. She stared down at the corpse.

"It should be moved to the death house."

"I would like you to come to the church." The priest spoke up quickly, he looked agitated, his eyes red rimmed as if he'd been crying. He wasn't shaved and his robe had been thrown on as if in a hurry. "Mistress, I think you should come to the church. I want to show you and the other members of the council something. Perhaps, mistress, if you haven't eaten, you could sup there?"

Kathryn accepted this kind offer, as did the rest, now ominously silent as they realised another ghastly murder had taken place.

"I think we're all in danger," the priest murmured.

"What do you mean, danger? Are we all in danger?" Walter asked, rubbing his paunch. "Is everyone in Walmer in danger?"

"I don't know," Father Clement murmured. "I just wanted you to come and see what I've seen, but first, we must finish here."

They left the chamber, went back through the kitchen and up the outside staircase. Kathryn noticed how steep it was. By the time she and Colum had reached the top even the Irishman was cursing quietly underneath his breath. She knocked at the door.

"Come in," the voice screeched.

Kathryn opened the door and went inside. The bedchamber was comfortable enough. The ceiling beams were rather low but the walls were covered in a creamy whitewash, and here and there hung a coloured cloth or a small tapestry. The bed dominated the chamber; the old woman lying there had the blankets piled high around her. She leaned against the bolsters gazing malevolently at Kathryn. She straightened up as her visitors entered.

"What's this?" she screeched. "Is all of Walmer invading my bedchamber? What is this?" She turned as if to pick up the large bell from the table next to her bed. She then remembered, took her hand away, and began to sob quietly. Kathryn went and sat on the edge of the bed. She could smell the spices Adam had used to cover the odours of a sickroom. She noticed the stained cup on the other side of the bed, as well as the pots and bowls for washing, and the dirty napkin that covered them. She glanced down the chamber, where chests lay opened, their lids thrown back. Large walking canes were placed carefully round the room so Mistress Mathilda could hobble out of bed and grasp one easily enough. There were two other doors and, by patiently questioning Mathilda and ignoring the rest as they clustered into the room, Kathryn established that the side door led down to the house whilst the other crossed a small hallway into Master Adam's bedroom. She received the old woman's permission to look there. The hallway itself was bare, small wooden pegs driven into the wall on either side, and then another door. Kathryn opened this. The chamber inside was very similar to Mathilda's but more tastefully furnished, clean and neat, nothing out of place. Kathryn returned to the sickroom. Mathilda was now crying through her fingers: what was to happen to her? Who would look after her now that her son was dead? Kathryn sensed there was little love between mother and son. Mother Mathilda was more concerned about herself than what had happened downstairs. Kathryn managed to subdue the hubbub and returned to her seat by the bed. Mathilda, however, was now glaring at Colum as if he was some demon from hell.

"I've never liked Irishmen," she whispered. "And I don't like them in my bedchamber." Colum shrugged, walked down the room and stood by the side door.

"Mistress Kathryn." Mathilda grasped Kathryn's hand while the old woman's rheumy eyes studied her carefully. "They say you're a physician. Can you cure me, physician?" The question was tinged with mockery.

"I can't cure you, mistress. I'm not here for that but to find out who murdered your son." Kathryn regretted her words. No sooner were they out of her mouth when the old woman threw her head back and begun to sob loudly, crying out "What will befall me, what will befall me?" Eventually Kathryn placated her.

"What happened here this morning?" she asked.

"I'm a very light sleeper." The old woman shook her head as if talking to herself. "Master Adam, well, he was up early, long before dawn. He came in here and told me about the deaths of Elias and Mistress Isabella." The old woman sniffed. "Good riddance to both, I never did like them. Master Elias, well, he always charged more than he should, you know?"

"Yes, mistress," Kathryn soothed. "What did Adam say?"

"He said he'd received a message from Lord Henry." Again she sniffed. "The two corpses were to be taken up to the manor. A physician, he must have meant you, had arrived and the corpses were to be examined, so away he went."

"And was that side door locked?" Kathryn asked.

"Oh yes. What Adam would do was lock that door, turn the key from this side, then leave by the outside stairs, and then go down, round to the back door." Mathilda talked as if Kathryn was hard of hearing. "He'd go in by the kitchen, he always made sure his precious chamber of powders was secured, then he'd leave. I'd hear him turning the key in the back door, then he'd go about his business as he always went about his business. I'm glad, mind you," Mathilda chatted on, "my son had some happiness before he died. That hideous wife of his, well, mistress, she was a slut, no better than a tavern slut."

"Hush, now," Father Clement broke in, "it is wrong to speak ill of the dead."

"This morning," Kathryn insisted, "your son, Adam, locked the inside door and went down the outside stairs. You heard him leaving?"

"I heard him securing the house, then I dozed for a while."

"And no one came up here?" Kathryn asked.

"Why should they? I told you I'm a light sleeper. If anyone came through that door or tried to turn that key I would have seen them, I would certainly have heard them!"

"And nothing suspicious happened during the rest of the morning?"

"No, mistress, I heard my son return. I thought he'd come up here but he didn't, so I thought, best leave him be. He liked a few moments to himself. Yes, that's right, I heard him in the kitchen, then walk along the passageway. I heard the door to the chamber of powders open and close. I thought, once he's finished there, I shall use my bell. It's good for a man, isn't it, mistress, to be alone sometimes?"

Kathryn reassured her and left the chamber, the others following. She went back down, inspected the kitchen, the beer keg and the jug of ale, then lifted the offending blackjack from its hook. It felt heavy in her hand. She took it over and placed it in a bucket of water.

"I think its best left there. Master Walter, you'll take careful account of what's in this house and seal the chamber of powders."

"I can't seal the house as I did Elias's," Constable Walter replied, "Mistress Mathilda still has to be looked after."

"I'll see to that." Amabilia spoke up. "Perhaps some of our flock will visit her."

Kathryn nodded and returned once more to examine the corpse. "Keep the others out," she whispered to Colum. He did so tactfully, making them gather outside the doorway as Kathryn returned to the chamber of powders. Once again she examined the corpse, the stool, and the pool of poisoned ale, its strong, yeasty tang which would have disguised the poison.

"You'll sup at the church?" Father Clement's voice carried into the chamber.

"Yes, yes, I will. I'll be honoured to be your guest," Kathryn replied over her shoulder. "And perhaps other members of the council? I'd like them there as well. I have certain questions to ask."

"There is something else," Kathryn whispered to herself. She moved the corpse over onto its back. A gasp of air escaped from his stomach. Kathryn tried not to look at those horror-stricken eyes as she felt along his belt for the ring of keys. Eventually she found them clasped on a small hook. She moved across to the poison chest beneath the table under the window. She'd glimpsed this before but had not mentioned it for fear of the constable's interference. She pulled the heavy chest out and carefully undid the three locks. The chest contained two trays, one beneath the other, each divided into small boxes. In each box was a pouch carefully tagged with the name of a poison. Kathryn was surprised. Adam was well stocked with red and white arsenic, belladonna, deadly nightshade, poison mushroom, tansy, mandrake. On the floor of the box was what Kathryn was really looking for—the poison ledger—a thick folio bound in black leather with a mandrake embossed on the front and held closed by a clasp. Kathryn opened it. The first parchment pages were yellow and cracked with age, the others more recent, smooth and white. Each page was the same, as the law directed, carefully laid out, providing details of every purchase in a fine clerkly hand: what was bought, how much, by whom, whilst the last two right-hand columns provided the price and date. Kathryn closed it and crossed to the doorway.

"I'll take this."

"You can't!" Walter protested. "Everything has to be sealed until the coroner has decided."

"Lord Henry is the coroner," Colum replied. "He will decide. Until then Mistress Kathryn will take the book."

Walter and the others were clearly agitated. Kathryn wondered how much they had to hide. The ledger she held was really a Book of Secrets. It might not only reveal the name of the poisoner but describe who in Walmer had been buying what. In a place like this everyone had secrets to hide. Kathryn stared back into the chamber. Someone had lit two rushlights but that made it look even more sinister.

"This is a fine house," she mused aloud, "and this chamber has been used as an apothecary's for some years. How did Adam obtain it?"

"He inherited it from his uncle," Mother Croul shouted from the back. "His uncle was a bad one, mind you, a wrecker, one of those Lord Henry hanged at Gallows Point."

"He also married well, his late wife, Margaret, was my sister." Ursula sucked on her teeth, glaring at Kathryn from head to toe. "We're not all peasants, you know. My father was a wealthy farmer, raised cattle he did, and sheep, sold the wool for export."

"I'm sure he did." Kathryn smiled. "But Adam was a widower?"

"My sister married him. Adam had been a scholar, went to the cathedral school at Ely. He was meant for the halls of Cambridge but his father brought him back. Had a good knowledge of medicine, did Adam, then he married my sister and inherited this house, that's how he could buy all these powders." Ursula sniffed. "Much good it did him!"

"And how long was he a widower?"

"About three years. Margaret died of stomach pains about three years ago."

Kathryn clutched the Book of Poisons closer to her. The more she stayed here, the more she felt this house to be a sinister, menacing place. The very fact that Ursula had indicated how her sister had died made her suspicious. She'd only met Adam for a short while but what she'd seen she hadn't liked. In Canterbury Kathryn was always perturbed by the number of deaths, quite sudden, from pains in the stomach or the back of the head. Unless a skilled leech or physician was present, someone could be quickly buried, their death dismissed as an act of God, rather than the work of man, the sin of murder. She decided that sometime very soon, she would ask Mistress Ursula a little more about Margaret's death.

"Well, we'd best go." Colum, thumbs thrust into his war belt, walked forward. The members of the Parish Council scattered like chickens before a fox. They'd studied Colum most closely and grown exceedingly wary of this tall, dark-faced Irishman with his deep-set eyes, firm mouth and chin, the way he swaggered, the war belt around his waist, the scabbard tapping against the top of his dark leather riding boots. The Irishman acted with authority, he was a close friend of Lord Henry and, therefore, a man of power. Moreover, the villagers remembered how, during the recent civil war, they'd met such men: Irish mercenaries loyal, body and soul, to the House of York. Colum stopped.

"You, sir." He pointed to Roger. The physician, pinched faced and watery eyed, glared back.

"Adam is dead," Colum declared, "his soul has gone to God so for him this world is over. You must take his corpse to the death house."

"Yes, you must," Kathryn agreed. "The poison will make his belly swell. He will not be a pleasant sight. I suggest he be washed and cleaned quickly. Father, his burial should take place soon, certainly by tomorrow morning, as should Elias's and Isabella's."

"It's my task," Walter intervened, "to remove corpses and decide when they're buried."

Colum smiled. "As long as he's removed and buried tomorrow morning, I couldn't give a fig, sir, what you decide."

"The body will be removed," Father Clement joined in. "I'll get an arrow chest sent down from the church." He turned to Simon the Sexton.

"Don't worry," the sly-eyed man replied. "The corpse will be moved as soon as possible."

They left the house, back into the street. The sparkle of the day had gone. Kathryn noticed how the sky was duller, the marketplace didn't seem so merry and bustling. A woman pushed by them, a dead chicken in her hand as she made her way back up to the town to the communal bakehouse. Across the alleyway a beggar on slats, drunk as a sot, kneeled against the wall, half-asleep, mucus draining from his mouth and nose. The trackway was rough and filled with slime and ordure. Kathryn, glancing over her shoulder at the villagers behind her, missed her footing. Colum caught her. He smiled lazily down at her. Suddenly, Kathryn felt angry. She shouldn't be here! She didn't want to be here. She should be back in Ottemelle Lane with Thomasina making sweet bread. She should be working in her herb garden with Wulf leaping about the grass, or in her spice room with Agnes cutting up different herbs and grinding them. She glanced down the lane at St. Swithun's with its four-gabled gate and, beyond it, the tower and nave soaring up against the darkening sky; the church's yellowish stone and red slate roof made it seem like a building glimpsed in a dream.

"There's been murder, has there?" Kathryn whirled round.

The preacher stood like a crow. No, Kathryn thought, a raven, sharp featured and clever eyed. He was gazing amusedly at her. He clawed at his tangled hair and beard as if trying to make himself presentable: his steady gaze held Kathryn's. She noticed how sunburnt his face was, whilst the hem of his black gown was encrusted with a fine white dust. Kathryn didn't like the way the preacher kept staring at her.

"*Est vous fatigúe?*" she said in French. "*Vous êtes un étranger ici?*"

"*Mais oui, madame.*" The preacher closed his eyes as he realised his mistake, then he opened them and grinned. He would have turned away but Kathryn caught him by the arm. He raised his walking staff but lowered it as Colum half drew his sword.

"Madame, you are observant."

"Your face is sunburnt," Kathryn replied, "I noticed the salt, the brine on your gown. Now, you're either witless and have been wading in the sea or you have recently been aboard a ship, lashed by salt water. I asked you a question in French: 'Are you tired? You are a stranger here?' and you replied immediately in the same tongue."

"As I said, you are most observant, madame."

"I just wondered why a preacher, who can travel across the narrow seas from France, should come to a village like Walmer? And yes, there's been a murder. Did you know the victim, Adam the Apothecary?"

"I talked to him about his immortal soul." The preacher sighed.

Kathryn tightened her grip on his arm. "Well, that's now with God, so why are you in Walmer?"

"To save souls, mistress." He gently freed himself from her grip, winked at Colum, and strolled away.

Kathryn and Colum, escorted by their small retinue consisting of Father Clement, Amabilia, Simon, Walter, Benedict, Ursula, and Roger the Physician, entered the High Road, passing houses where the doors were thrown open, dogs and children ran about, the clack of spinning wheels whirled through the air. Old men sat in the sunlight, perched on stools, their feet resting on wooden chests containing a pot of glowing charcoal to keep them warm as the air was turning chilly. The smell of baking bread and roasting salted meat mixed with the stench of sour vegetables, wet wood, and the slops piled high in a heap in the centre of the high road where mewling cats and reckless crows clashed in bitter conflict. Kathryn walked as if in a dream. These people resented her as a stranger and an intruder. The news of the violent deaths must now be common knowledge as was the news that the lord of the manor had intervened to send these strangers to poke and pry.

On the corner of Carter Lane Walter paused self-importantly to consult, as he put it, with his bailiffs preparing to place a line of beggars and malefactors into the finger, head, and arm stocks. The groans of these men and women were pitiful. The sight of two red-faced and flustered women who'd been caught playing naughty and were about to be placed across a barrel to be birched, deepened Kathryn's agitation.

"Master Walter." She gripped the Constable's arm. "Master Murtagh and I are enjoying our wedding days. We are the honoured guests of Lord Henry." She gestured at the ragged line of miscreants. "Perhaps a pardon? Compassion for them?"

"The law is the law, mistress." Walter's chest puffed out like that of a pigeon preening itself. "Justice must be done and seen to be done."

"Read this." Colum opened his wallet and thrust a cream-coloured square of parchment bearing green and red seals into the constable's fat fingers. "Read it, go on."

Walter undid the parchment and stared down, lips moving slowly.

"It's written to all sheriffs, bailiffs, and officers of the Crown, that what the bearer of that document has done, he had done for the good of the King and the welfare of his realm." Colum paused. "And if you can't read it, it's signed Edwardus Rex, and carries the mark of his personal signet ring and that of his chancellor. Now," Colum raised his voice, "I declare this day, the Feast of St. Michael, a holy day, a kind of jubilee! Constable, free the prisoners!"

Walter's lower lip trembled, even as the prisoners raised ragged cheers at their good fortune. The constable stepped forward, thumbs beneath the leather belt around his paunch. Colum's hand fell to the hilt of his sword. Walter hastily stepped back.

"Free the prisoners," the constable bawled. "Now, sir." He flicked his fingers at Colum. "Down here."

With Father Clement murmuring praises at Colum's mercy and Amabilia eloquent with ejaculations such as 'Praise be the Lord and have mercy on all of us,' Kathryn and Colum followed Walter as he waddled down Carter Lane. This was a broad thoroughfare lined with stalls on each side, selling cloths and leather goods. Most of these were now closed, guarded by apprentices. The sons and daughters of the owners there had retired to the nearest alehouse, cookshop, or one of the great taverns, The Silver Swan, or Blue Boar for a pot of ale and something to eat. At last they reached Elias's yard. The rear gate was bolted and covered with the constable's seals. Still huffing and puffing, Walter tore these seals off, lifted the bar, and led them into the cobbled yard, a large open space with a cess pit in the centre for the filth to drain away. The yard reeked of burnt hair, charcoal, and the heavy tang of horse manure. The smithy itself was a large open shed at the back of the house: anvils, hammers, pincers, and bent nails lay about. The forge door hung open, grey ash spilling out to cover a pair of powerful bellows. Halters and horse collars hung from hooks on the upright beams. Kathryn, ignoring the rest milling about, stared at the dust-filled forge. It seemed to symbolise this empty, ghost-haunted yard. She shivered as she recalled the words uttered by the priest on Ash Wednesday. "*Remember, man, that thou art dust and unto dust you shall return.*" She felt full of life, of the love between herself and Colum: she was confident, at peace with herself and those around her, yet this dirty, deserted yard was a powerful reminder of the fickleness of life.

"Kathryn?"

She patted Colum's arm and walked towards the shattered butt. Its slats lay about and the copper bowl it once held had been turned upside down. She picked up a stick, turned the bowl over, and sniffed carefully at the rim. It was now odour free. She sighed and passed through the forge. A blackjack lay by a stool. She plucked this up by the handle and sniffed; a nasty odour like old fat burnt on a skillet made her recoil. She glanced back. The others were clustered about just inside the gate, gossiping amongst themselves. Colum, tired of their company, was admiring a horseshoe, running his finger around the curve. The copper container glinted in the weak sunlight like a beacon drawing her into the hideous acts committed here. Yesterday evening the water butt had stood in its barrel near the gate, a wire mesh over it to keep out the dirt and dust so it would only collect the purest rainwater, fresh as from any spring. The gate to the smithy's yard would be open, people would be coming and going. It would be so easy for the assassin, during that twilight time, to slip through the gate, cross the yard, and pour the poisonous powder through the grille into the water. She could imagine the blacksmith bawling for his blackjack of water, he drinks two stoups and Elias's soul is for the dark.

Kathryn took one further look around the smithy, put the blackjack down, and approached the rear door, sealed with dirty blobs of white wax bearing the constable's mark. Kathryn broke these seals and pushed open the door. The kitchen inside was dank and dark, its window shuttered. Kathryn pulled these aside, when a sound behind made her whirl round. She stifled her gasp. Two grey rats nosing among the food left on the table scampered to the edge; one rose on its back legs, its pointed snout sniffing the air. Kathryn grasped a pewter cup and threw it, and the rat scampered away. She heard a furious scratching on the kitchen door and hurried across to open it: a long, black-haired tomcat burst into the room in hot pursuit of the rats, streaking through the half-opened buttery door like the shadow of death. There was a clatter, a hideous squeal, and the cat came loping back, a large rat dangling from its jaws. It slipped through the half-opened back door just as the constable, accompanied by the rest, rushed in. Walter was all ready to protest, so Kathryn ordered Colum to keep him and his companions outside. The Irishman closed the door and Kathryn went slowly round the kitchen.

The beef left on the table was rat gnawed, and flies buzzed about it. She noticed the three-branched silver candelabra, the fine pewter plates and goblets. On the floor lay the cup from which Isabella had drunk, still reeking of a bittersweet odour. Kathryn studied the wine cask resting on its wooden trestle, squat and sinister, the peg in the bunghole waiting to be turned. Kathryn crouched down and twisted the crude wooden peg, and the wine poured out splashing onto the floor. She took a pewter cup, filled it, and raised it to her nose. The Bordeaux was rich and strong, yet she still caught the bittersweet taste of almonds. Poor Isabella, agitated and distraught, shocked by her husband's brutal death, would not have realised what was happening. She'd have broached the cask and drunk deep of her own death. Kathryn straightened up, wondering how and why the wine was poisoned in the first place.

"Kathryn, Kathryn, are you well?"

Colum was standing at the doorway, hand on his sword hilt.

"The Parish Council"—he grinned sheepishly—"are becoming restless and hungry."

"So is God, Colum." Kathryn half smiled back. "He's hungry for justice, for these bloody mysteries to be resolved and justice carried out for the victims." Kathryn winked at him. "Please ask them to wait a little. Fasting will be good for both their bodies and their souls."

She returned to examine the cask of wine. She glimpsed the stamp, letters burnt into the cask that proclaimed it came from the vineyards of the Castle of Mauleon on the borders of Gascony. She could find nothing else. So, where had the wine been poisoned? Here in the house or elsewhere? Kathryn knew the bunghole of any wine cask could be opened and resealed, that it was a well-known trick of importers who wished to water down the wine and make a greater profit. Kathryn stared around the dank kitchen. But how, and why, had Isabella chosen that particular cask, for that particular day? She let the wine from the cask run out onto the kitchen floor. It was best if the cask be emptied and later burnt. She'd tell Walter the Constable the same.

Kathryn left the kitchen. In the passageway outside she discovered a battered door leading down to the cellar. It creaked open on its leather hinges. Kathryn returned to the kitchen, lit a tallow candle, and walked slowly down the steep stairs, clutching the coarse guide rope pegged to the cellar wall. The cellar reeked of filth: when she reached the bottom a slight scuffling alarmed her. She reached out the thick squat tallow candle and stifled a scream. On the floor, at the bottom of the stairs, Elias and his wife had placed a wooden board covered with a thick glue, a common device to trap rodents and cockroaches, after which the board was removed and burnt. This plank of wood bore the corpses of vermin, beetles, a rat and a number of mice, one of whom was still alive flailing about weakly. Kathryn stretched out her boot, kicked the board away, and stepped down. The cellar ceiling was low; slightly hunching, Kathryn raised the candle and gazed about.

"A place of ghosts!" she murmured, trying to ignore the sound of that gruesome scuffling. She was aware of that awful stench! Kathryn covered her nose and mouth, wishing she had a pomander. She breathed in again deeply, trying to dispel the feeling of nausea. She smelt the perfumed cream she'd rubbed into her hand that morning and relaxed. She must concentrate on this cellar, no more than a square with dirty lime-washed walls. Old tools stood stacked in one corner, some broken furniture, a barrel of ale already broached, its tap still dripping slowly. A pile of old clothing, cracked jars and discarded pots and pans lay next to this. Kathryn found a pole and sifted through the rubbish. She eventually found the wine store, but these were only a stack of sealed jars brought from some vinter—she could find no other cask.

Kathryn was glad to flee the cellar and continue her search of the rest of the house. The place was comfortable but she sensed a lack of care, an absence of warmth. The paved stone floors were dirty, the rushes none too clean. The solar was well furnished but the candlewicks were untrimmed and the air reeked of cheap oil lamps. The tapestries were of poor quality and slightly moth-eaten. In the far corner of the solar Kathryn discovered a narrow door leading to a small cubicle that contained a stained desk, a high-backed chair, and a stool. A narrow place with an arrow-slit window high on the wall, this must have served as a writing office. There were a few manuscripts but no books. Kathryn sifted amongst the grease-stained parchment and found a calfskin-bound, yellow-edged ledger in which Elias kept his accounts. Kathryn put this outside the door to collect later and went up the corner stairs to the rooms on the second storey. One was completely bare, the other had two trestle beds, stools, a table, and a broken crucifix hanging on the wall with some pegs driven in just beneath it. Kathryn guessed this must have been where the maid and the apprentice slept. It was stripped bare of all possessions. Kathryn recalled how Lord Henry had promised that he would take the two children in to his own care, allocating them posts in his kitchen.

The principal bedchamber was more comfortable with its four-poster bed that boasted blue-and-gold hangings. A triptych on the wall displayed scenes from the life of St. Dunstan, the patron of blacksmiths. A large ambry full of clothes stood next to a chest of personal belongings, trinkets, and jewellery. Kathryn went through these but found nothing amiss. She pulled back the shutters of the window and stared out through the thick leaded glass. The street below was empty, people were still enjoying their midday rest after a frenetic morning's work. A child raced by chasing a dog, followed by an old man tottering on his cane. He made his way across, pulling at the leash of two tamed weasels who seemed more intent on fighting each other than following their master.

Kathryn turned away and stared around the bedchamber. The counterpane of the bed was of blue-and-gold worsted, a tawny dress with a white kirtle lay on the side. Was Isabella preparing to change that fatal evening? Kathryn walked across to the lavarium. The bowl was empty but the jug was full of water on which dust and dirt now settled. On the edge of the bowl were two white napkins, neatly folded, and a bar of precious castile soap. Kathryn picked this up and sniffed, savouring the rich, sweet smell. She put this back and wiped her fingers on a napkin. Isabella had definitely intended to wash and change, but why? To celebrate the Feast of St. Michael? Kathryn recalled the kitchen, the small rib of rat-gnawed beef in its dripping pan on the table. Yes, some sort of celebration, but was there any connection between St. Michael and the Guild of Blacksmiths?

Kathryn sat down on the edge of the bed. She felt as if the ghosts of those two hapless victims were close by, reluctant to leave this place. She closed her eyes and whispered the requiem. What she'd sensed here was a sadness, of two souls whose lives had been riven by suspicion, anger, and spiteful argument. Elias was, undoubtedly, a good smith, a craftsman, but his house showed little wealth apart from his wife's clothing and that small coffer of jewellery Kathryn had found in the great chest. Had Elias drunk the profits and, in fits of generosity, tried to placate his wife with costly gifts, dresses, robes, trinkets, and castile soap? Kathryn opened her eyes and smiled grimly. She recalled her first marriage to the drunken Alexander Wyville. He had been the same, aggressive and violent, but then tried to soothe her with some bauble bought from a goldsmith. She'd not kept any of them. As soon as Alexander left to join the Lancastrian lr-bird, she'd sold the lot to a local goldsmith.

When Kathryn stood up, the heel of her boot hit the jakes pot beneath the bed. She crouched down and pulled this out. It was clean and scrubbed. Kathryn glimpsed the sack wedged tight between the floorboards and the bed. She tugged and dragged this out, took the small knife she carried in her wallet and cut the thongs around the neck and emptied its contents out onto the floor: a war belt with decorated scabbard. The handle of the dagger was of polished wood embellished with silver stars. The sword scabbard was of costly leather stiffened with gold studs along the rim. The sword itself had a silver handle. Kathryn pulled this out and exclaimed in surprise at the shimmering blade, slightly bluish as she turned it toward the light. She had seen enough weapons in the armoury at Kingsmead to recognise a work of craftsmanship from Toledo or Milan. She pushed this back and studied the war belt. How did Elias, a blacksmith, have something so precious, the property of a knight or a retainer in some lordly household? She picked up the belt and her curiosity deepened. The belt was emblazoned with a colourful heraldic device, a golden falcon against an argent background above a red portcullis with a black bar sinister across it. Kathryn recognised the arms as those of a leading Lancastrian, the Bastard of Faucomberg, who had tried to hold London against Edward of York, only to lose both the city and his head.

Kathryn searched the sack; she found a good linen shirt slightly rent and frayed. Elias and his wife had been rather unsuccessful in trying to wash the bloodstains away. Kathryn recalled Colum's story of fleeing Lancastrians who'd been cut down in Walmer. Did this war belt belong to one of those? She placed the items back in the sack. She walked down the stairs, collected the ledger, and rejoined the others standing sullenly in the cobbled yard. Walter noticed what she was carrying and opened his mouth to protest, then thought otherwise, loudly snorted, and turned away.

"What are those?" Colum came over.

Kathryn stood on tiptoe and kissed him full on the lips. "The ghosts are gathering, Colum," she whispered, "spilt blood cries for vengeance! God is beginning to take notice."

Chapter 4

This world nys but a thurghfare, ful of wo and we been pilgrymes,
passynge to and fro.
—Chaucer, "The Knight's Tale,"
The Canterbury Tales

Kathryn put the ledger in the sack and handed it to Colum.
"Just hold this for a while," she said to him. "I wish a word
with you," she called to the rest. They gathered round. Mother
Croul made her way from the other side of the yard where she'd
been standing by herself. Kathryn looked at their faces. Mother
Croul with her clever eyes, gentle Father Clement, Amabilia, her
merry mouth now pulled down at the corner. Roger the Physician, lean and sour, playing with the ring on his finger. Benedict
and Ursula, close together, the notary's face pasty, eyes watery.
Ursula had lost some of her arrogance as if this place of death
had sucked the energy from her. Walter the Constable still
preened himself like a cock with his red bulbous face and piggy
eyes, his greasy hair standing out like black spikes. He was still
very unhappy at his authority being challenged and kept glaring
around, eyes darting, as if trying to summon help against these
intruders. Only Simon the Sexton was absent. Kathryn was
about to speak when the church bell began to toll.

"The sexton has laid out the corpses in front of the altar," Father Clement said. "The time of mourning has begun."

"Mistress, must we stand here?" Amabilia asked.

"I would like to meet you all," Kathryn replied, "where the

booming clang of the bell doesn't stifle conversation." She shrugged. "Perhaps this is not the time or the place."

"We should satisfy our hunger," Amabilia said. "I have made a stew we could eat in our refectory." Her words were greeted with murmurs of approval, Kathryn included, and they left the yard. The lane was growing busy again as the poorer sort flocked around the makeshift, tawdry stalls where secondhand clothes were sold. Further on, the butchers were preparing to wash down their benches, emptying scalding buckets over the wooden planks, clearing away any offal, whilst their apprentices kept back the yapping dogs and the rag-garbed poor, desperate for free scraps. The street narrowed, and the preacher, black gown flapping, passed across like a ghost from one alleyway to another. He didn't even bother to stop, turn, or acknowledge them, but hurried on, a scrap of bread in one hand, a lump of grilled meat in the other. Kathryn watched him disappear down the darkness of the needle-thin alley. She noticed how his staff was pushed through the cord round his waist the way a fighting man would carry his sword.

Father Clement was eager to go on. They reached a strip of common land which stretched to the high brick cemetery wall. In the centre of this soared the huge four-gabled lych-gate. Kathryn and Colum followed the priest into the cemetery, a great expanse of long green grass, shrubs, wildflowers, and the cool shade of ancient, twisted yew trees. The graves were neatly tended. Some had a simple wooden cross frayed by the weather, others bore carved headstones. Kathryn noticed how clean these were kept, as they were in her old parish church of St. Mildred in Canterbury, the moss and lichen scraped away. The cemetery lay in a quiet trance, broken only by the call of a bird or the clicking of grasshoppers. The sweet smell of wildflowers such as ladies' mantle and pea flower hung like a fragrant mist.

"God's acre," Father Clement murmured. "I try to enforce canon law. I insist that this is a holy place and only allow occasions such as tasting church ales or prayers and pageants during Rogation Days. Don't you agree, mistress?"

Kathryn nodded as Father Clement led them up the pebbledashed path. Out of the corner of her eye Kathryn glimpsed a young man and his sweetheart, suddenly roused from the long grass, creep from their love nest towards the cemetery wall.

"I see you, Master Ralph, and you, Mistress Alison," Father Clement called out. "This is not a taproom."

The young man and his lover fled to the cemetery wall, which they quickly climbed. The priest's remark and the sight of the two lovers fleeing provoked laughter.

"It's the same in any churchyard, isn't it?" Father Clement smiled at Kathryn. "People lie here, but not all of them are dead."

Kathryn smiled at the priest's witty but gentle observation. She recalled that of Father Cuthbert, her own confessor, at the Poor Priest's Hospital: *"More children were conceived amongst the dead than amongst the living."*

They passed on towards the church with its impressive nave, black-slated roof, and stained-glass windows, some with intercepting, others with panel tracery. The stone used, Father Clement explained, was good sandstone, which gave off a soft golden hue. The bell tower, which had now fallen silent, was a late addition to the church, as was the great porch door, over which a mason had carved a terrifying tympanum showing Christ coming in judgement on the Last Day. On his right, angels with swords of fire and on his left the scorpions, dragons and monkey-faced demons who symbolised the power of hell.

"A dire warning," Father Clement warned, "but come, mistress, look." He took her closer to the door and pointed out the stone gargoyles, each with a demonic face, popping eyes, snub noses, and smiling mouth, yet both wore a bishop's mitre.

Kathryn translated the inscription carved in stone beneath each gargoyle: " 'May his days be short and his bishopric go to another.' "

"A strange inscription for a church." Kathryn remarked.

"St. Swithun's was built during the troubled times of King John," Father Clement replied. "The local lord, who owned the rights of advowson, would only appoint priests hostile to the local bishop."

"And does Lord Henry still have those rights?" Kathryn asked. "Is he responsible for appointing the priests here?"

"Yes." Father Clement peered shortsightedly at her. "However, during the recent troubles, the local lord was changed so often, with Lancaster appointing this seigneur and York appointing another, that matters lapsed." He pulled a face, then smiled, and Kathryn noticed how clean his teeth were, his breath sweet. "But Lord Henry immediately confirmed my appointment for life. He was only too happy to. You see, mistress," he hurried on, drawing closer so that the others couldn't listen, "I'm constructing a tomb in the crypt for his wife, the Lady Mary."

"You're a builder?" Colum asked.

"A stonemason, sir," the priest whispered, ignoring the constable's loud exclamations of how hungry he was. "I used to be a stonemason, a very good one, a member of the guild in Dover." Father Clement straightened up. "That's before I realised that the Lord had called me to be a different builder, to raise His church in a more spiritual way. I travelled to Canterbury and was accepted for holy orders by Archbishop Bourchier."

"Ah, Bourchier," Kathryn teased back. "His Grace is now well past his eightieth year. He seems to have been old for so long."

"Well, he ordained me," Father Clement declared, "he appointed me to Hardleston, and then for the last sixteen years to Walmer. However, old habits die hard. I love the feel of stone, I love to cut it. Come, I'll show you round the church."

He led them off, stopping at the narrow corpse door, explaining how the Galilee Chapel had been built by a later lord and how he'd tended the brickwork. They rounded the church. Behind it, ringed by trees, stood the priest's house, a two-storey mansion with wings added on either side to form a cobbled courtyard. The buildings were black-slated with rounded windows, some filled with glass, others with stiffened linen panels. Father Clement explained how one wing served as stables and outhouses, the other as his workshop. He told the others to follow Amabilia into the house—they needed no second bidding— while he took Kathryn and Colum into what he called his house of stone, a long low building with a wooden hammer-beam roof. In the centre stood the great workbench littered with tools, axes, chisels, plumb lines, compasses and, all around, blocks of ashlar, high-quality sandstone, and buckets with instructions for making mortar clearly painted on their side: two parts sand and one part lime.

"You have the stone delivered?" Colum asked.

"Oh yes, behind here you'll find loaded carts. Lord Henry is a generous patron. He has told me that he will bring stone from Oxfordshire and Portland in the west country, as well as the best rubble the market can provide." He led them out. Kathryn stumbled in the doorway, knocking off the lid of a milk churn. She stooped down, picked this up, and went to replace it when she noticed the almost rancid smell. The milk had not only curdled but begun to dry. Father Clement apologised and took the lid from her, explaining how, due to what had happened, they had not really tended the house. Nevertheless, he chattered on, the meal Amabilia had prepared would be delicious.

"The corpses are laid out." Simon the Sexton came striding across the courtyard. "Though God knows where their souls are!" Simon cradled a tankard in his hand. He was undoubtedly a toper but, with his flinty blue eyes and hard face, the sexton was no fool.

Amabilia stood in the doorway waving at them. "You must come, everything is ready."

Kathryn and Colum walked across as Simon led Father Clement away to whisper in his ear.

"What is in this sack?" Colum asked.

"You'll see." Kathryn winked back. "I suspect we are going to discover a number of secrets, Colum. Our good parishioners have a great deal to hide."

They entered the priest's house. It was comfortable and homely: no rushes strewed the floor, instead the paving stones were scrubbed and pots of herbs stood in the corners. It was really a long hall that had been partitioned off. On her right, through a half-opened door, Kathryn glimpsed chairs and stools with cushioned seats. The refectory lay to the left, a long chamber that led off to the kitchen. A mantel stood on the back wall but this was now covered with a decorated screen. Above the wooden panelling, to either side of the fireplace, hung paintings, tapestries, and hangings. The long trestle table was scrubbed. Amabilia had laid out platters, horn spoons, and pewter mugs. The meal she served, beef diced and spiced with bowls of vegetables, tasted delicious, whilst Amabilia proudly declared she had brewed the ale herself. The bread was slightly stale but Kathryn ate hungrily, watching the others fill their stomachs. She and Colum sat on either side of Father Clement, Amabilia next to her, and the rest ranged on each side of the table. They all ate as if starving. The constable pushed the food into his mouth, now and again raising his head to glare at her. Simon the Sexton drank more than he ate. Benedict and Ursula first picked at their food as if reluctant, but eventually began to eat, chattering between themselves. Mother Croul and the physician remained silent throughout. At the end of the meal Amabilia, helped by Kathryn, cleared the platters away. She then served a portion of pear tart in white Rhenish wine, which tasted sweet. Afterwards, Kathryn dipped her fingers into the water bowl and wiped her hands and mouth.

"I'm afraid I do have certain questions to ask you." She put down the napkin and picked up the leather sack. Clearing away her bowl, she emptied the contents of the sack onto the table, ignoring the exclamations of surprise. Colum got to his feet, picked up the war belt, and strapped it round him. He drew the sword, raising it to catch the light, causing consternation amongst the parishioners. "I found that in Elias's bedchamber," Kathryn declared. "Why should Elias have such a valuable weapon? Why should the blacksmith own something which must have belonged to one of the Bastard of Faucomberg's principal retainers?"

"You know why," Roger spoke up.

Kathryn regarded the physician as a silent, rather furtive man, but now that his belly was full of ale and food, Roger had apparently decided to show his annoyance at this course of events.

"Mistress, you've had us dancing round you all morning."

"I have not had you dancing!" Kathryn snapped. "Three people have been foully murdered."

"And what makes you think," Ursula said, "that we should know something?"

"Because you are all members of the Parish Council. I'm sure you realise all three victims were also members of the Parish Council. You hold positions of authority in this village. You know about Elias, Isabella, and Adam the Apothecary. On your allegiance to the Crown, not to mention your loyalty to God, if you have information which could resolve these mysteries, you are legally bound to hand that over. So, I'll ask my questions. I may suspect the answers but I'd like to hear them from you."

"Then I shall answer." Roger half stood, glaring down the table at Kathryn. "A year has gone since the end of the war. We are villagers, the little people of the land. We go about our business while the great ones, with banners flying, go to war and fight each other for the Crown, for possessions, for lands and estates. Walmer was a Lancastrian stronghold, not because we wanted it that way but because that's the way the great ones of the soil wanted it. Now Edward of York strikes back. He destroys the House of Lancaster at Barnet and Tewkesbury, and every Lancastrian not killed or captured is sent fleeing for his life. The three who fled here were a danger to us; we declared our loyalty to the Crown and pursued them."

" 'We'?" Colum broke in.

"We were all at the killing!"

"I wasn't," Mother Croul shouted.

"Nor was I," Father Clement said sharply, "neither was my sister."

"Sit down, physician," Colum declared. "I know about men of war, I also know about physicians. Have you read your Chaucer? 'Nowhere in all the world was one to match him.' "

"You're a student of the tales?" Father Clement asked.

"I find Chaucer amusing and interesting," Colum remarked. "I know many of his verses by heart. However, we're not here to discuss poetry, are we, Master Physician? What happened when those three Lancastrians came here?"

His question was greeted by silence.

"Tell me." Kathryn pointed at Benedict sitting opposite her. "Tell me what happened that day."

"As Roger the Physician said"—Benedict bared his lips and cleaned his teeth with the tip of his tongue—"we little people were going about our normal business. News came of great battles, one to the north and the other in the west country."

"I received orders," Walter the Constable broke in. "Proclamations from the sheriff of Kent that all Lancastrians trying to flee the country were to be regarded as traitors, and if they did not surrender they were to be cut down."

"Master Constable, perhaps you should tell the tale," Kathryn offered.

"There is nothing much to tell." The Constable shrugged. He picked a crumb from the table and popped it into his mouth. "Three horsemen entered Walmer. They dismounted and entered the tavern, where they asked for tankards of ale. We could tell they were men of war, their horses were blown, they were covered in mud and dirt. One of them was wounded here, in the left arm."

"Describe them," Kathryn intervened.

"One was a young squire perhaps no more than twenty summers, the other two were archers, much older, but the squire seemed to be the man of authority. He was well dressed in half armour, that sword belt wrapped about his waist. Anyway, Elias the Blacksmith was in the Silver Swan, as usual, quenching his thirst. He became mischievous, got to his feet and raised his tankard. 'I give you Edward of York,' he declared. The three Lancastrians simply stared at him. 'I give you his Grace Edward of York,' Elias repeated. The young squire slammed his tankard down on the table, got up and left. Elias and the others followed. All of us were in the Silver Swan, apart from Father and Mother Croul. Elias, who was drunk, became angry. He asked why they didn't return the royal toast. The squire told him to be damned and mind his own business. Elias picked up a piece of wood and struck the squire as he was about to mount. The two archers

90

tried to draw their swords. Elias and the rest of us gathered round. I suppose," Walter said with a sniff, "we'd all drunk deeply. The three men were unable to mount their horses, which shied away, so they fled and we pursued them. The hue and cry were raised. We were all shouting, 'Harrow, Harrow.' The squire seemed to know where to go. He went down to mercery, fled across the common land, and into the cemetery. He hoped to seek sanctuary. We caught him there." The constable was now anxious, beads of sweat glistened on his vein-streaked cheeks. He stared furtively around, but the rest kept their heads lowered except for Mother Croul, who was smiling quietly to herself. Kathryn sensed the constable was lying but wanted to hear his story for what it was worth.

"By now we'd picked up weapons, clubs, anything," the constable continued. "The three Lancastrians were tired and wounded. Adam and Elias struck the squire with a hammer and axe. The young man collapsed. The two archers tried to flee, they became separated, they were pulled down and knifed." Walter seemed unperturbed by the bloody events he was describing. "Afterwards their corpses were stripped and laid out at the market cross until Lord Henry and others arrived. Ah"—Walter pointed at Colum—"I thought I'd seen you before, you were in Lord Henry's company."

"I was there."

"And what happened to the corpses?" Kathryn interrupted.

"I returned the following morning," Father Clement replied, openly troubled at the violence of his parishioners. "By then Lord Henry had ordered them to be placed in shrouds and buried in the Poor Man's Plot on the western side of the cemetery—that's where we bury strangers and beggars who die suddenly without kin. I blessed the graves . . ." His voice trailed off.

"And no one ever came here to reclaim the corpses?" Kathryn declared. "And the possessions of these men?"

"As I said, Elias was our leader," Walter replied. "He was full of ale. When Elias was angry he was a bad man to cross, and Adam was no better."

"You helped yourselves, didn't you?" Kathryn accused. "And in doing so, broke the law. The goods of such men are to be handed over to an officer of the Crown."

"We thought," Benedict declared, "we'd cut down three traitors."

"Were they given the chance to surrender?" Kathryn asked. "Doesn't Chaucer talk about how well read you lawyers are supposed to be? Don't you know the law, Master Benedict?"

"My husband knows the law," Ursula retorted. "These were traitors carrying arms. They were cut down, their bodies stripped. Master Murtagh, haven't you ever plundered a battlefield?" She shrugged. "So, three strangers, enemies to the Crown, were killed trying to flee the King's justice. What does that have to do with Adam's death, or Elias?"

"Perhaps nothing," Kathryn replied, "or perhaps everything. I want to find out more about this village. Lord Henry has been given estates around here. He is lord of the manor."

"Aye, so he is," the physician gibed. "We all know the great Lord Henry, he owns fish ponds, pastures, woodland, arable land and a lot more. We all pay him his dues."

"He is a good lord," Benedict intervened tactfully. "He is a good lord. Mistress, again, we ask you, what does all this have to do with the murder of Adam or Elias and his wife?"

"As I said, I want to know as much about your village as possible. So these three Lancastrians, traitors as you describe them, were killed and lie buried in the Poor Man's Plot. What else has happened since, anything untoward?"

"'*Mene, Mene, Tekel Parsin,*'" Father Clement murmured. "Isn't that what was written, sister?"

Amabilia, who'd been in the kitchen since Kathryn had emptied the sack out onto the table, came over and sat down. She glanced at Kathryn and nodded.

"Father, what are you referring to?"

"There's a painting in the church," the priest explained, "that shows the prophet Daniel at the feast of a Babylonian King. God's hand appeared at that feast and wrote a warning on the wall."

"And?" Colum asked, sitting down next to Kathryn.

"The same words were scrawled on the floor in the entrance to our church." Father Clement bit his lip in anger.

"So it was someone who could write?" Kathryn asked.

"The letters were crude." Benedict spoke up. "Anyone could have copied them. Last Sunday morning, when we entered the church for Mass, we found those words scrawled on the floor: we don't know by whom or why."

"They could have been written anytime." Father Clement sighed.

"I locked the church just before midnight the previous day," Simon the Sexton explained, "and I opened it before dawn. The light inside is poor." He shook his head, "I wouldn't have noticed it, but you know who it was, Father!"

Kathryn glanced at the priest.

"The preacher," Father Clement said, and blinked. "He was seen in the church late Saturday evening. He's always quoting the Scriptures, but there again, so can Satan, whilst the devil can appear as an angel of light."

Both the priest and his sister were visibly agitated. Father Clement was pale faced, and Amabilia kept dabbing her eyes.

"There's something else, isn't there, Father?" Colum asked. "You mentioned as much before. Something you wish to show us?"

Colum's question was echoed by the others. The priest crossed himself, got to his feet, and left the refectory. His guests were murmuring amongst themselves as he returned grasping a square of dark, greasy parchment. He handed this to Kathryn. The parchment looked as if it had been torn out of a folio, jagged at one end, yet unused except for the words etched in deep black ink. It reminded Kathryn of the writing in the apothecary's ledger. The words were boldly drawn:

"Who shall rid us of this pestilent priest?"

Below it, Kathryn recognised a misquotation from one of the prophets:

"I shall smite the flock and then the shepherd."

"I found these nailed to the door of my house last Sunday

morning," Father Clement murmured. "Which is why I was so angry when I preached after Mass."

"Who?" Kathryn asked. "Why?"

"I know." The Sexton broke the silence, his face aggressive. "And so do you, Father. I told you not to—"

"I let the preacher sleep in the death house on Saturday evening," the priest confessed. "I gave him a blanket, some wine and food. I was trying to be Christian. He seemed friendly enough, asking about the doings of my parishioners." Father Clement pointed at the notary. "Especially you, Benedict."

"Busybody!" Ursula snapped as her husband coloured slightly, fingers going to his lips.

"If it was the preacher," Colum asked, "where did he get the parchment, quill, and ink?"

"The apothecary." Father Clement shrugged. "This morning Adam told me that the preacher had visited him late on Saturday evening. He noticed his fingers were rather black, as if he'd been handling charcoal. He begged Adam for a quill, a pot of ink, and a scrap of parchment. Adam agreed, the fellow sat outside on a plinth, where he wrote something, then left."

"Yes, that's it." The sexton smiled triumphantly around. "Adam used that parchment to wrap powders in, whilst the writing in the church was done in charcoal. Of course," he crowed. "Didn't Adam mention, at our Parish Council meeting, something about the preacher visiting him?" His question was greeted with nods.

"He should be arrested!" the constable declared. "Father, why didn't you mention this before?"

"At first we thought it was all some cruel jape," Amabilia declared. "The preacher is a stranger, Master Constable, he isn't a scapegoat."

Colum and Kathryn agreed.

"Hideous murders have taken place," Colum declared, "it would be wrong to point the finger without firm evidence."

"So." Kathryn picked up the pewter beer jug and pressed it against her hot cheek. "Three Lancastrians, unknown men, are killed and buried here. Elias, one of the leaders of the posse who

94

killed them, takes their most valuable possessions and hides them, hoping to sell them at an appropriate time. Last Sunday, a warning from a painting in the church is scrawled on the floor. Father Clement is threatened and the preacher acts suspiciously. Let's now move to the death of Elias. Did he have enemies?"

"Let's ask another question." The physician scoffed. "Did he have friends? To put it bluntly, mistress, Elias was foulmouthed, hot-tempered, and free with his fists. He was violent towards his wife and his neighbours. Many in Walmer would have liked him dead."

"And Isabella?" Kathryn asked.

"She was pretty," Ursula intervened, "in a sort of full-blown way."

"She was lecherous," Roger declared in a mock whisper, "God rest her soul, but Isabella was hot eyed, generous with her favours."

"To you?" Kathryn asked.

The physician simply wiped his mouth on the back of his hand.

"To any man here?" Kathryn insisted. Benedict glanced down at the table, biting his dry lips.

"Master Benedict, did you know the blacksmith's wife? I mean, in an intimate way?"

"How dare you!" Ursula screeched. "How dare you accuse my husband of going with such a leman!"

"She's dead," Father Clement intervened. "Whatever sins she committed, may the Lord have mercy on her."

"I simply asked your husband a question," Kathryn said softly. "He can confirm it or deny it."

"I did not know her!" Benedict glanced up. "I did not know her in the way you mean. I would pass her in the street and exchange greetings. I would talk to her about the crops, the weather, the doings of the great ones of the soil." Again, that nervous chewing of his lips. "But nothing else."

"If you're looking for a guilty party," Walter declared, "well, mistress, you have just seen his corpse."

"Adam the Apothecary?"

"Adam the Apothecary," the constable replied. "He and Isabella were well known for creeping off into the woods. Isn't that right, Mother Croul?"

The old woman at the end of the table seemed more interested in her food and drink than the company.

"We're all sinners," she declared. "Everyone in this room is a sinner. Isabella was no different. She sinned, but the Lord is compassionate. Her husband was a violent and dangerous man. If Elias hadn't been poisoned in some tavern, this year or next, he would have been stabbed." The violence of her remarks surprised Kathryn. Mother Croul stared down at her. "Now you're here, mistress, asking questions. I know the path you're following. That warning in the church, the words copied there, are a warning to all of us. God is going to take vengeance for sins committed here."

"What sins?" Colum asked. "Why should Walmer be any more sinful than any other place in the kingdom?"

"I don't know," Mother Croul answered. "If I did, I'd tell you. Whoever killed the blacksmith and his wife, not to mention the apothecary, will strike, and strike again. You believe that, don't you, mistress?" She pointed a bony finger at Kathryn, who nodded in agreement.

"So, let's cut to the quick." Mother Croul's voice grew stronger, "Ask your questions, mistress. Elias was violent, Isabella hot eyed, and Adam the Apothecary . . . well, yes, I saw him in the forest with Isabella, as perhaps did you, Master Physician."

Roger just waved his hand, picked up crumbs from the table, then buried his face in his tankard.

"On the night Elias was killed . . ." Kathryn resumed her questioning.

"There was a parish meeting, late in the afternoon," Father Clement answered, "here in this room."

"And who was present?"

"Everybody here. Amabilia was busy in the kitchen. We always serve members of the council some sweetmeats and white wine."

"But Elias and his wife didn't come?" Kathryn asked. "Why is that?"

"They excused themselves," the priest replied. "They sent a message that they were busy, and that is true. They said they were going to celebrate. I believe they were preparing for today's feast."

"Did any of you enter the blacksmith's yard that day?" Kathryn asked. Her question was greeted with shakes of the head. "Are you sure?" Kathryn asked. "If I can prove that anyone in this chamber was in the blacksmith's yard, and is now denying it, you fall under suspicion."

"I did visit Elias early in the day," Benedict retorted, "but it was because Elias wanted to draw up an indenture with a supplier of nails. I did not enter the yard, I met him in the kitchen. Oh, it must have been about an hour before noon."

"Did you notice anything untoward?"

"Nothing!" The notary shook his head. "Except the preparations. I asked Isabella what she intended. She replied, 'Elias and I shall feast like kings and queens tonight,' that was all."

"Did you see the tun of wine," Kathryn asked, "a small cask? Master Constable, when you go back to the house you'll find the wine has drained away on the kitchen floor. The cask should be burnt, it contained the poison."

"I checked it this morning, that cask was freshly broached, it was almost full. The only people who'd broach that cask of wine would be Elias or Isabella." Walter pulled a face.

"You're correct, Master Constable. I suspect that wine was poisoned before it was ever delivered to the blacksmith's house." Kathryn's statement was greeted with exclamations of surprise.

"It's been done before," Kathryn continued, "it is well known for wine importers to remove the bunghole, empty some wine out, pour water in, then reseal it. If it can be done by a merchant, why can't it be done by someone else, only this time poison put in?"

"Was it the same poison?" old Mother Croul asked.

Kathryn shook her head. "The poison given to Elias would take some time to work, depending on its strength. He was very strong but the Juice of Almond, with its bittersweet potion, is a true killer. Within a few heartbeats, the victim is already dying. The other vexing problem is that whoever poisoned Elias also intended to poison his wife at the same time. He, she, or they, intended the blacksmith and his wife to leave this world at the same time."

"But, but . . ." The notary pulled back the sleeves of his gown. He was mocking Kathryn, acting as a lawyer would in court with a rather doubtful plaintiff.

"But this is impossible, mistress. How could the poisoner know that Elias and Isabella would, at the same time, consume a poisoned drink?"

"It's possible," Kathryn replied. "Everybody here knows how, at the end of a day's work, Elias always drunk two stoups of clear rainwater from his special water butt. As for the blacksmith's wife, how many people here, preparing a banquet or feast, would take a sip of wine? Only Isabella did not take it in celebration but more to calm her mind, to give her strength after the death of her husband. Let us say"—Kathryn stared at the notary—"for the sake of disputation, as they say in the courts, that Elias did not drink his water on that particular evening and joined his wife at the kitchen table. The cask would have been broached, the cups filled, and they would have still died together, the only difference being they'd have shared the same poison. Now, their cask of wine was the best Bordeaux from Mauleon on the borders of Gascony. Did Isabella or Elias ever talk about anyone giving them such a gift?"

Again, silence.

"Does anyone know where that cask came from?"

"Mistress, most of us buy our wines from the Silver Swan or the Blue Boar," Benedict remarked. "Of course, there are those who bring wine in without paying the custom due."

"So this could have been a cask of smuggled wine?" Kathryn asked.

"I doubt it," Mother Croul responded. "Ever since the wreckers were hanged there's been no more smuggling in these parts. I would know; I rarely sleep, and I go out at night."

"As do other witches," Roger whispered. Mother Croul ignored him.

"That cask of wine was given to Isabella by someone who wanted to poison her and her husband." Mother Croul clicked her tongue. "The villagers round here are in great terror of Lord Henry, they'll not risk smuggling again. I know, my second husband was one of those hanged by the great lord."

"And he deserved it," Roger snapped.

"You need not curse my late husband," Mother Croul remarked. "God assoil him. Black of heart and black of soul, he met God's judgement. Good, honest sailors died at his hands. I do not weep for him, so why should you? Mistress, there is no smuggling; that cask was given to the blacksmith's wife as a gift."

Kathryn glanced down the table. "Does anyone here know anything about the deaths of Elias and his wife? If not, let us turn to Adam the Apothecary. Mistress Ursula, he was married to your sister."

"He was."

"A happy marriage?" Kathryn asked.

Ursula pulled a face.

"And your sister died how long ago?"

Ursula stared down at the table, "Three years," she whispered. "Oh, *Domine miserere!*" Her fingers to her lips, she said, "Oh, *Domine miserere!*"

"What?" Kathryn asked.

"My sister, Margaret, died three years ago this very day, the twenty-ninth September, the Feast of St. Michael. Oh!" The woman half rose, her husband gently pushed her back.

"What did she die of?" Kathryn asked. She ignored Roger's sarcastic loud whisper, "Lack of breath!"

Benedict, however, leaned across the table, shaking his fist at the physician. "When you talk about the dead, sir—" Roger made a rude sound with his lips, passing his tankard from one hand to the other, his watery eyes never leaving those of Benedict.

"Why not tell our questioner," the physician murmured, "how your sister-in-law died?"

"She died of stomach pains," Ursula offered.

"I tended her," Roger declared. "Some wound inside, perhaps a tumour or a cyst, there was nothing I could do."

"There never is," Benedict remarked.

"So she fell ill in the early summer, for how long?"

"For a few months," Ursula replied. "Then she fell into a fever," she added quickly, "there was nothing we could do."

"What are you implying?" The sexton had drunk deeply and sat swaying half-asleep. "What are you implying, Mistress Swinbrooke?"

"It's a coincidence, even more so," Kathryn replied, "that Adam should die on the same day as his wife and that he should die of poison. Master Roger, you are a physician, I am sure a very good one; were you ever suspicious about Margaret's ailments?"

The physician put the tankard down and placed his hands to his face.

"Why not tell her," Benedict declared, "you were sweet on my sister-in-law."

"Margaret was a gracious woman." Roger took his hands away. "I am sorry about my earlier remark. It was meant to hide my own grief. Yes." He measured his words carefully. "I liked Mistress Margaret. I found Adam the Apothecary rather sinister. So yes, the thought did cross my mind that Adam may have had more than a hand in his wife's death." He ignored the exclamations of the rest, as well as the shriek from Ursula, who clung to her husband, staring at Roger as if he were some ghoul from hell.

"You never told me this," Benedict declared, "you never voiced anything?"

"How could I?" The physician spread his hands. "Adam was as sinister and as violent as Elias. Do you remember those three Lancastrians? Adam had their blood on his hands, he enjoyed it, I could tell that by the look on his face. He, and Elias, were the leaders in that bloody affray. How could I voice my suspicions about such a man? I had no proof. When Margaret died, her body was immediately sheeted, coffined, and buried."

Kathryn listened to the hubbub of conversation break out,

each giving their own judgement on Margaret and Adam. She stared down at her hands moving the ring Colum had given her. It caught the light from the window behind her. Walmer, she reflected, is no different from Canterbury. People lived their lives and hid behind masks; only in times of trouble are the masks plucked away.

She glanced sharply at Father Clement. He was holding his tankard swirling the ale around. Amabilia had risen and left to go to the kitchen. She came back with the fresh jug of white wine. Kathryn realised that they had all eaten and no one had been worried about poison. Yet, she was sure, some people in this village knew as much about poisons as she did.

"Mistress." Benedict broke through the clamour. "Do you think Margaret's death was suspicious?"

"As I said," Kathryn replied, "it is suspicious that Adam and his wife died on the same day. I have listened to Margaret's ailments described. There is a possibility she was poisoned. Certain poisons, as some of you may know, such as arsenic, either the red or the white, can be given in increasing dosage, so death can take weeks, even months. I've heard of such cases."

"But can it be proved?" Benedict banged the table.

"Master Notary, you are a lawyer. I have attended the exhumation of a corpse. Once, as a young girl, my father took me along. A woman had died in rather strange circumstances but no one dared voice their suspicions. My father, however, knew the properties of arsenic. He maintained how, when someone died of arsenic poisoning, the body did not decompose quickly and was often preserved."

"And when the corpse was exhumed?" Simon the Sexton asked.

"It was almost as fresh as the day it was buried," Kathryn replied.

"According to canon law," the priest replied slowly, "I have to cooperate with the lawful authority. If Lord Henry gave the order for Mistress Margaret's coffin to be exhumed, then Simon and I would see to that: the Church has a ritual, which must be followed."

"For the moment," Kathryn replied, playing with her ring,

"let us leave Mistress Margaret and return to Adam. His death is just as mysterious as Elias's and Isabella's. Here we have an apothecary who returns from the manor house. Father, you were with him. What happened then?"

"The corpses of Elias and Isabella were loaded back on the parish cart, the one used for funerals. We bought them down here and handed them over to Simon to be taken to the death house. He shrugged. "After that, Adam went home, the alarm was later raised, and Adam's corpse found."

"So when he returned to his house, he would enter by the back door," Kathryn remarked. "He goes into the kitchen, takes down a blackjack, and fills it from a jug of ale. He then takes that blackjack along to his chamber of powders, locks and bolts the door, drinks the ale, and, unfortunately, dies of the powerful potion the ale contained. Now," she said with a sigh, "we know the ale was poisoned, yet the jug is free of any taint—so that means that the poison was placed in the blackjack. But if that's the case, how did the poisoner know that particular blackjack would be the one used by Adam? There are four of them hanging from hooks, it could have been days, weeks, before Adam reached for that particular blackjack to quench his thirst. There's another mystery: How did the person enter the house? According to what you have told us, as well as common report, Adam kept the rear door of his house firmly locked. So his mother's chamber can only be reached by the outside one, and that is on the latch?"

"Oh, yes." Amabilia was moving round filling cups. "Always kept unlocked, Adam was frightened of his mother knocking a candle over and not being able to get out, or anyone else being able to get in. According to Adam, anyone who entered that chamber would be seen or heard by his mother. She slept lightly, her handbell always nearby."

"So," Kathryn asked, "someone could enter through the outside door, but they'd have to cross the old lady's bedchamber, unlock the other door, and go down into the house."

"If anyone tried that," Simon the Sexton slurred, "Adam's

mother would have raised the hue and cry. We'd have heard the shout of 'Harrow' from one end of the village to the other. Frail as she looks, Mathilda can scream, as we all know to our cost."

"She's a foul-tempered scold," Ursula said, "no one enters that bedchamber unless they have to."

"But still the mystery remains," Kathryn insisted, "how did someone enter that house? How did they know that particular blackjack would be used by Adam? How did they know they wouldn't be seen or heard by Adam's mother? And why was Adam poisoned? What had he done? Whom had he offended?"

"If Elias was alive," Mother Croul added, "I'd say it was the blacksmith, but as his body is rotting and his soul has gone to God . . ."

"Did the apothecary have other enemies?" Kathryn asked.

"He was arrogant," Benedict declared, "and secretive. He dispensed his precious powders as if he was the holder of great secrets."

"I have his ledger."

"I don't think that's a faithful record," Roger the physician pointed out. "Adam enjoyed a reputation for giving love potions or powders to some young girl who'd conceived and wished to miscarry. He came from bad blood, the apothecary: his father was a leech, his uncle used to be the apothecary before Adam. . . ."

"He was also a wrecker," Mother Croul declared. "He and my late husband were of the same coven, killing and pillaging to their heart's content. Lord Henry had them strung up on the gallows like a farmer would rats."

"Did anyone here visit Adam's house?" Kathryn asked, raising her voice. "I mean, in the days before he died?"

"We all visited the apothecary." Amabilia retook her seat. "I would go there to give his mother some comfort."

"And I would take the viaticum," Father Clement declared, "but not often. Mistress Mathilda has a vicious tongue. She would often use such occasions to regale me with all the gossip. I didn't think it was appropriate for receiving the Eucharist."

"And I would visit her," Ursula offered, "because I felt sorry for her, but not recently. It was something I regarded as a duty, rather than a pleasure."

The rest also agreed. Roger described how he'd visited the apothecary's house for some powders on the previous Thursday and then gone upstairs to see Mistress Mathilda. The rest made similar claims and Kathryn realised her questioning was elucidating very few facts.

"Father, I thank you for your hospitality." She leaned across and patted the priest's hands, clasped before him on the table. She noticed how soft and smooth the skin was, the lacerations from the stone cutting neatly healed. "Father, I have to go. However, I must ask all of you a very important question and one which doesn't need an immediate answer. It's in two parts. The first is, why would someone poison three villagers in Walmer at the end of September, for no apparent motive? And the second part is, if the poisoner has murdered three times, why not again and again? I trust you'll all be very careful about what you eat and drink."

Chapter 5

So wnynge in moral vertu was his speche and gladly wolde he leme and gladly teche.
—Chaucer, General Prologue,
The Canterbury Tales

Father Clement coughed and got to his feet. "Mistress Swinbrooke, I must show you and Master Murtagh my church. I suddenly remembered," he smiled down the table, "we were all so hungry, so eager to eat we forgot to say grace. So, '*In nomine Patris et Filit.*'" Father Clement made the sign of the cross and intoned the grace after meals.

"We give thee thanks, Almighty God," the rest joined in. The priest bestowed the blessing and pointed to the sack Kathryn had brought.

"You'll give those to Lord Henry?"

"I have to," Kathryn replied. "They are the goods of a rebel, God rest his soul. Whilst Lord Henry is the justice in this area, I'm sure he'll either have them sold and the money given to the village, or . . ." She let her words hang in the air. "It is a matter for him to decide."

The rest thanked the priest for the meal, nodded at Kathryn, and left. Amabilia cleared the table. Father Clement took Kathryn and Colum out across the cobbled yard, around the church, and through the main door. They paused in the porch, almost a room in itself. Father Clement explained how he'd personally carved the water stoup as well as the inscription above it:

When you come to this Holy Place
Sprinkle Holy Water in your face

"It's a reminder." The priest smiled. "My parishioners are entering the House of God and the Gate of Heaven." He opened the second door and led them in. Immediately, on the wall facing them was a picture of St. Christopher carrying the Christ Child, very similar to the one in St. Mildred's in Canterbury. Kathryn recalled the legend how, if you looked at the image, you were promised a safe and peaceful journey that day. She crossed herself.

St. Swithun's was an impressive church. Its stonework and woodwork were painted and gilded. The windows high in the wall glowed sapphire, gold, and silver, colours becoming very popular in church decoration. Here and there were small chantry chapels, each protected by a wooden screen that contained a small altar beneath a statue of a certain saint, the most prominent chapel being that of Swithun. The nave was long with pillars on either side whilst, at the end, a large carved rood screen led into the sanctuary. Before this, draped in funeral cloths and ringed by purple candles, lay three coffins on their trestles. Father Clement sketched a blessing in their direction and took them round the church explaining how successive priests, including himself, had hired painters to cover every inch of the wall in a vivid array of wall paintings: the Virgin with the crucified Christ, the wolf who had guarded the severed head of St. Edmund the Martyr; the Seven Deadly Sins vying with the Cardinal Virtues; an owl being mobbed by two magpies (illustrating how idle chatterers can disturb wisdom).

Father Clement accompanied them, explaining how the church had been well favoured by the local lords, not to mention the profits from the many bequests to celebrate Requiem Masses for the dead. Eventually he led them into the sanctuary. Its floor was covered in soft Turkey carpets, as were the steps leading up to the high altar, where two great brass candlesticks stood at either end. Behind the altar, up further steps, hung the pyx, which contained the host. Before it a red lamp glowed, a dull glow of fire. The church smelt of beeswax polish and scented candles, the ever-pervasive incense a constant reminder of how this was a holy place.

Kathryn let the priest chatter on—so enthusiastic about his church, its paintings, carvings, and statues. He led them into the sacristy, showing them the copes and chasubles, the stoles and albs, as well as the great carved wooden chest that contained the parish documents.

"The painting?" Kathryn intervened. "The one about Daniel."

"Ah yes, come, I'll show you that." Father Clement led them back down the nave to the walls on either side of the main door. Here the artist, crudely yet in eye-catching colours, had described the story of the Prophet Daniel in the Old Testament. How he'd been the King's Councillor, how he'd been placed in the lion's den and escaped and, on the far wall, the famous pagan feast when God's hand had written those words condemning the pagan King and all his kingdom to destruction: "*Mene, Mene, Tekel, Parsin,*" etched in black against a silver background. Kathryn resolved that even an illiterate person could have copied down the symbols.

"But how would anyone in the parish know what such words meant?" Colum asked. "In a tongue I've never heard."

Kathryn pointed to the bottom of the painting where, in gold writing against a green background, the words had been translated:

> *I have numbered,*
> *I have weighed in the balance,*
> *I have found wanting!*

"They were scrawled on the paving stone over there, just inside the church door," Father Clement explained. "Neither Simon nor I saw them. Benedict, he was the first to arrive for Sunday Mass; he noticed them and raised the alarm."

"And why do you think they were written, Father?"

"I don't know." The priest ran his hand through his thinning hair. "I really don't. Nor why I should be worried, nor why the preacher, if it is he, should have any grievance against me. You've broken bread with me, mistress, sat at my table, listened to the chatter of my parishioners. Any parish is like a still pool, calm and quiet on the surface. But take a stick and start digging, and all sorts of hideous things come floating to the top." He pointed to a great chair placed on one side of a pillar, a prie-dieu on the other. "I sit there, Mistress Swinbrooke, and hear their confessions. You'd be surprised what happens in a village like Walmer, the intense hatreds, resentments, and jealousies. The scores to be settled, old grudges polished and sharp, bitter words honed like an archer does an arrow. God have mercy on us all. They are good people, they are generous, they attend Mass, they try to lead good lives, it's just like . . ." He peered into the darkness. "It's as if things go wrong, mistress, because they go wrong! That's what St. Augustine said, didn't he? We want God, we pursue the good, but we're always out of harmony with ourselves, with our neighbour, with our world, with our God. It's no different in Walmer. To answer your question bluntly; no, I don't know why those words were scrawled, or that message sent. Perhaps someone was settling a grudge with me or someone else. I was angry at the time. I delivered one of my severest sermons. However, by the time the Parish Council met, my temper had calmed. Amabilia always soothes what used to be a fiery tongue."

"And Lady Mary?" Kathryn put her arm through the priest's, pulling him close, a gesture of friendship he appreciated. He took her hand with his free one and patted it.

"Father, you've been most hospitable," Kathryn apologised, "I hate to ask about the tittle-tattle of the village, but a year ago Lady Mary fell from the cliffs."

"An accident, poor woman!" Father Clement shook his head. "Amabilia dressed the corpse, you know. Her face was all battered, terrible wounds to the stomach and legs. You see, she'd been caught between the rocks and the sea, pushed backwards and forwards. In a sense, Lord Henry was fortunate. If it hadn't been for the rocks, her corpse could have been swept out to sea and God knows where it would have floated."

"Was it Lady Mary?"

Father Clement took away his arm and looked at her in alarm. "Well, the face was badly damaged, but of course, the same height, and colour of hair. I remember Amabilia talking about a mark on her arm, she'd seen it before on Lady Mary's arm, just beneath the elbow. Lady Mary used to come down here with flowers for the altar. She'd like nothing more than to arrange them in baskets in the sanctuary. She'd often pull back the sleeve of her gown, that's when Amabilia noticed it. Oh yes, it was Lady Mary."

"Was Lady Mary happy in her marriage?" Kathryn asked abruptly.

The priest carried on walking, shaking his head. "Mistress Kathryn, you ask impertinent questions. Some I can answer, others I cannot. I heard Lady Mary's confession, but I cannot reveal her secrets."

"I don't intend that, Father. I apologise if I gave offence."

"Not really." The priest glanced at her from the corner of his eye and smiled. "Lady Mary came from a wealthy family, she adored Lord Henry. I'm not too sure whether he loved her in the same way. He may have married her for her wealth and position or to promote his interests at Court. Oh, he was kind enough, never once did she ever complain about his lack of generosity, but there was a lack of fire. She once said he treated her as he would a favourite horse—kind, considerate, gentle, but no fire, no spark."

"Do you think she slipped?" Kathryn asked.

"Do I think Lady Mary took her own life? No, I do not. She was too religious, too spiritual, and too aware of the presence of God."

"And Lord Henry's young squire. You may recall him Father, William Marshall, spruce, quick of wit."

"I remember William," the priest agreed, "he would often accompany Lady Mary down here as her man-at-arms, protector, or guardian. Sometimes the byways and highways can be dangerous, it's known for a pedlar or tinker to attack someone vulnerable. Yes, William was educated, a scholar, he could talk in different tongues, he particularly enjoyed the paintings and would often come and watch me sculpt."

"Did he ever talk about Lord Henry?"

"Never, he was Lord Henry's man, body and soul."

"Did Lady Mary treat William with any special affection?"

"Oh, Mistress Swinbrooke, what a nose you have for sin." The priest laughed. "The relationship between Lady Mary and William was that of a squire with his lady, courteous, as Chaucer would say *'parfait'* in every sense of the word. Never once did I catch anything hidden, a glance, a smile, a touch or a look. No, William Marshall was Lord Henry's man. He never discussed the business of the manor or what he and Lord Henry did, either at court or abroad." Father Clement led them into the transept leading down to the crypt.

"And the wreckers?" Kathryn asked.

"Oh, that was a dreadful time." The priest paused, slipping his arms up his sleeves. "A violent gang from Walmer and the farms around—heartless, sinful men. They would light false beacons on the clifftops, particularly when the weather turned foul, draw ships in and wreck them on the rocks. I would have nothing to do with them. I refused Adam the Apothecary's uncle, one of the leaders of the wreckers, both the Eucharist and Absolution. In fact, one Pentecost, I excommunicated them all with bell, book, and candle, cursing their eating, their drinking, their sleeping, even their shitting! They were devils from hell. Outside in the cemetery, the Poor Man's Plot must contain at least thirty to forty corpses, poor sailors and travellers washed up on the rocks. I gave them peaceful burials. It was I who petitioned His Grace the Archbishop Bourchier to raise these matters at Court. Of course, it took the death of Lord Henry's elder brother for the vengeance of the King to be felt. Those were lawless times! York against Lancaster, one family against another, truly the words of the Gospel had come true, brother against brother, father against son. Demons, like the wreckers, enjoyed all the liberty they needed."

110

"Did any of these wreckers escape?" Kathryn asked.

The priest stepped closer. "Elias had a hand in that mischief, as did some of the others—Benedict the Notary, Roger the Physician, even our sexton. During the reign of the wreckers these men and their womenfolk grew remarkably wealthy. They could afford luxuries, good wines, clothing, and furnishings for their houses. The wreckers were a secret coven, they took oaths of loyalty to each other. On the fringes of them were others who took their gold and silver coins to look the other way."

"And Lord Henry?" Colum asked.

"Oh, he arrived in Walmer like the anger of God. At first we didn't even know he was here. He stayed in a farm further inland. One night he struck. The beacons were lit but Lord Henry was prepared, there was even a war cog out at sea, and he'd ordered the sheriffs to raise their levies. The whole coastline was cordoned off. Lord Henry moved in. The wreckers tried to make a stand on the beach. Some were cut down, the rest were tried as if they were traitors taken in battle. Lord Henry dispensed judgement from horseback, using his sword as a cross. He cursed them, in the name of the King declared them guilty, and ordered sentence to be carried out immediately. He hanged two dozen of them on a great gallows, one after the other. Their bodies were tarred and left there, as a warning to others. The week following he hunted down the rest. Some were killed, others fled the area. They became outlaws, wolfheads living in the forest. None of them returned to Walmer. Since then there's been no further disturbance of the peace."

"But resentments must run high," Kathryn asked.

The priest pulled a face. "I don't think so, mistress. The wreckers were outlaws, hated and feared by their own kind. What they did was mortally sinful, worthy of hell. Do you think honest farmers, peasants, and tradesmen like to see bodies drenched in sea water, faces bluish white, eyes gaping, being brought up from the coast to be given burial here in our churchyard? No, Lord Henry was regarded by many as a saviour. He is a good lord, just and merciful. Only those who broke the law had anything to fear. But come, I'll show you something."

He took a candle from before the Lady Altar and led them down the dark steps. The crypt was stone cold and silent. Father Clement used the candle to light the pitch torches fixed into the wall at the entrance to the crypt and a large candle in front of the statue of St. Swithun standing in the far corner. The crypt was really nothing more than a square chamber supported by columns. In the centre stood a tomb chest of beautiful golden sandstone at least five feet high and a yard across. The stone was cleanly cut, with a smooth tabletop and ribbed sides. The walls of the crypt were covered with most vivid paintings, of scenes from the Old and New Testament all involving the sea: Jonah being cast up by the whale, Christ walking along the water, Peter and the Apostles fishing. The final painting showed sinners being woken from their long sleep in purgatory, underneath the verse proclaiming: *And on That Day the Sea Shall Give Up Its Dead*. Even in that dim light Kathryn could see the paintings were fresh in texture.

"Lord Henry saw to that," Father Clement whispered, "a memorial to all those lost at sea. He had the statue of St. Swithun carved and brought here from Leominster. I offered to do it myself but he'd seen a statue there which he favoured. However"— he tapped the paved floor—"this is where he laid Lady Mary to rest and above this is her tomb chest."

He took them round and showed them the weepers carved in their niches on either side of the tomb chest, the front and back being reserved for the arms of Lord Henry and Lady Mary. Kathryn openly admired the sculptured figures; some were sharp, others unfinished, illustrating the birth of Jesus; Joseph and Mary presenting the Divine Child in the Temple; Jesus, as a boy, helping his Mother in different tasks.

"It's a work of art," Kathryn murmured. "Father, my congratulations, you must be pleased."

The priest smiled modestly. "Well, I do relish working in stone. I love its texture and colour. The ability to create something, not out of nothing but something that wasn't there. I look at a slab of stone and think, 'Ah, I know what you can be.' Perhaps that's the way God looks at us."

"And Lady Mary is buried here?"

"Yes, beneath the paving stones. She'll have a worthy memorial when it's finished. This used to be the ossuary, when the graveyard was emptied the bones were piled here. Lord Henry provided a plot in the nearby woods as an extension to the cemetery. The bones were given an honourable burial there whilst he turned this into a chantry chapel of remembrance for his wife."

"Does Lord Henry come here often?" Colum asked.

"On Sundays he attends Mass in his own chapel," Father Clement replied. "Once a week he comes into church and kneels here before the tomb, no more than an hour. He makes his devotions, shares a cup of wine with me, then leaves."

"Has he ever talked about his wife's death?"

"Never!" the priest replied. "But I can see he's distracted, something's worrying Lord Henry." Father Clement smiled thinly. "Try as I might, he will not share his secrets with me."

Kathryn would have liked to ask the priest more questions yet she'd trespassed on his hospitality and kindness long enough and did not wish to alienate him. She and Colum, who was still clutching the sack, made their farewells. They left the church, walking through the cemetery.

"Well?" Colum asked, as they stood at the edge of the common, staring out watching two ragged boys playing with the hoop from a barrel, rolling it backwards and forwards between them. "Are you any wiser, sweetest wife?"

"Savage Irishman," Kathryn murmured, "I'm more mystified than knowledgeable. As the good priest said, this is a community with its secrets, its hidden passions, stark jealousies, and brooding anger. Something has happened and I don't know what. Whoever killed Elias and the others is a skilled poisoner, someone who knows a great deal about herbs."

"In which case our noble physician must be at the top of our list of suspects."

"Possible," Kathryn agreed.

"And Father Clement?" Column asked.

"Perhaps."

Kathryn watched the two boys intently. One of them looked like Wulf the foundling. She idly wondered what he was doing.

"Kathryn," Colum advised, "the priest is a skilled mason, a gentle man who, perhaps, at times can be quite ruthless. Nevertheless, I saw nothing in his house which would indicate that he was skilled in herbs and potions or knew anything about the power and potency of certain powders. He has talked to us the most but, there again, he is their priest, their leader."

"I agree, Colum, this poisoner could be any of those we sat at the table with, or someone we haven't even met. The murders of Elias and Isabella are particularly mystifying. Where did that wine come from? How was the poisoner so certain it would be drunk that evening? The same is true of Adam the Apothecary's murder. Colum, I feel as if I've been stumbling around a dark room. I've touched things, I've seen things, but nothing which would prick my wits or alert my suspicion. The problem is," she added, "I did not expect to be doing this during our wedding days!" She grasped his arm. "Colum, here we are—"

"Deeply in love!" he finished her sentence.

She stretched up on tiptoe and kissed him on the cheek. "We are passionately in love, Irishman! So what are we doing here, outside a cemetery, talking about poisons, going back to be greeted by a manor lord who has as many mysteries as his villagers have?"

"Yes." Colum tapped the toe of his boot on the ground. "And we are soon to have a great dinner. Lord Henry has decided to lavishly entertain his guests in more relaxed circumstances."

"In which case," Kathryn replied, clasping Colum's hand and, lifting it to her lips, kissed it, "we should return. I need to rest and think."

"I don't care much for those Frenchmen," Colum mused. "Sanglier looks like a fox but has the temperament of a weasel. Could the poisonings in Walmer have anything to do with him?"

"I'd like to say yes"—Kathryn laughed—"but the French have their own dark secrets, they would not be bothered with the doings of villagers."

They walked back down Mercery and along the High Street where stall owners were finishing the day's trading. The constable was there with his posse of bailiffs, they all looked hard eyed as Kathryn and Colum passed, giving no greeting.

"Do you think Walter the Constable is a man of violence?" Kathryn asked.

"I know Walter the Constable is a man of violence," Colum replied. "I've met his sort so many times in camps up and down this kingdom. Bully boys who've been given a bit of power and the opportunity to wield it with relish."

They crossed the now emptying marketplace. Beggars whined for alms, children played waiting for their parents. Kathryn glimpsed the preacher sitting on the steps of the market cross. He lifted his head as they passed, and sketched a blessing in the air. Kathryn nodded in acknowledgement.

"Now, there's a man who has questions to answer." Kathryn let go of Colum's arm and walked back. The preacher sat, head down.

"Sir?"

The preacher crossed himself and glanced up, Ave beads wrapped round his fingers.

"I was praying." The preacher squinted up at her. "I was praying for guidance, mistress."

"Are you a native of Walmer?" Kathryn asked.

"I'm a native of all towns and villages, wherever God sends me."

"I asked you a question, sir. Are you a native of Walmer?"

"I come and go where the wind blows." He glanced shrewdly at Colum, who'd followed Kathryn back. "But, to answer your question, mistress, I'm of the west country."

"And what has brought you to Walmer?"

"God's work. Why, mistress, do you suspect me of these hideous poisonings? I assure you, search me. I have a few pennies for a loaf of bread and a cup of watered wine. If you give me something, perhaps I will eat better tonight."

Kathryn dipped into her purse and took out a silver coin.

"You spoke to one of the poisoner's victims?"

"Aye, the apothecary—but only for a short while about matters spiritual."

"And you have an interest in Benedict the Notary?"

"Only because he is a man of the law." The preacher smiled up at Kathryn. "A wandering preacher is always wary of the law."

"Why did you obtain a sheet of vellum from the apothecary? A similar sheet, with a warning written in black ink, was pinned to the priest's door last Sunday morning." Kathryn leaned down and touched the preacher's black, dusty fingers. "Another warning was scrawled on the church floor."

The preacher, no longer smiling, rose to his feet, "Aye, mistress, and I have slept near the church, but"—he spread his hands—"my hands are black because of the charcoal I gather for a fire, whilst the sheet of vellum was used for a sermon."

"Where is it now?"

"I later burnt it on the fire." He glowered at Colum. "I have done no wrong. No evidence can be laid against me."

Kathryn handed him the coin.

"Why, mistress, thank you." The preacher bit the coin. "I'll drink your health and pray for you. Mistress, I know nothing of this village, its people, or, indeed, their sins. If I do I shall search you out and tell you." And, grasping his staff, he walked away.

"He's not a preacher, Colum," Kathryn murmured as they left the marketplace, following the trackway curling up towards the manor house.

"Why do you think that?"

"Look at his hands and wrists, Colum, all scarred. He's a swordsman, and the callus on the fourth finger of his right hand—he's also strung many an arrow. A soldier, I think."

"I've met the like," Colum agreed. "Taken a knock on the head, seen some vision and turned to God."

"I don't think he's turned to God," Kathryn replied. "I think he's up to mischief. I have no proof, just those eyes. Our preacher has a weakness not only for a cup of wine, watered or not, but a pretty face. We should also question Lord Henry more closely. We must confront him with the mysteries which seem to concern him as well as those threatening his villagers, but not today." They walked on up the path, standing aside as carts trundled by, back to the village.

"Lord Henry is buying in supplies," Colum explained. "I think he wishes to impress his guests."

When they returned to the manor house, Colum went to check on their horses. Kathryn returned to their chamber on the first gallery, a spacious room. Its walls were almost covered by beautiful wooden panelling, the strip of plaster above painted a brilliant white and decorated with triptychs, crosses, and thick cloth of gold. The bed was the work of a craftsman, hung in dark blue velvet, with the sheets and bolsters of the finest linen. There were chests and coffers, stools and tables, even an elegantly carved writing desk for Kathryn and Colum to use. On the table beside the bed, a servant had placed two goblets with a jug of wine, each covered with a white napkin bearing the Lord Henry's arms. Kathryn removed the napkin and sniffed at the wine. It smelt clear and strong but Kathryn felt that, if she drank, she'd sleep, and she wanted to think. She decided to remove her bracelet: she opened the great coffer at the end of her bed and paused. Everything was in order, yet Kathryn knelt down, opening her jewellery casket. She moved to the box of cosmetics lying next to it.

"I'm sure," Kathryn whispered. She stared at the door they'd left unlocked for the servant. Was it one of them? Kathryn was sure someone had been into this coffer, moved some of her clothes and opened the caskets, yet nothing was missing. Perhaps a curious servant? Kathryn closed the coffer and walked to the window and opened its small door of mullion glass. The chamber provided a clear view of the clifftops and the sea glinting in the late afternoon sun. She followed the line of the countryside, the green grass of the moorland, the dusty track leading up to the scaffold. A figure moved along it, Kathryn was certain it was Mother Croul.

"I wonder." Kathryn murmured. "I wonder if you can tell me more."

She went across to the lavarium, splashed water on her hands and face, and opened one of her perfume jars and dabbed a little on the side of her neck. She changed her soft leather shoes for riding boots, grasped her cloak and, going down to the stables, searched out Colum. He was deep in conversation with one of the ostlers, admiring a saddle on its frame.

"The work of a craftsman," Colum declared, patting it. "Kathryn, why are you here?"

"I want to go for a ride."

"By yourself?"

"Just up to the clifftop," Kathryn replied.

Colum went across the yard and took out a gentle cob. He saddled it, helped her up, then stood with one hand holding the reins, the other on her knee.

"Now, promise me you won't go far, just to the clifftop and back. I'll have a servant standing in the gatehouse to watch you. He'll be there until you return." He grinned. "Where you go, danger always seems to follow."

Kathryn leaned down and pinched his cheek. "Unhand me, Irishman, I have to leave!" She urged the horse on, Colum's warning still ringing in her ears. Once out of the cobbled yard, Kathryn turned her mount, following the line of the wall. As she did so, the three Frenchmen, sitting in the shade sharing a pannikin of wine, got to their feet brushing crumbs off their doublets. Kathryn reined in.

"Mistress." Sanglier bowed, the other two followed suit. "If we'd known you were riding out alone we would have asked to accompany you."

"Sir, if you'd accompanied me, I wouldn't be riding alone, would I?"

The Vicomte laughed. "Mistress, enjoy your English weather. They say the sun will soon disappear."

Kathryn gathered up the reins and stared at the three Frenchmen. They must be out here because no one could eavesdrop on their conversation.

"I understand Lord Henry has more trouble in the village," Sanglier declared, "one death after another. Ah well, the Lord giveth and the Lord taketh away."

"What do you mean?" Kathryn asked, and leaned down. "My lord, what do you mean by that?"

"Oh, don't you know?" The Frenchman stroked his moustache. "The village of Walmer belongs to the lord of the manor. When a man dies, his estate returns to Lord Henry. If these deaths continue he'll be a richer man by the end of the week."

"Lord Henry has wealth enough." Kathryn resented the mockery in the Frenchman's voice. "He doesn't need dead men's goods." She urged the cob on. Behind her one of the Frenchmen laughed, but Kathryn didn't turn. Out of the corner of her eye Kathryn glimpsed the stone wall of the manor rising up against the blue sky. Sunlight flashed in the windows, to her right the sea shimmered as the sun began to dip. A beautiful afternoon, Kathryn thought. The grass and gorse from the cliff was rich and sweet smelling with wildflowers of various colours. Above her a gull screeched. A rabbit scampered across her path. Ahead of her Kathryn could see Mother Croul kneeling beside the scaffold as if it were a statue. She only moved when Kathryn dismounted and hobbled the cob. She sat back on the grass beneath the scaffold, and Kathryn joined her, staring out across the sea.

"So quiet, isn't it?" Mother Croul peered as if she were trying to glimpse something beyond the far horizon. "Look at the sea, mistress, like glass. I love to watch the sunset when the sea turns red."

Kathryn stared up at the three-branched scaffold, a soaring monstrosity of black wood and cruel eye hooks. A piece of rope dangled from one of these.

"It's peaceful enough now," Mother Croul confessed, "but I was here, mistress, when they hanged them. One cart after another, ladders up against the scaffold. Men scampering up, nooses around necks, and the carts pulled away, leaving the bodies to dance and jerk. It was bigger than this, the other scaffold, six branches in all, though this one's gruesome enough. Anyway, enough of death. You are enjoying your stay at Walmer Manor?"

"I thought I would." Kathryn smiled back. "The village is beautiful. The sea is so serene, I can hardly hear the waves."

"Come back in winter and you will." Mother Croul laughed.

"Thunders like a giant trying to break in. So, have you recently exchanged vows at the wedding door with that strapping Irishman? They are fearful of him, you know, the villagers, but there again, they would fear an Irishman. There were plenty here during the recent wars, men of terror!"

"The cowl doesn't make the monk," Kathryn replied, quoting from Chaucer.

"I know what you say, but, still, your Irishman is a fighter. I can tell that. The way he lifted that sword in the hall, I thought he'd take all our heads."

Kathryn laughed. "In battle a warrior," she replied, "in peace a perfect, gentle knight."

"Men aren't gentle," Mother Croul disagreed, "they're violent. No, that's wrong, my first husband was gentle and kindly: he wouldn't hurt a fly and would tend the broken wing of a bird. My second—ah, mistress, we women can be foolish. Wild he was, and worse. Sometimes, mistress, I believe we're like horses; you can have a horse and it's basically good. Find another, and there's something wicked about it. So it was with my second husband. He joined the wreckers, not just because he wanted the profits, he liked to kill."

"So, why do you come here?" Kathryn asked.

"I used to lay flowers," Mother Croul replied, "light a candle. Eventually I thought, what's the use? Sometimes I just come here to make a vigil, to say the Requiem, and to pray." She brought her hand up, prayer beads curled around her vein-streaked hand. "Sometimes I just come here to meet his ghost."

"You loved him, didn't you," Kathryn asked, "your second husband?"

"God forgive me, mistress," Mother Croul whispered, "but you're right, I did love him, and such a death! Now and again, you meet a man who couldn't give a damn about God or man." Her voice trailed away. "But you're here to ask me questions about these hideous deaths."

"Tell me about Walmer, please."

"So you regard me as the village gossip?"

"I regard you as a wise woman," Kathryn replied, "who climbed these cliffs and hoped I might come and join you."

Mother Croul laughed, then fished in the pocket of her dark brown robe; she took out a piece of cheese, broke it in two and offered half to Kathryn, who took it. The cheese was delicious and fresh.

"I make my own," Mother Croul observed, "and, as for the villagers, well, there's the priest, Father Clement, a man who lives in his own world, carving his stone and saying his prayers. A gentle priest but I recognise something strong in him. He can be harsh and deliver a powerful sermon. To the penitent sinner he is good and kind. To those who resist God's grace and the warnings of Holy Mother Church, hard as flint. He's been here sixteen years. He cursed the wreckers from the sanctuary and bolted the door of the church against them. He belled, booked, candled, and cursed the devilish crew all the days of their lives. I heard that curse. I told my husband he was excommunicated! He only laughed. I knew then Satan would come to claim his own."

"And Amabilia?" Kathryn asked.

"A gentle soul. Sometimes I wonder if she's right in the head. Oh, there's been gossip how she and her brother are as close as man and wife, you know how tongues clack, but it's only nasty minds and spiteful mouths. Father Clement's a good priest, a shepherd interested in the sheep rather than their wool."

"And Benedict and Ursula?"

"Ah!" Mother Croul put her hands together, licking her fingers, eager to take every crumb of cheese. "Now, there's two peas from the same pod, narrow of mind, hard of heart. Benedict is not from these parts but further north. He'd an understanding with the wreckers. He was of their coven but on the edges, between the shadow and the light. He made himself most amenable to Lord Henry. Does legal work over this and that and carries messages for him everywhere."

"Is he an assassin?" Kathryn asked. "Could he kill?"

"Oh yes. He has grasping hands. He'd whip me from here to London just to earn a groat."

"And his wife, Ursula?"

"Airs and graces, mistress. She's as hard as he, but acts the great lady. There was always rivalry between herself and her sister."

"Do you think that Adam the Apothecary poisoned his wife?"

"No, mistress, I don't think. I know."

"You're so certain?"

"I have no proof, yet Adam was a nightmare soul. Looking back down the years I wonder how many he helped into the darkness. There again, that's only the chatter of an old woman. Adam must answer for his crimes before God's Court. And, before you ask, mistress, the sexton's a toper, full of ale and malice. He has his own secret, hidden pursuits. You saw the two lovers in the churchyard?"

Kathryn smiled.

"A common occurrence," Mother Croul continued. "Simon likes nothing more than to spy on them. He thinks it's a secret which he nurses to his heart. I've seen him there, like a stoat amongst the grass, watching young lovers couple. He takes great pleasure from it, not to mention the power it gives him. On more than one occasion he's threatened some young maid that he will reveal all unless she does exactly what he wants."

"And our constable?"

"Fat Walter." Mother Croul paused as a gull swooped, screeching over her head. "I always think that the calls of those birds are the voices of ghosts, but that's fanciful. Walter is a flawed man, one with talents, but he's a bully boy. He and his bailiffs like nothing better than to hound some beggar to the parish boundaries, or birch the buttocks of some wandering whore or tinker's girl."

"And finally we come to our physician."

"Roger is a gifted man but one with secrets. He's not from these parts but from London. According to gossip, he once lived in a great mansion, silver and gold trickled through his fingers, but something happened. A wandering chapman told me how Roger had given a wrong potion to a powerful merchant's wife.

Roger had to flee the city and bury himself in Walmer. In many ways he's a good physician, sharp-eyed, keen of wit, always prepared to distil a potion for this or a powder for that, and, as long as he's paid, doesn't really care. A man nursing grudges, bitter and twisted." She turned and gazed fully at Kathryn. "We're not comely, are we? Not in God's grace, but, there again, don't we all have secrets? I'm sure your Irishman has witnessed scenes he'd prefer to forget. And what about you, mistress?"

"Kathryn, please call me Kathryn."

"Well, Mistress Kathryn"—Mother Croul grasped her cane, got to her feet and stared down at her—"what secrets do you have?"

"A loveless marriage," Kathryn replied, "at least before this, a drunken husband."

"Ah." Mother Croul patted her gently on the head. "We all have our past like sacks piled upon our back, sometimes the very weight can break us."

"Tell me," Kathryn asked, getting on to her feet, "these three Lancastrians, fleeing for sanctuary or refuge—were you party to their deaths?"

Mother Croul, resting on her cane, shook her head. "Poor men," she said pitifully, "they made a mistake of coming to Walmer and going into the Silver Swan. They should have ridden their horses to one of the fishing ports. No, I wasn't present at their deaths, but I heard what happened, Elias and the rest, baying like hounds, pursuing them through the streets. I heard rumours how the young squire tried to surrender. When they reached the cemetery he threw his sword down and held up his hands. I don't know what truly happened except Elias and the rest showed no mercy. They were eager to prove to Lord Henry, and everyone else, how they were loyal to the King." She peered at Kathryn and drew close. Kathryn smelt the faint lavender from her clothing. "You think that's important, don't you?"

"Perhaps," Kathryn replied. "The death of those three strangers might be, in some way, connected to these poisonings. It's a wild guess. I'm floundering in the dark."

"Then you'd best get back." Mother Croul laughed. "The real

darkness will soon be upon us. This clifftop can be a dangerous place. Walmer covered in shadows, hidden by the night, is not what it is during the daylight hours. Come, I'll walk with you."

Kathryn unhobbled the cob and returned to the path. Mother Croul began to point out different plants, how farmers once tried to plough this clifftop.

"But the earth is too salted," she said, "the wind blows in from the sea. Listen, mistress, you can only hear the waves murmur now. In winter the wind is a fury, few people come up here. Anyway," she said, grinning, "they say it's haunted, how the ghosts of the wreckers spend their purgatory here."

"How many people know about herbs?" Kathryn asked. "I mean, in the village?"

"We all do, mistress, you know that. Roger the Physician, Benedict, even Walter, and, of course, Adam the Apothecary had a treasure house, a list of powders for everything."

Kathryn glanced sharply at her. "Including murder?"

"You have said it, mistress, including murder."

They reached the entrance to the manor house. Mother Croul made her farewells and Kathryn walked into the cobbled yard. She stopped in astonishment. Everyone seemed to be there. Lord Henry was proudly showing off a recently purchased pedigree falcon, a beautiful blue-grey bird, its pointed dark face masked by a little hood. It sat on its stand, jesse bells ringing like those from some elfin kingdom. Lord Henry was showing the bird off to Sanglier, Cavignac, and Delacroix. Colum was making his own contribution, comparing the quality of this bird to the others. Ostlers and grooms stood about but, in the corner, Kathryn was surprised to see the preacher sitting on a stone plinth, a cup of claret in one hand, a lump of bread in the other. He was eating lustily, slurping from the cup, peering across as if watching a scene in a mummer's play. Kathryn handed the reins of the horse to an ostler. Lord Henry greeted her. Kathryn noticed how his eyes were bright, his mouth merry, the first time she'd seen him so happy since she'd arrived in Walmer.

"I'm just showing off the bird, Mistress Kathryn, a noble falcon. Colum believes that the merlin can be faster, more deadly. Is it true, my lord,"—he turned to Sanglier—"that your master's mews in Paris holds every type of hawk under the sun?"

"His Grace is a keen falconer," Sanglier replied, "and loves to hunt, particularly down near the marshes."

"We all love hunting." Lord Henry stroked the breast of the bird with his finger. "There, there," he soothed, "my beauty."

"What's he doing here?" Kathryn asked, pointing at the preacher.

"I wondered the same," Sanglier spoke up, "I've seen him striding around like a judge come to judgement."

"You're sharp-eyed, my Lord Vicomte."

Henry handed the peregrine to one of his grooms, clapped his hands, and called the preacher over. The fellow rose, finishing his bread, washing it down with a final gulp of wine. He tossed the cup to one of the servants, came across and clasped Lord Henry's hand, who pulled him closer, putting an arm round his shoulders. Such a gesture of friendship surprised even Colum. The three Frenchmen stared narrow-eyed.

"Here is a man of God," Lord Henry began sardonically, "known as the preacher. He travels here, he travels there, even across the narrow seas to France."

"In which case," Sanglier broke in harshily, "next time he visits Paris I can entertain him. My lord, this man is a spy."

"He is a collector of information." Lord Henry was openly revelling, "And has recently returned from Paris. His real name is Richard Blandford, Clerk of the Green Wax. Once, like you sir"—he gestured at Delacroix—"he studied for the priesthood before he realised that God called him to another path. So, his knowledge of the Scriptures and the Fathers is plentiful."

Blandford stood enjoying the discomfort of the French.

"Now, Master Blandford is hot from Paris, where he lived with the vagabonds. I believe, sir, there is what you call the Guild of Pecheurs, the fraternity of sinners, that's one way of translating it," Lord Henry continued, "but it can also be the Guild of Fishers, they search the Seine for valuable objects, they take corpses washed into the reeds, or along the mud banks."

"And?" Sanglier demanded.

"Marshall's corpse has been found. He was recognised by the ring on his hand bearing my insignia." Sanglier stepped back, Delacroix and Cavignac grouped behind him.

"What is this?" Sanglier demanded.

"We have news," Lord Henry repeated himself, "William Marshall's corpse has been found. It has been given to the Filles de Dieu, the Good Sisters, who run the Mercy Convent near the Porte Saint Denis, for burial."

"And?" Sanglier demanded.

"William Marshall did not drown," Lord Henry continued evenly, all humour gone from his face. "Marshall had been killed, his throat a jagged slash, opened from one ear to another, gaping like another mouth. He was murdered."

"You do not lay his death at my master's door?" Sanglier protested. "Or believe that any of us had a hand in this? Paris, like London, is full of thieves. Monsieur Marshall should not have gone fishing in the Seine."

"Who told you that he'd gone fishing?"

"You did."

"Ah yes, my Lord Vicomte, but fishing for what?"

Lord Henry turned to his spy, patting him on the shoulder; small clouds of dust rose from the coarse, black cloth.

"Tell them yourself."

"I stayed three months in Paris." The preacher's voice was harsh. "Amongst the pecheurs there was a great deal of rivalry to discover the corpse of William Marshall, the Englishman who drowned. There were others, I don't know who," he added sarcastically, "also offering gold and silver if the corpse and anything on it was found."

Sanglier gazed back stonily.

"Was anything found?" Cavignac spoke up.

"Nothing! Poor Marshall was found in the clothes he wore, a few coins in his wallet, but the dagger from his scabbard was gone."

"A good man, William Marshall." Lord Henry's voice stilled the clamour in the yard. "His death will be avenged." And, stretching out his arm, Lord Henry demanded that the favourite peregrine be placed on his gauntleted wrist. He bowed to all his guests and walked back across the courtyard and in through a narrow door leading to his own private quarters.

Sanglier and his companions immediately withdrew, talking amongst themselves, making for the gateway well away from any eavesdropper. Colum stood watching the stable boy unsaddle the cob Kathryn had taken out.

"Well, I never!" he breathed.

"Well, I never what, Irishman?"

"Lord Henry is keeper of the Secret Seal because, behind that smooth, calm, handsome face is a brain which writhes like a box of worms." Colum shook his head. "He's sly and cunning, more than a match for Sanglier."

The preacher sauntered up, winked at Kathryn, and followed Lord Henry into the manor.

"I'm not sure what's happening, Kathryn," Colum murmured. "Lord Henry devised a game and, whether they like it or not, Sanglier and his companions must play their parts."

"So, Marshall was murdered," Kathryn declared. "The important question is, by whom? The French?"

"Enough questions." Colum grasped her hand and kissed her fingers.

"So the preacher is a spy and a liar," Kathryn insisted, "and what's more—"

"Enough!" Colum smiled. "Enough for now!"

Chapter 6

He yaf nat of that text a pulled hen. That seith that hunters ben nat hooly men.
—Chaucer, General Prologue,
The Canterbury Tales

A maid had wheeled a capped brazier into their chamber, its glowing charcoal, strewn with herbs, gave off a deliciously fresh smell. For a while Kathryn sat on the edge of the bed and studied a bestiary that Lord Henry had placed there as a courtesy gift from his library. She leafed through the coloured parchment, looking at the dark reds and greens. She stopped at a strange-looking creature the artist had depicted in a blueish purple.

The Irishman was now stripping, ready to wash. Kathryn tapped the page. "Did you know, Colum, the wild ass lives in Africa, and one male will dominate an entire herd of females." She smiled. "According to this, the male is so jealous of any new-born colt, he will bite off its testicles. On the eve of twenty-fifth March, the Feast of the Conception of Christ, the wild ass will bray twelve times during the night and twelve times during the day. Yet at the same time, it represents the devil, because the wild ass doesn't know the difference between day and night." She turned the pages and stared at the strangely sketched camel. She pointed at the picture. "I saw one of these when my father took me to the Tower of London. According to the writer, it chews the cud like an ox and can cover hundreds of miles in one day." She closed the book and placed it on the bed.

The Irishman was now dipping a napkin into the bowl, washing his body. Kathryn noticed the crisscross scars on his side and back.

"How many wounds do you have, Irishman?"

"More than I care to count. Some are from battles, others from fights in dark streets and stinking alleyways. Do they repel you?"

"Nothing about you repels me, Irishman." Kathryn would have continued the teasing but abruptly, on the evening breeze, came the sound of a tolling bell.

"Simon the Sexton," she explained. "I wonder what's wrong now." Then she remembered the three corpses. "They must be blessing them," she remarked quietly, "Elias, Isabella, and Adam. They'll be incensed just before dark. Father Clement will sing the Requiem Mass tomorrow. By the end of the day they'll lie buried in the God's Acre. Isn't it strange, Colum, how swift life can be?" She opened the book and pointed to a picture of a lion. "That's what death's like, a devourer, a beast striking from the grass or a hawk winging from the sky."

Colum put on a clean shirt, came over and touched her under her chin. "In which case, my little philosopher, we should enjoy the day while it lasts. Are you happy, Kathryn?" He sat down on the bed beside her. "Or does your mind still dwell in the past?"

"If it dwells in the past, Irishman"—she put her arms around his waist and leaned her head on his chest—"it's because I'm so happy, such a contrast, yet, listening to that funeral bell, sometimes I have nightmares that Alexander Wyville doesn't lie buried in some lonely churchyard in the west country but, like the devil, he wanders around seeking mischief. One day he might come back and, like a housebreaker, burst into my life."

Colum stroked her hair. "If he does, then he'll find the house closely guarded and a wild Irishman with sword and buckler ready."

"That's my ferocious soldier," Kathryn murmured. They began to kiss. Colum rose, locked the door, and came back. They lay making love. Outside the darkness fell and the sounds of the manor faded. Kathryn fell asleep, head resting on Colum's chest. When she woke, night had fallen. The Irishman lay sleeping beside her. She got to her feet and went to the window. Outside in the courtyard below, pitch torches flared against the darkness, the flames whipped up by the strengthening breeze. She opened the casement window. The sound of the sea was stronger now, and the cold night air carried the tang of salt. She dressed quickly, went into the gallery and down the stairs. She passed Lord Henry's writing office, where the door was ajar. The sound of a flute playing intrigued Kathryn. She peered through the crack of light. At first she couldn't believe her eyes. The writing office was as costly and well furnished as any chamber in the manor but Lord Henry wasn't writing. He stood in his shirt and hose, boots off, doing a jig, the sort a man would do in a tavern, while the preacher played the flute. Lord Henry sensed he was being watched. He turned and Kathryn scampered away as the door crashed firmly shut. The faint tune followed her as she went down the stairs into the long hall. This was deserted but the servants, busy with tomorrow's feast, had laid out a collation of cold meats, freshly baked bread, pots of butter and honey, and jugs of wine, malmsey, and ale. Kathryn filled a platter with strips of lamb, goose, pheasant, and two manchet loaves. She took this and two napkins up to her chamber where Colum had already stirred, sitting bleary eyed on the edge of the bed. Kathryn opened the shutters wider and urged Colum to eat.

"It's so strange," she mused. She stared across at the six-branched silver candelabra; Colum had lit this while she was out of the room, and placed it on the window ledge, well away from any drapery or tapestries. The flames danced in the breeze that crept through the cracks in the windows or under the door, casting shadows that rose and fell with the bend of the flames.

"What's strange?" Colum sat on the other side of the table picking at a piece of meat. Lifting the goblet up, he admired the line of gems around the rim.

"Lord Henry," Kathryn declared. "He's the King's confidant, a master clerk, a man skilled in the ways of war as well as the chancery. He rises in the King's favour, a warrior, he's sent to Walmer to seek justice for his brother, and carries out vengeance against a gang of wreckers. A wealthy man who has drunk deep of the cup of life. He's given this manor house and the estates around. He's married to a lovely wife, though a marriage of convenience rather than love"—she leaned across and tipped Colum on the nose—"unlike others I know! Now, a year ago, Lady Mary died of a fall from the cliffs at Gallows Point. I went out there today, Irishman, to meet Mother Croul."

"I know." The Irishman smiled. "My sentry told me exactly whom you'd met. You sat on the grass gossiping."

"I never asked her about Lord Henry. I didn't think it as appropriate. Sitting at the edge of that cliff, I could see how a distraught woman could easily slip. The ground is flat and suddenly dips. If someone agitated, anxious, took an unwary step, a fall would be easy to imagine. Whatever he is, I don't think Lord Henry is a cold-souled murderer, nor do I believe his wife would commit suicide. Her death was an unfortunate accident. Six months later Lord Henry and his chosen man-at-arms, a favourite clerk, were despatched on the King's business to Paris. According to the accepted story, Marshall went fishing on the Seine. However, I'm sure if I made further enquiries, I'd find Marshall was not interested in fishing. He went to meet somebody. He was on some errand from Lord Henry and disappeared."

"And the Book of Ciphers?" Colum asked.

"I'm not too sure whether he was carrying the Book of Ciphers." Kathryn sipped at her wine. "Do you seriously think, Colum, a man as skilled as Lord Henry, or a clerk as experienced as William Marshall, would carry, in the heart of the enemy camp, such a valuable document?"

"Yes, I did wonder about that."

"Anyway, Marshall disappears, and Lord Henry, distraught, returns to England. A short while later a strange letter, apparently written in Lady Mary's hand, is sent to the Chancellor, Archbishop Bourchier, in which Lord Henry is accused of being guilty of the murder of his wife, Lady Mary; that she did not suffer an accident but was pushed, though there's little evidence to substantiate that. The letter, which you have in your possession, was apparently in her hand. I'm sure, if you compare it with other documents, this would be true—it also carries her seal. Bourchier has asked you, and thereby me, to investigate this matter.

"Now we come to Walmer, the beginning of October, the year of our Lord 1472. Three French envoys have arrived in England to treat for peace. Lord Henry acts agitated, discomforted, worried about his clerk and the Book of Ciphers. The French seem to be enjoying themselves. Oh, by the way, Colum, did they bring a great retinue?"

"Men-at-arms, but, as with all these matters, armed men are not allowed into this manor, they're billeted at a farmhouse further inland."

"Matters proceed," Kathryn continued. "The preacher arrives, but he's no more a preacher than I am. He is Richard Blandford, an English spy from the Office of the Green Wax, used by Lord Henry to take messages to his agents as well as collect information in France. The preacher arrives in Walmer. He acts his part, though God knows what he is doing here. At last he enters Walmer Manor, where Lord Henry introduces him as his spy, which means that Blandford can never go back to France now that Sanglier has this information. Lord Henry believes such a revelation is worth the price of informing his opponents that William Marshall did not suffer an accident but was foully murdered." She paused and bit into a piece of tender venison.

"What are you saying, Kathryn?"

"Early this evening, I went down to the kitchen. I was hungry, I wanted something to eat for both myself and my sleepy-headed Irishman. I pass Lord Henry's writing office. He's cloistered with his clerk, Richard Blandford, who is playing the flute whilst Lord Henry, boots kicked off, jigs as any merry tinker would in a tavern. He was celebrating, rejoicing about something, but what?"

"And?" Colum asked.

"This is what I believe, Colum, though I have little proof." Kathryn wiped her fingers on a napkin. "First, Lady Mary died a tragic but accidental death. Lord Henry may feel guilty about it but he wasn't responsible. He's also innocent of the death of William Marshall, though intrigued by the fate of his comrade, his most skilful of clerks. He therefore instructs the preacher, his agent in France, to stay in Paris and discover the truth. He apparently achieves this. At the same time Lord Henry invites Sanglier, one of Louis XI's most trusted councillors, together with two high-ranking clerks, to England, to negotiate over a possible peace treaty here at Walmer. They arrive. Lord Henry acts as if defensive, disconcerted. More importantly Lord Henry knows that Sanglier has learnt a great deal about him, especially the mystery surrounding Lady Mary's death."

"Is that so?" Colum exclaimed.

"Now, the picture I paint"—Kathryn chewed on the corner of her lip—"is indistinct, but my conclusion is that Lord Henry himself wrote that letter."

"What!"

"Yes, I believe that Lord Henry wrote that letter to Bourchier."

"But why?"

"For two reasons. Lord Henry may have felt responsible for his wife's death, we don't know why but such a confession might purge his soul. The second reason is, I suspect, he wanted the French to find out."

Colum pushed himself away from the table. "Kathryn, this does not make sense, it's not logical."

"No, listen," Kathryn retorted, "the letter was in Lady Mary's hand but Lord Henry is a most skilled clerk, so erudite he's keeper of the King's Secret Seal, a scribe, a man versed in letters. It's not impossible for him to imitate his wife's hand, her style of writing, her phrases, nor is it inconceivable that he kept one of her seals and used it for that letter."

"But how would the French find out?"

"There's a notary in the village," Kathryn replied, "Benedict. Lord Henry uses him to take messages here and there, both at home and abroad."

"Ah, I see." Colum smiled. "He would ask Benedict the Notary to take the letter to Bourchier in Canterbury . . ."

"A short while later, Benedict is despatched to France where, in some tavern, he would divulge all the gossip he knows to one of Sanglier's agents. Lord Henry, however, is a most cunning man, he is deliberately misleading the French. He wants to make them think that he is weak, vulnerable, disconcerted, worried about the stories concerning his wife's death, Marshall's disappearance, the Book of Ciphers. He issues this invitation—"

"And the French rise to the bait."

"It's no coincidence," Kathryn agreed, "that the preacher arrived at the very time Sanglier and those two precious clerks are at Walmer. Lord Henry is leading them a merry dance. Now they are here, they have to obey his tune, but I wonder where he is leading them."

"Shall we confront him?" Colum asked.

Kathryn shook her head. "No, I may have it wrong. Though I believe we're on the right path, only the good Lord knows where it will lead. Now," she said as she returned to her food, "I thought we may have had a letter from Thomasina."

"I'm sure all is well in Canterbury." Colum shook his head. "Thomasina will be quacking under her breath, going round the house, doing this and doing that or out in the garden wreaking vengeance amongst the weeds. Agnus and Wulf will either be teasing each other or driving her to distraction."

"And my patients?" Kathryn asked.

"Your patients." Colum stretched across and clasped her hands. "There's Father Cuthbert at the Poor Priest's Hospital. We are enjoying our wedding days!"

"Are we, Irishman? Is that why you brought me to Walmer?"

Colum's hand fell away. "This business in the village?" he asked, scratching his head.

"The poisonings." Kathryn ran a finger round the rim of her goblet. "Colum, I don't think it has anything to do with the business here at the manor. Someone is intent on vengeance but I don't know why or for what purpose. All I know—a feeling, a guess—is that these murders are connected to those three Lancastrians killed in the churchyard. You know they may have tried to surrender?"

"In which case," Colum replied, "those who killed them are, in theory, guilty of murder."

"You came here, Colum, you saw their corpses. Didn't anyone ask why they were here?"

"Walmer is on the coast." He shrugged. "Perhaps they hoped to hire a fishing smack, flee across the narrow seas to Hainault or Brabant. During that time the fishing men and merchants of England did a most profitable trade taking exiles abroad."

"But these three," Kathryn asked, "were on no proscription list, were they? They weren't enemy commanders but little people. Soldiers who fought for the wrong cause. I just wonder, Colum, if they came to Walmer for a different purpose." She gazed around the chamber.

"The sword belt we found?"

"I have given it to Lord Henry. He says it's the property of the Crown and should be sent to the Exchequer in London."

"And the two ledgers?" Colum pointed to the chest next to the bed.

"I intend to study them," Kathryn remarked. "Perhaps they may hold something, though I don't know what." Kathryn rose to her feet and stood by the window for a while. She could just make out the outline of the scaffold against the night sky and, turning to her right, glimpsed the pinpricks of light from the village.

"Should I have words with Lord Henry?" Colum asked harshly.

"Keep your counsel, Irishman," Kathryn replied, "though I would be delighted to know what is happening."

"So I shall find out for you," Colum grinned, as he turned and left the room. Kathryn sat down and finished her wine. She looked at the chest at the foot of the bed. "No," she whispered, "I can wait until tomorrow." She got to her feet and undressed, putting on her night shift, just as Colum came back through the door.

"Lord Henry and the preacher are dining in the hall by themselves. They seem happy enough. When I entered they were discussing hawks and hounds. Lord Henry was promising Blandford that, now he was home to stay, he'd take him hunting."

"Have you met Blandford before?" Kathryn asked.

"No, but I have heard his name, a trusted clerk, one of those men who live in the twilight, who move from Court to camp. I had friends, comrades, who did the same. Some were captured by the French and hanged. Others were killed by Lancastrians, a few just disappeared, only God knows where their bones lie."

"And the Frenchmen?" Kathryn asked.

"Neither sight nor sound." Colum grinned. "Apparently they're cloistered in Sanglier's chamber discussing matters of great import. The rest of the household is preparing for tomorrow's great feast. I'm sure Lord Henry intends to bait them. Sanglier is now insisting that the proper negotiations begin."

"In other words," Kathryn remarked, "Sanglier wishes to leave."

"I think so." Colum sat on the edge of the bed staring at her. "He realises he's been trapped and wishes to return home. Now, come, let your hair fall down."

Kathryn put her arms around his neck. "Why, Irishman." She fluttered her eyelids. "What do you intend?"

Kathryn started awake. She'd lain between the sheets naked. She'd fallen asleep feeling warm and passionate but the night air had turned cold. Colum had doused the candles and the sparkle of the braziers had dimmed. She moved the blankets aside, found her night shift, put it on, and, taking a cloak, wrapped it round her shoulders and walked to the window. She reckoned it must be well after midnight. The manor lay quiet. Pitch torches flared in the courtyard below. The night was truly beautiful, a full moon in a cloudless sky, whilst the stars hung like bright gems against a dark blue curtain. Kathryn could still make out the path leading to the clifftop. She pressed her hand against the pane and listened to the sounds of the sea, the tide closer, clashing against the rocks. She opened the casement window to feel the breeze. Autumn was dying, winter would come. She thought of the snow falling, thick and heavy, clogging the lanes and alleyways of Canterbury; of Colum, struggling through the drifts, concerned about his precious horses at Kingsmead.

She closed the window and looked over her shoulder. The

Irishman was deeply asleep. Kathryn stared down into the court-yard. She thought she'd seen a shadow move but perhaps it was a cat or one of Lord Henry's guards. Such nights like these, she reckoned, would be short-lived. The weather would turn, the rain come, the biting wind, the cold, the time for fires, braziers and warming pans, of clasping hot cups of posset.

"I should take advantage," Kathryn whispered. She felt re-freshed, unable to sleep. She found a pair of soft leather boots and put them on. She took a heavy cloak to wrap round her shoulders, a walking cane from the corner of the room, and slipped out of the chamber. The manor house lay silent. Capped candles glowed everywhere. A lantern, hanging in the stairwell, provided enough light to go down the stairs. In its dim light the paintings on the wall assumed a life of their own: the Apostle Peter stared sorrowfully down at her; in another, St. Sebastian writhed as he was shot to death by arrows. Kathryn reached the foot of the stairs and started as a cat padded across her path. A sleepy-eyed porter, near the side door, struggled awake, almost falling off his stool. Kathryn pushed him gently back.

"Don't worry." She raised the latch. "I'll see myself out and in again." She crossed the courtyard, where the sentry was more vigilant and challenged her. Kathryn replied and the guard has-tened to open the small postern gate, which led out onto the moorland. She slipped through this and braced herself against the full force of the night wind. In the silvery moonlight the grass and gorse bent and all around her rose the cries and calls of the night. An owl, like a feather-winged ghost, floated before her and disappeared into the blackness.

Kathryn walked onto the pathway leading to Gallows Point. She stared back at the manor house. Here and there a candle glinted or a lantern glowed. She walked on, revelling in the night breeze's freshening effect. She felt hungry and wondered if the kitchen was still open for bread and meat, perhaps a little wine. She glanced down the trackway, half listening to the murmur of the sea. A sound made her look up and she almost screamed at the figure which blocked her path.

"I'm sorry, mistress." The preacher uncovered the lantern he carried and gazed merrily at her.

"You're like a cat!" Kathryn snapped. "Don't you know better than to appear so quietly in the dead of night, out here on a lonely moor?"

"If you're going to talk about knowing better, mistress, do you know how dangerous it is to be out here by yourself?"

"Oh, I know the dangers," she retorted, stepping closer, "but"—she raised her walking cane—"I can defend myself."

"Such beauty by moonlight," the preacher murmured.

"Why are you here?" she demanded.

The preacher shuttered the lantern and lowered it. "Like you, mistress, I find it difficult to sleep whilst there is business to be done."

"Lord Henry is pleased, isn't he?" Kathryn asked. "Now you've come from France with news."

"He's not pleased about Marshall's death," the preacher remarked, turning back and looking at the manor house. "He grieves for him but, there again, his grief is six months old. Now he comforts himself that he knows the truth, or some of it."

"Is Lord Henry baiting a trap?" Kathryn asked. "Is he expecting Sanglier and the other two to step into it? Will the door close behind them?"

The preacher laughed, turned suddenly, and, with his free hand, grasped Kathryn's, raised it to his lips and kissed her fingertips.

"Lord Henry has talked about you, mistress." He resisted Kathryn's tug. "Sharp as a knife, keen as a cutting blade; I can see he's right. What you must do, mistress, is as you should at a mummer's play, sit back and enjoy what will happen."

"There'll be hunters out tonight." Kathryn pointed to the moon. "You know the old proverb, Master Preacher, 'The hunter must always be careful that he does not become the hunted.'"

"I'll remember that." He stepped round her, wished her good night, and walked off into the darkness towards Gallows Point.

Kathryn returned to the manor house through the postern gate. Just before she did so she turned. The hair on the nape of her neck prickled, a shiver of cold ran across her shoulders. Was there someone else here? Was that a sound of the night or the scrape of a boot? She took a sharp intake of breath. Had the preacher gone out to be alone or to meet someone? Kathryn no longer felt hungry. She thanked the sentry, crossed the courtyard, and returned to her own chamber.

Kathryn woke late the next morning. Colum had already risen and been out. On the bolster beside her she found a white rose, freshly cut and drenched in dew. She got out of bed, stripped, washed, and put on fresh clothes, a white smock with a green sarcenet dress gathered high at the neck. She put on woollen stockings and slipped her feet into sandals, fastening their thongs. She stood in front of the piece of burnished copper that served as a mirror to comb and dress her hair, piling it up at the back before covering it carefully with a white stiffened veil. She examined herself carefully. Her skin was soft and wrinkle free, her eyes had lost those dark shadows.

"No great beauty," she murmured, "but still the love of his life." She left the chamber and went down the stairs now thronged with servants running hither and thither preparing for the evening feast. The air was sweet with the smell of pies and pastries being cooked in the ovens of the bakehouse.

She found her way to the chapel. No one was there so Kathryn knelt before the high altar and, as always, prayed for Colum, the repose of the souls of her mother and father, and the welfare of all those she knew in Canterbury. She also recited the Requiem for those who had died in Walmer.

She became distracted and wondered what had happened the night before. Why was the preacher striding out into the night? And was there someone else hiding near the wall? She returned to her prayers, made the sign of the cross, rose, and then knelt on the prie-dieu before the Lady Altar. She murmured the Ave Maria and lit a taper for Thomasina and the rest of her household in Canterbury.

Afterwards, she went out to the great hall where Lord Henry, Colum, and the three Frenchmen were in heated argument. They fell silent as she entered. Sanglier and the rest rose to greet her.

Lord Henry insisted that she sit in his chair at the head of the table while he slid onto the bench beside Colum. A scullion carried across a trencher bearing cheese, dried meat, freshly baked bread, pots of butter and honey, and a blackjack of honeyed milk.

"You slept well, mistress?"

"I slept well enough." Kathryn smiled at Lord Henry. "Why the silence?" She gazed round. "When I came in, there were heated words."

"The preacher has disappeared," Colum declared. "His bed hasn't been slept in, he's gone, no trace of him."

"I met him last night," Kathryn confessed. "I decided to go out and enjoy the night air. I thought I was safe enough. The preacher met me on the trackway. He was carrying a lantern. We exchanged words. He seemed calm enough. He went his way, and I went mine."

"Yes," Lord Henry agreed, "my watchman saw you go as he did you, my lord." He turned to Sanglier.

The Frenchman shrugged. "If I wish to take the night air, then that is my choice. If Mistress Kathryn can walk out under the stars, then why can't a Frenchman? I'm your guest, Lord Henry, not your prisoner."

"And you enjoyed the night air?" Kathryn asked.

"Very much. It's a good time to think, mistress. I did not meet your preacher. Did he not proclaim, my lord, that he came and went like any . . ."

Kathryn was sure he was going to say "rogue."

"Like any such person," Sanglier finished tactfully. "I'm sure he will return." Lord Henry seemed not so sure. He'd lost some of the bonhomie, the lazy charm and ill-concealed happiness of the day before. He pushed away his trencher, got to his feet, and, nodding at his guests, left the hall. Sanglier and his two companions followed shortly afterwards. Kathryn couldn't decide what their mood was: they were calm, but closed faced, as if troubled and concerned themselves.

"I didn't know you left in the dead of night," Colum teased.

"Well, sir, you were fast asleep and good for nothing," Kathryn teased back, "so I thought I'd enjoy the night, although

I returned soon enough, parched and cold. Do you think the preacher has disappeared?"

"It's possible." Colum rubbed his eyes.

"But Lord Henry believed he was here this morning."

"A sea of mysteries," Colum murmured. "God knows the truth." He paused as a bell tolled from the village. "The Requiem Mass will take place within the hour. Lord Henry is attending and I've agreed to join him. Kathryn?"

She shook her head. "I've spent enough time with the villagers. I wish to stay, Colum. I need to reflect."

Distracted, she returned to her food. Colum got up and kissed her on the forehead, Kathryn absentmindedly responded. A short while later she left the hall for her chamber. Colum was already booted and spurred, cloak over his arm, strapping on his war belt.

"You stay within," he declared. "I would prefer it if you did, Kathryn, now the preacher has disappeared."

Kathryn agreed, kissed him good-bye, and listened as he went down the stairs. She opened her writing satchel, laying out the tray of pens, a capped pot of ink, and sheets of parchment kept within two strips of hardened leather. She sat down, undid the ink cap, and began to write. Kathryn decided to ignore the doings of Lord Henry and what had happened at the manor, instead she concentrated on those macabre murders in the village.

Primo, she wrote, "*Mene, Mene, Tekel, Parsin*"—*why were those words copied onto the church floor? Apparently they were first seen on the Sunday morning but, there again . . .* Kathryn stopped writing. The church had remained open after nightfall so the words could have been scrawled there the night before and only seen in the light of day. They were definitely a warning and one which angered the parish priest, especially as he had received his own threatening proclamation. Was the preacher the author of these dire warnings? If so, why? What connection did that mysterious stranger have with Walmer? Kathryn now regretted questioning the preacher on this, but as a man used to deception, he would have denied everything.

Secondo—*What were the blacksmith and his wife preparing to celebrate? Where had that tun of wine come from? How had it been poisoned? Why did Isabella open it on that particular evening? Who had slipped into the yard and placed that poison in the water butt?*

Tertio—*Adam the Apothecary*—*he'd apparently returned home from taking the two corpses to St. Swithun's; he'd entered the rear door, taken the blackjack down and filled it with ale and locked himself in his chamber of powders. Why had he chosen the blackjack which contained the poison? How had the assassin arranged this as well as entering the house without being seen?*

Kathryn sat back in her chair. She'd seen so much yesterday—glimpses, looks, items she couldn't place, like a jumble of words on a piece of parchment. They'd only make sense if they were put into their proper place.

The bell in the village tolled again, a sign that the Requiem Mass was beginning. Kathryn closed her eyes. She could imagine the three coffins under their funereal drapes, lying before the high altar, ringed by purple candles in their black oaken holders; Father Clement beginning the Mass, the sprinkling of holy water, the homily, and the coffins being taken out through the corpse door to lie in God's Acre until the resurrection. Kathryn paused at a knock on the door.

"Come in," she called. A servant entered carrying a tray, a jug covered with a napkin, and a silver plate with hot diced meats sprinkled with herbs.

"Lord Henry told me to look after you." The servant placed the tray on the table just inside the door.

Kathryn absentmindedly thanked him. Once he'd gone, she took the tray and brought it over to the table near the window and cleared away the manuscripts and pens. She tested the meat and ale. "*Circumspecte agatis*," she whispered to herself. "At all times act prudently." Both food and drink seemed well enough. Kathryn, lost in her thoughts, absentmindedly picked at the meat, sipping from the ale as she stared out of the window towards that lonely gallows, stark against the sky.

In her cottage on the edge of the wood, Mother Croul was preparing her midday meal. She crouched at the makeshift hearth slowly stirring the cauldron, watching the water bubble, the pieces of tender rabbit she'd shredded mixing with the herbs and vegetables placed there.

"Add a little spice and salt," she murmured to herself, "and all is well." Beside her, the two cats, Gog and Magog, stretched out, enjoying the heat after a morning's hunt. Mother Croul depended on these. Gog, in particular, could bring back a young rabbit, on one occasion still alive, to the door of her cottage. Some people would call this magic. Mother Croul stared down at the cat.

"You like playing with your victims, don't you, cruel one." Mother Croul went back to her stirring. She kept thinking about the physician, the woman from Canterbury, sitting with her high on the clifftop. Mother Croul trusted her. Kathryn Swinbrooke had an honest, open face whose clear eyes missed nothing.

"But she's in love," Mother Croul whispered sarcastically to herself, "she's blinded, I'm sure, not thinking properly. There's so much I could tell her. All those things I've seen."

Mother Croul paused again as the bell of St. Swithun's tolled, a sign the Mass was now finished and the corpses were being taken out for burial.

"God have mercy on them," she whispered. Suddenly, one of her cats rose. Mother Croul heard a sound and whirled round, but the figure coming across the floor was striding too fast. Mother Croul glimpsed the glint of the blade, then it was deep inside her, twisting into her stomach, the assassin's hand going behind her scrawny neck to pull her close. Mother Croul screamed at the pain, watching the assassin's eyes through the black visor. She knew who it was, even as the light faded from her own eyes, screwed up against that terrible circle of pain. She was back on the clifftop, her husband was there, the wrecker, the man they were going to hang. Mother Croul felt a second dizzying shock of pain—she flailed her hands out. She was aware of her cat mewling and, all the time, that terrible pain, the pressure bulging in her belly. She coughed, tasted her own blood. She did not have time to whisper *"Miserere mei"* before she slipped into the darkness. The assassin let her drop and pulled the dagger out. The cats fled. The assassin took a pannikin of oil and the fat tallow candle from its holder—the final touches to hide the murderous work done in that derelict little cottage by the wood.

Kathryn was woken by the tocsin of a bell. She had decided to rest, going into a deep sleep. The clanging of the bell was so insistent, she jumped from the bed and ran to the window. Why was the alarm being raised? Had another poisoning taken place? She went to the door and opened it. Servants throughout the manor had also been alarmed and were gathering below at doorways and windows, wondering what had happened. Sanglier came striding out from Lord Henry's library, Delacroix and Cavignac sloping behind like two shadows. They talked rapidly in French before asking a servant if he knew what was happening, but the man spread his arms and shook his head. Kathryn went back to her bedchamber and dressed quickly, putting on her boots and her cloak. She'd reached the courtyard when she heard the clatter of hooves. Colum and Lord Henry and a group of retainers galloped into the yard. Colum swung out of the saddle and hastened towards her.

"I think you'd best come, Kathryn."

"Another death?"

"Yes, but not of poisoning. Mother Croul! We were burying the bodies in the graveyard when the alarm was raised. We could see the fire above the trees, the black clouds of smoke. You'd best come."

Lord Henry agreed to accompany them. Once Kathryn's cob was saddled, they left as hastily as possible down the trackway into the village. The day's trading had been suspended because of the funeral but now the streets were full with people gathering in doorways and outside the two great taverns and alehouses. Lord Henry had left certain retainers to keep the curious away. By the time they'd reached the cottage the fire had been brought under control, not so much because of the water or dust used but because there was nothing left to burn. The cottage and the area around it were a smoking, scorched circle of cinder and ash. Here and there a beam still glowed, sparks fluttered and fragments of ash were carried on the breeze to sting the back of the throat and clog the nostrils.

Kathryn gave the reins of her cob to Colum, opened the wicker gate, and walked down the path. The ground where the cottage had stood was blackened ash, even the makeshift stables had been scorched and buckled under the heat. The ash was still hot to the touch when Kathryn trod on it; more sparks flew up, drawing warnings from both Colum and Lord Henry. Kathryn withdrew.

"Mother Croul?" She called over her shoulder. "Is she? . . ."

"She did not attend the funeral," Lord Henry replied, "she never did. She always claimed she'd witnessed enough deaths."

Kathryn watched the great swell of ash sizzle under the splashes. More sparks flew up but eventually the heat lessened. Lord Henry came up and asked her a question but she was too engrossed in the dreadful sight to answer. Colum walked away and came back with a large stick, which he thrust into her hand.

"I found that near the stable," he said. "Do you want me to come with you?"

"No, only the good Lord knows where the poor woman's remains are. It's best if as few people as possible walk over the ashes, until her remains are found." She patted Colum's arm. "If you could stay?"

She grasped the stick and, covering her mouth and nostrils with one hand, walked over the sea of ash and cinder. Smoke spiralled up. Flakes of dirt swirled, sparks of fire shot up to sting her face. Colum and Lord Henry shouted their offers of help but she shook her head. She took her hand away from her face. The smell of fire and smouldering ash was strong but, beneath it, there was something else, as in a kitchen when oil has been left to burn in an empty skillet. She used the pole to sift amongst the ash. Here and there were dark grey patches, though there was little left, just twisted pieces of pewter and pottery, the neck of a jar, the blade of a knife. The deeper she sifted the more her suspicions grew.

The fire must have been intense, certainly in the centre of the house, well away from the hearth now reduced to a mass of crumbling stone. If the fire had started near the hearth there'd be proof of this. Instead, all the evidence indicated that the heart of the fire was in the centre of the room. It must have been started deliberately. She knocked aside a blade, an axehead, and a spigot, and found the remains of Mother Croul, hardly more than skull and bones. The skin had shrivelled, there was no sign of the left arm, patches of blackened flesh still clung to the bone.

Kathryn knelt down and murmured a prayer. She turned over the skull looking for a break but could find none; the same with the ribs, though the one she touched snapped under her finger. The smell of oil was all-pervasive.

"She must have been covered in it," Kathryn whispered to herself. "Killed, probably stabbed or garrotted. Her killer drenched the corpse in oil . . ."

"Kathryn, who are you talking to?" Colum shouted.

"To myself," she called back. She turned the bones over and, as tenderly as possible, grouped them together. She recalled St. Augustine's description of a human person, a living soul full of thoughts and desires, memories and experiences; yet these had all gone, in the blink of an eye, like a candle snuffed out. Kathryn had liked this old woman, sharp-eyed and keen witted.

She glanced around, now used to the sparks, the ash, and the acrid smell. All about the cottage, people had gathered to watch, gossiping among themselves. A peasant and his wife, hugging a sack of grain intended for the local mill. A girl, shepherding a goose, stood sucking her thumb. A verderer emerged from the forest, a line of rabbit corpses hanging from the rod he carried. She looked to her left, where others had arrived—Father Clement, Amabilia, Benedict, Ursula, Walter the Constable, and Simon the Sexton, drinking so fast from a beer jug, he splashed his fat bleary face. The priest, without being asked, covered his mouth and nose and stumbled across to say the prayers. He nodded at Kathryn and knelt down but the heat was too intense so he got to his feet. Kathryn asked Colum to bring a plank of wood; the Irishman did, laying it carefully beside Mother Croul's remains. Again the priest knelt down, crossed himself, and intoned the prayer often recited as the corpse was taken out of a church to be buried: "Go forth, Christian soul, and may the company of angels . . ."

Kathryn had seen enough, she turned and retreated to the wicker gate. Simon and the constable brought across an arrow chest and, once the priest had finished his ministrations, began to load the makeshift coffin with the pathetic remains. Father Clement walked away, and as he did so, the constable cracked a joke and the sexton, still slurping from his beer jug, laughed raucously. Lord Henry shouted at them to show more respect, an order the priest reinforced by coming back and whispering hoarsely at them. Kathryn shook the debris and ash from her gown while Lord Henry brought across a pannikin of water.

"Is there anything I can do, mistress?" he asked. She shook her head and drank. "In which case, God rest her. An accident?"

"No." Kathryn sighed.

Lord Henry closed his eyes. "God have mercy," he murmured. "Another murder! You are sure?"

"Mother Croul was sharp-witted," Kathryn replied. "It would be easy to think the fire started in the hearth, but it didn't, it started in the centre of the room. An assassin undoubtedly killed her, then saturated the corpse in oil. The remains are pathetic."

"And the assassin?"

Kathryn pointed to the silver cross hanging on a gold chain round Lord Henry's neck. "Only the good Lord knows."

"When I get to know," Lord Henry replied, "I'll make sure the misbegotten wretch hangs from the highest gallows." He turned on his heel and walked away.

Chapter 7

No wher so bisy as a man as he ther nas,
and yet he seemed bisier than he was.
—Chaucer, General Prologue,
The Canterbury Tales

Colum put his arm around Kathryn's shoulder. She felt her horror at what had happened dulled by a fierce determination to bring the malefactor to justice. The doings of the great ones— Lord Henry's Office of the Secret Seal, the machinations of Sanglier—such things were part of the fabric of life. Like the poor, they would always figure in man's existence. Elias and Isabella she had not known, and the same was true of Adam the Apothecary. They seemed unlikable people, used to the violence that had claimed them, but this old woman had died not because of anything she'd done or said but simply because of what she was, a woman with a sharp memory and a keen eye. Kathryn believed she'd been murdered to be silenced, just in case she'd remembered something. The assassin obviously saw her as a danger. Kathryn quietly vowed she'd reflect on everything Mother Croul had said to her, and wondered if the assassin had watched them meet at Gallows Point the day before.

"What happened?" Father Clement, bleary-eyed from the smoke, his face smudged with ash, came over, Amabilia resting on his arm. Behind him clustered the rest of the Parish Council.

"I don't know." Kathryn decided to say as little as possible. "I was at the manor house when the alarm was raised."

"I was conducting the funeral." Father Clement turned,

coughed, and spat. "We were lowering the coffins into the ground. I was throwing in a clod of earth, giving the last blessing when Amabilia raised the alarm, didn't you?"

His sister, pale faced, nodded in agreement. "I saw smoke rising above the trees. At first I thought it was some woodman's fire, but then the flames came."

"Were you all at the funeral?" Kathryn asked. "Did any of you leave?" All she received were blank looks.

"Did any of you leave the funeral, either the Mass or the burial ceremony after it?"

"Of course not!" the constable snapped. "We were all there, we can all vouch for each other. What are you implying? The fire could have been an accident."

"If Mother Croul's death was an accident," Kathryn retorted, "then flowers don't grow and pigeons don't fly." She gestured at the arrow chest now lying just beyond the carpet of ash. "Who'll pray for her?"

"I will," Amabilia spoke up, "and my brother will say a Mass."

"Say three," Kathryn opened the purse and took out two silver coins. Father Clement refused but Kathryn pushed them into his hand.

"Say Masses for the dead, Father. Sing the Requiem for her. Make sure she's not buried in that chest but in a proper coffin, good wood with a silver-gilt cross on it. And a headstone. I promise I'll pay you before I leave."

The priest agreed, grasping Kathryn's hand warmly, thanking her for her generosity.

Kathryn and Colum left, walking back through the village where people still stood, gathered at doorways muttering at the awful events of the day. Along the High Road came a group of travelling mummers, their possessions piled high on brightly coloured carts on which garish faces had been daubed. The lead cart was pulled by a great grey horse with a hogged mane and tawdry-looking harness. The horse was guided by a man wearing a gargoyle mask. Small boys, their hair dyed yellow, coloured streamers attached to their motley rags, ran alongside it. On the cart, holding the reins, sat a woman with a demon's mask. She glanced towards them, and beneath the mask her painted lips parted in a black-toothed smile. Others in the troupe were dressed macabrely in black and green with jester bells attached to their jackets of dyed sheepskin and battered leather. On the second cart rose a mock gallows. From its three branches dangled the stuffed corpses of cats and rats. Above this a banner curled in the breeze and on it, scrawled in white paint: *Timor Mortis Conturbat Me*—The Fear of Death Disturbs Me.

Kathryn hid a smile. This uncanny group of travelling players with their strangely caparisoned horses, garishly painted wagons, and devilish costumes, seemed to sum up the atmosphere in the village—of murder walking the streets, haunting its alleyways, dealing out sudden death, but for what reason?

She and Colum stood aside to allow the mummers to pass. Some of the villagers shouted greetings, others laughed, a few hurled abuse, which was returned in good measure. All the time the moon players kept up their dance to the sound of flute and the clatter of a drum. Small boys raced by with baskets, begging for coins or scraps of food, most of their requests being coarsely refused. Kathryn and Colum watched the mummers go and the villagers drift back to their doorways.

"They'll not stop here," Colum murmured. "Once they learn about the deaths. They'll receive little welcome and move on. So, you believe Mother Croul was murdered?"

"Yes, I do," Kathryn replied. "Not by poison. I suspect she was strangled or stabbed—it would have been very sudden. The place reeks of oil; the fire was deliberate."

"And the killer?" Colum asked.

"Only the poisoner knows, whoever he or she is. A deliberate act, Mother Croul's soul sent into the dark, and now the assassin hides as cleverly as before."

"But who?"

"That is the mystery—you were in the cemetery Colum, what happened?"

"I was standing at the edge of the crowd, Lord Henry some distance behind. I was watching Father Clement more than anything else. Funerals always fascinate me, Kathryn, the coffin slipping into the ground, sprinkled with holy water, blessed with incense before being covered with soil. The same thought always occurs to me, it's like watching a door being closed. I always wonder if there's anything beyond. Anyway, I was muttering the prayers like the rest when Amabilia came running from the church pointing at the smoke. Consternation and chaos broke out. Father Clement shouted for peace while he finished the ceremony. Once he did so, he sent a young boy running to discover the truth. The lad came back gasping and spluttering, Mother Croul's cottage was on fire but there was no sign of the old woman. For the rest, Father Clement ordered Adam's grave to be filled in, and returned to the church, the others went to see for themselves. Lord Henry and I returned to the manor—the rest you know."

Kathryn glanced up at the sky. The day was turning grey. She noticed how the leaves whirling along the patch were a golden brown.

"Lord Henry asked 'Who?'" she whispered. "I might be mistaken, perhaps the murderer is someone else, a villager we haven't met. But Colum, in your mind, go back to the cemetery—you're standing in God's Acre, Adam the Apothecary is being buried, the clods of earth have been thrown in. Father Clement is chanting the death prayers, sprinkling the coffin with holy water—you must have looked round. Did you see anyone leave?"

Colum stopped walking and closed his eyes. He recalled Father Clement's black-and-gold chasuble, the white alb beneath being whipped up by the breeze, the altar boys in their surplices, one carrying the cross, the other a stoup of holy water and the asperges rod, a sea of faces, with people whispering and talking.

"I remember nothing untoward," he confessed. "Adam's coffin was lowered by labourers. I remember Father Clement giving them the coffin penny after they finished dragging the ropes up. But nothing, Kathryn. The funeral Mass was an hour long, St. Swithun's has many doors, the corpse door, the Galilee porch. Anyone could have slipped out. I understand it's only a short distance to Mother Croul's cottage through the woods. I'm not sure where Lord Henry was. I stood by myself, leaning against a pillar in one of the transepts. I was busy watching the ceremony, listening to the words of the Mass, admiring the wall painting on my left. Kathryn, for all I know, any one of those villagers could have left that Mass, gone to Mother Croul's, killed her, doused her cottage in oil, and started that conflagration. I just don't know."

They reached the manor. Colum insisted that she accompany him into the hall, where the servants had laid out a collation of meat, bread, apples, and cheese. The three Frenchmen stood in a cluster, wine goblets in their hands. Lord Henry was having words with them.

"He's worried," Colum whispered, "he has already sent out riders to look for the preacher and, so far, with little success."

Kathryn took wine and a platter of food from a servant. She didn't like the way Sanglier kept staring across at her. Now and again he would turn to Cavignac and whisper something, followed by giggles, as they turned their back on her. She noticed how Sanglier would place his hand on Cavignac's arm or shoulder, a gesture of confidence and reassurance. Lord Henry had moved away, talking to servants about the banquet planned for that evening, declaring that, despite the funerals in the villages and the death of Mother Croul, the feast would still take place.

Kathryn returned to her chamber to finish her meal. Colum joined her and said that he must go back to the stables. Kathryn sat on a stool. She ate little and sipped the wine, the best claret she'd tasted for many a day. Outside the day was now turning a dull grey and the wind had strengthened, bringing in the muffled thunder of the sea against the rocks. Kathryn recalled what she knew about Mother Croul's death. She could make no sense of it. As for the preacher—she remembered Sanglier's laughter and felt like confronting him. What was the Vicomte doing out so late at night?

Eventually she realised she was making little progress, so she opened the chest, and took out the ledgers she'd found in Elias's house and that of the apothecary. She went through these carefully. Elias's were simple enough: goods bought, horses shod, pieces of iron mended, but nothing to provoke suspicion. On the day he died he'd been busy, one horse after the other, owned by this villager or that, new horse shoes fashioned, a box of nails sold to a passing tinker. Search as she might, Kathryn could find no mention of a tun of wine amongst the goods bought in the market during the weeks before they died.

"Nothing at all," Kathryn murmured, closing the book and putting it down beside her. Adam's ledger was different. Here the hand was more clerkly and neat but, there again, nothing to provoke suspicion. A list of customers and the different herbs they'd bought: black mustard, which, if crushed and mixed with honey and beeswax, took away marks and spots, softened bruises or the roughness of a scab. Parsley to cleanse the urine, saffron to clear wounds. Even the occasional poison dispensed—Adam made careful note of this—"for the extirpation of rats and vermin." Powders to make someone sleep, starwort to lessen a swelling in the groin, knapweed for a sore throat or to staunch bleeding. Fennel juice, if dissolved in wine and dropped in the ears, would ease pain as well as reduce the agony of a sore tooth. Kathryn scrutinised each entry. The poisons sold provoked no suspicion; some of the buyers she didn't even recognise. Now and again Adam made an entry in a cipher known only to him. Kathryn was sure that these were potions given to some young woman as an aid against pregnancy. Yet there was no sign of an assassin, of someone amassing deadly powders. She closed the ledger and placed it aside.

"But, of course, the assassin would be stealthy," she spoke to herself. She walked across to her writing desk and sat, head in hands. She went back in her mind's eye to that cottage. Why should Mother Croul be killed? she wondered. Because of what she knew! What did she tell her yesterday? Nothing, apart from gossip—that's how Kathryn would describe it: the villagers, the fate of the wreckers, the temper of Lord Henry, but nothing extraordinary.

Colum returned from the stables, reminding his wife it would soon be time for the banquet. Kathryn opened the travelling chest and took out the gown she'd wear, her dress of the finest scarlet and gold damask with a white high collar and matching ruffs, a stiffened kirtle beneath and buskins of dark silver velvet. She would not wear a veil but leave her hair uncovered. She opened her jewellery box and took out hair clasps, earrings, a bracelet and the loving ring Colum had bought her. Again, she was sure someone had sifted carefully through these, yet there was nothing missing and she did not wish to alarm Colum, who would certainly raise the matter with Lord Henry. She laid the jewellery out on the bed and went across to the lavarium. She took off her dress and the kirtle beneath and carefully washed herself. When she'd finished, she turned, and blushed with embarrassment. Colum was sitting on a chair watching her intently.

"We are man and wife, Kathryn."

"We are bride and groom!" she corrected him.

Going across, she took her kirtle and hastily put it on, covering her nakedness. She also took out a jar of perfume, small and costly, and undid the stopper. She closed her eyes at the beautiful fragrance. Colum had purchased it from a merchant in London who claimed to have bought it in Alexandria in Egypt.

"What was the name of this perfume, Colum?"

"Kiphye," Colum replied. "They say it's distilled from the blue lotus."

"It's beautiful," Kathryn murmured, "so fragrant." She dabbed a spot on her finger and applied some behind the ears, along her neck, drying her hands on her kirtle. She then sat before the mirror and began to apply her face paint carefully. She looked down at the box of belladonna—the black eye-liner some ladies used. Kathryn still kept it but now never used it. She'd read in a treatise about eighteen months ago how the powder, although used for makeup, could still be poisonous, how the skin somehow absorbs it into the body and so it damages the vital humours.

As she dressed and prepared, Kathryn kept going back to Mother Croul's death. A servant came up with a tray of wine, two cups and a plate of freshly baked bread and strips of delicious cheese. Kathryn sipped at her wine.

"I think she was killed—just in case."

"What are you talking about, Kathryn?"

"Mother Croul—she died just in case she knew something. That's how ruthless the killer is, Colum. We must take warning from that. Whoever this poisoner is, he or she is determined to kill and kill again. Mother Croul was removed as an obstacle but, for the life of me, I don't know why."

"And the business here at the manor?" Colum squatted down beside her to use the mirror to shave his cheeks. Kathryn got up.

"You'll cut yourself," she warned, "sit down on the stool and do it properly. I believe Lord Henry is playing a game, a clever subtle ploy, to trap these Frenchmen. He brought them and the preacher back here. Now something has gone wrong, but I don't know what."

Colum, answering in grunts, more concerned that he looked presentable, donning a white shirt tied high at the neck and a tawny jacket with hose to match. He slipped a ring on his finger and wrapped a dagger belt around his waist, pushing his feet into soft black boots.

"Well," he breathed, "that's the best I can do. Just look at you, Kathryn." He came over, clasped her by the hands, and knelt before her.

"We're like those paintings in a church, aren't we? When you see Virtue and Vice. You have the beauty and I have the ugliness."

Kathryn kissed him softly on the mouth. "To me, Irishman, you shall always be all that's fair and good in human flesh. But come, I'm sure our host is waiting."

The banquet was not to be held in the hall but in Lord Henry's private solar, a sumptuously decorated chamber. Gorgeous tapestries hung above the dark panelling depicting scenes from the classics: Jason and his Argonauts, Achilles on the island of Chios, the Wooden Horse being pushed into Troy, Ulysses on his voyage home. Lord Henry was waiting for them, only too eager to describe each tapestry in detail and show them the rest of the solar. The royal banners of England and France draped down from the rafters. The room was well lit by pure beeswax candles;

dark opened cases with frontings of pure glass reflected the glowing light. The chairs and stools, even the benches, were of the finest oak, all polished to a shimmering gleam. In the minstrel's gallery at the far end of the solar, musicians were preparing. A young boy with a voice like an angel was rehearsing the hymn *"Dulce Mater."*

Lord Henry was dressed to match such glory in a doublet and hose displaying the colours of the royal household—scarlet and gold—with a collar of office around his neck. His blond hair was combed and oiled, his beard and moustache neatly clipped. He took them over towards the fire, where logs crackled giving off the sweet smell of pine. He served them glasses of white wine while waiting for the Frenchmen. Despite Kathryn's best efforts he would not discuss the doings in the village but curtailed the conversation to different items in the chamber. He explained how he loved the feats of the ancient Greeks and how his great ambition was to lead an embassy to the great Turkish Emperor. Eventually such chatter ended as Sanglier and Cavignac swept into the chamber.

The Vicomte and his clerk were dressed in the blue, white and gold of the French royal household. Jewellery glittered around their necks and at their fingers. They'd prepared well and brought a present for Lord Henry, a psalter with a beautiful, jewel-encrusted cover, which they formally presented on behalf of their royal master. Lord Henry received this gift, observing the protocols and niceties. He thanked them for their generosity and, once again, welcomed them formally to his manor in the hope that they would eventually negotiate a lasting peace between the Crowns of England and France. Once such ceremony was over, Lord Henry ushered them to the round wooden table in the center of the room. He seated Kathryn on his left, Sanglier on his right, gesturing at the others to take their places.

"Where is Monsieur Delacroix?" he asked.

Cavignac shrugged.

"Has he not come down, my lord?" Sanglier murmured. "We knocked at his chamber. I'm sure he will be with us shortly."

Lord Henry glowered at such lack of etiquette, but raised his hand as a sign for the banquet to begin. In the ministrel's gallery the young boy began to sing in a soft fluting voice, the beautiful hymns *"Dulce Mater"* and *"Virgo Pia."* The servants appeared carrying trays of capon roasted in white almonds, salmon cooked in a wine sauce and coated in cinnamon. Lord Henry was intent on displaying both his wealth and his power. Each guest had damask napkins, and knives and spoons with amber handles, their sheaths picked out with silver threads. Lord Henry declared they were his gifts to them and could be taken from the table. Gold-chased ewers and jugs were brought round by servants so that they could wash their hands, and Kathryn savoured the sweet smell of rose water.

The second course, pottage from a golden bowl, was served, yet still Delacroix had not appeared. Lord Henry, however, chose to ignore such discourtesy and regaled them with stories about his travels to Hainault, Brabant, and the cities of the Rhine. He joked about how his royal master would love to seize another English traveller, Henry Tudor, the last Lancastrian claim to the English throne, who was suspected of being sheltered in France. Sanglier refused to rise to the bait. Partridge—the third course— was served, and this time the pewter goblets were replaced with gold-chased cups and long-stemmed glasses of precious Venetian glass. At last Lord Henry acknowledged the empty seat. He raised his hand, silencing Sanglier's story about a French jester, and called his chamberlain over.

"Go up," he said, "to Monsieur Delacroix's chamber. Tell him his host is waiting."

The chamberlain hurried off, and the meal continued in silence. The chamberlain returned in a fluster.

"My lord," he waved his hands, "there was no answer. I tried the door, but it seems locked and bolted."

Sanglier scraped back his chair, as did Cavignac.

"There must be something wrong," the Vicomte murmured. "Delacroix is never late. I'm sorry, my lord."

The meal ended abruptly. Lord Henry insisted that he accompany Sanglier and Cavignac to Delacroix's chamber on the second floor. Lord Henry climbed the stairs, his anger apparent. He stopped at the chamber and knocked. Kathryn and Colum had followed. For a while all was confusion, Lord Henry, followed by Sanglier, trying his best to evoke a response. Then Lord Henry's anger disappeared, a look of worried concern on his face. Sanglier was insistent that the door be broken down. Eventually Lord Henry agreed. Servants brought up logs from the woodshed and, under Lord Henry's direction, hammered the door. Eventually it snapped, the locks at top and bottom broke free, and the door crashed back on its leather hinges. One of these sagged, hitting Lord Henry as he tried to enter. Sanglier insisted that he go first.

"My lord, this may be your house but this chamber was the residence of an accredited French envoy."

The door was pushed aside and made secure, and they entered the chamber. It was as tastefully furnished as the rest of the manor. An oil lamp glowed on the table. Even as Sanglier hurried round the high-back chair facing the window, Kathryn could distinguish the outline of a head and one drooping arm. Sanglier shouted for the oil lamp to be brought. Kathryn hurried across.

Delacroix was dead. His face was white as snow, eyeballs rolled back in his head, which sloped to one side, his body all relaxed, one arm on his lap, the other hanging over the chair. Kathryn picked up the wine cup from the floor and sniffed at it.

"Bittersweet," she declared, and although wearing her best dress, she crouched down and sniffed at the wine dregs on the polished floor. She smelt the same odour as in the cup. Getting to her feet she walked over to a side table bearing the wine jug, but as Cavignac standing nearby declared, this was free of any taint. Kathryn noticed a small pouch lying next to the wine jug, its cord undone. She picked this up and sifted the contents out onto her hand, ignoring Sanglier's protest about the Frenchman being an accredited envoy. Kathryn couldn't care less; a man had been poisoned. She sniffed carefully—a bitter acrid odour.

"Is that poison?" Colum asked coming across.

Kathryn shook her head. "No, no." She sniffed again, picked a few grains on top of her finger, and gingerly tasted. "No, this is nothing more dangerous than valerian."

"Delacroix liked that," Cavignac spoke up. "He always took some to help him relax or sleep."

"Common enough," Kathryn agreed.

Lord Henry however was striding up and down the chamber. He'd unsheathed his dagger, as if expecting some secret assailant to jump out from behind the arras, or be lurking in some corner. Sanglier stood before the chair staring down at the corpse. Kathryn went over. She felt the dead man's cheek, ice cold. She pressed her fingers and noticed how the muscles of the face had begun to harden. Delacroix was still dressed in the same garments he'd worn when she had seen him in the hall.

"He's been dead some hours," she declared, "the corpse is cold, the body is beginning to stiffen. I would guess at least three to four hours. The wine was poisoned."

"Impossible!" Lord Henry declared. "You were all served from the same jug in the hall. My lord." He turned to Sanglier. "You were there, Delacroix carried his goblet."

Kathryn listened to the argument and stared at the dead man's face, harsh featured in life, now with a ghastly sallow look, half-opened eyes, lips quite stretched, hardening in the final rictus of death. Kathryn placed the poisoned wine cup on the small table beside the chair.

"My lords." She clapped her hands. Sanglier and Lord Henry broke off their discussion. "It might be best if we leave and continue our conversation downstairs."

The Frenchmen reluctantly agreed. Sanglier protested at how an official French envoy had been poisoned in Lord Henry's household, but the English lord would have none of it. He declared his innocence, adding that Delacroix's death had nothing to do with either him or anyone at Walmer.

"That," Sanglier declared as he left the chamber, "is to be proven."

By the time they reached the solar Lord Henry and Sanglier were hurling accusations and counteraccusations at one another. These exchanges made Kathryn aware of the deep, lasting enmity between these two men, who hid their hostility behind courtly etiquette and diplomatic protocols. It was Colum, banging on the table with his own cup, who eventually restored some semblance of order.

"My lords! This is no way to proceed."

Cavignac quietly murmured in agreement. Lord Henry took a deep breath and sat down in his chair, eyes closed. Sanglier picked up his wine cup, thought again, and slammed it down on the table so hard the wine spilled out.

"There's no need for that, my lord," Lord Henry opened his eyes and stretched out his hand. "My lord, you are my guest. I protest, I had nothing to do with your comrade's death."

Sanglier did not accept his hand but acknowledged the apology. Lord Henry ordered the solar and minstrel gallery to be cleared. Once this was done he had fresh goblets brought and a new cask of wine broached. He drank from it first to assure the rest, then served them all. The food was now forgotten. Lord Henry asserted himself, pointing out that the poisoned wine cup had been taken from the hall by no less a person than Delacroix himself.

"He returned immediately to his room, didn't he?"

"I did not go with him," the French clerk declared, eyes watchful in his girlish-looking face.

Kathryn noticed how the collar of the Frenchman's shirt was edged with lace. He'd oiled his black hair, bringing it to curl round the side of his face like that of a girl. He wore an earring in one lobe whilst jewellery flashed on his long delicate fingers. Cavignac smiled at Kathryn.

"I assure you, mistress—and I know you already with your severe gaze—Delacroix went to his chamber by himself. He was carrying his wine cup. It is common practice, and my Lord Vicomte will agree, to be careful what we eat and drink in a foreign household." Lord Henry glared at him. "In such a place," Cavignac continued blithely, "we sip our wine and refuse any cup which does not taste right. Moreover, my comrade, like me, kept his hand over the cup at all times, it's a common enough practice." Even Lord Henry agreed to this.

"So, he returned safely to his chamber?" Kathryn asked.

Lord Henry picked up the small bell that lay hidden behind the goblet on his table and shook it furiously. The chamberlain appeared and Lord Henry rapped out an order. A short while later an armed retainer came swaggering into the hall, dressed in the livery of Lord Henry, sword belt clasped around his waist, a pair of gauntlets in one hand, the other resting on the hilt of his sword.

"Ah, Stephen." Lord Henry beckoned him over. The man went to go down on one knee but Lord Henry shook his head. "You were on guard outside Delacroix's chamber?"

"Yes, my lord."

"And you saw him return there?"

"Yes, my lord."

"And he was carrying a goblet of wine?"

Again, the retainer agreed. "And, my lord, it wasn't tainted."

"How do you know that?" Sanglier demanded, eyes screwed up, fingers furiously combing his closely cropped beard.

"My lord, he handed the cup to me as he unlocked the door. I was thirsty. The Frenchman said if I wanted, I could have a sip. I did so; only then did I realise . . ."

"That you were tasting it for him?" Kathryn broke in.

"Yes, mistress. The Frenchman took the cup back and smiled at me. He said that he never trusted long-tailed Englishmen, and slammed the door shut. I heard the bolts being drawn and the lock being turned. I stayed there until the bell for Vespers rang, that's when the Captain of the Guard had said I would no longer be needed as the Frenchman was coming down here to attend the banquet."

"And you left your post?"

"Yes, my lord." The retainer gestured at Sanglier. "Even as he and the other came along the gallery. As I went down the stairs I heard them knocking on the door, calling the Frenchman's name. I thought he had gone to sleep. My business was finished."

"And no one visited Delacroix's chamber?" Kathryn asked.

The retainer looked at Lord Henry who gestured at him to reply.

"Mistress, while I was on guard, no one entered that chamber, nor did the Frenchman leave. I heard him moving about, then silence."

Kathryn recalled the chamber, the polished floorboards, the heavy furniture.

"My lord, there is no other entrance?"

"Of course not!" Lord Henry replied, dismissing the guard.

"And the windows?" Kathryn continued.

"Are full of glass and too narrow for a man to enter."

"Whilst the pouch of powder found near the wine jug contained nothing but valerian, a potion which would make him relax and sleep, but certainly not stop his heart."

"What are you saying, Mistress Kathryn?" Sanglier was now all courteous, though staring curiously at her.

"My Lord Vicomte, I am stating the obvious. Monsieur Delacroix leaves the hall. He's drinking wine which is untainted, otherwise he'd have felt its effects even as he climbed the stairs. Actions like walking or climbing often hasten the effects of poison. He handed the guard the goblet of wine and, half teasing, asked him to sip. So Delacroix was certainly on guard against any poisoning. You must have heard about the events in the village?"

"Of course we have," Cavignac snapped, "and the death of that old woman."

"Now, Delacroix," Kathryn continued blithely, ignoring the Frenchman's interruption, "upon entering that chamber, probably took out his pouch of valerian and added a little to his cup. He wanted to relax, to sleep before the banquet tonight. He drinks the wine and dies, not of natural causes but of a potent poison, as deadly as viper venom. There was not much wine left. I suspect he took a deep draught, he may have even been falling asleep when the poison made its presence felt, so he was unable to shout or cry for help. The poison administered, particularly in such a strong dose would have . . ." Kathryn paused. "Yes, like a fire sweeping through his body, a seizure of the heart, an inability to breathe, followed by a loss of consciousness."

Kathryn stared down at the silver platter edged with gold; on all four sides a precious stone winked.

"Did any of you visit Delacroix today?" she asked.

"We both did," Sanglier replied quickly. "What are you implying?"

"Nothing." Kathryn turned to Lord Henry. "If you could ask your guard to return?"

Lord Henry agreed. The chamberlain brought the retainer back. Questioned by Kathryn, he insisted that he'd been on guard an hour before noon and only left when he thought the Frenchman would be joining his companions for the banquet.

"You know I was there." He nodded at Sanglier. "You came down and knocked on his door. There was no answer. You said he was asleep and continued on your way to the banquet."

"And did either of these two gentlemen," Kathryn pointed at the two Frenchmen, "visit Delacroix after he brought his goblet of wine up from the hall?"

"No, no, they did not."

"We were getting ready ourselves." Cavignac spoke up. "Like Delacroix we rested, changed, and washed. Afterwards, as the guard says, both of us came down. We knocked at Delacroix's door, there was no answer. We thought he was asleep and would soon follow us."

Kathryn thanked the guard, and Lord Henry dismissed him. Kathryn studied a tapestry depicting the Passion of Christ; on a scroll underneath, the words: *Expectans, Expectavi, Dominum.*

She recognised the quotation from Psalm 39. "I have waited patiently for the Lord and He has turned His eye upon me." She closed her eyes momentarily and prayed for guidance.

"Truly a mystery." Sanglier seized the initiative. "Here we are, French envoys in the kingdom of Edward the Fourth, yet we are not safe."

"Nonsense!" Lord Henry snapped.

"We are not safe." Cavignac took up his colleague's remark. "We are here as envoys. Delacoix was our friend, a colleague. Now he has been foully poisoned. Isn't it true, my Lord Henry, that members of your village have been poisoned?"

"Are you saying that the same poisoner is loose in this

manor?" Lord Henry retorted. "That's ridiculous! You have no proof that Delacroix's death can be laid at the door of any Englishman."

Sanglier's lips parted in a false smile. "Are you implying this murderous act can be put down to me, to Cavignac, or to both?"

"What my Lord Henry is implying," Colum intervened, "is that there has been a most unfortunate, regrettable death. Monsieur Delacroix has been poisoned. We don't know whether he took his own life, was poisoned by someone who is also killing people in the village, or by someone else here in the manor."

"Why should Delacroix take his own life?" Cavignac taunted. "He loved life, he drank the cup to the very dregs. He was happy, contented."

"But not contented enough to sleep well," Kathryn remarked quietly. "The pouch of valerian powders?"

"Monsieur Delacroix had difficulty sleeping. He had scruples, mistress. You know the way he dressed?"

"Ah," Kathryn remarked, "I observed that, more like a Dominican friar than an envoy of the French King."

"Delacroix was intended for the priesthood," Cavignac replied.

Kathryn noticed how his English, like that of Sanglier, was almost word perfect. She wished she knew more about these two clever Frenchmen, and was mystified by their reaction. On the one hand they seemed concerned about their colleague's death, yet apart from their initial outburst, they remained controlled, calm, and poised.

"And?" Kathryn asked.

"Delacroix did not become a Dominican friar as he vowed to his parents. They died before he took solemn vows, so he left the order. Delacroix always felt uneasy on that matter. During the day one couldn't ask for a sharper mind and keen wits." Cavignac sipped from his own wine. "But, at night, or on his own, he was different. Hence," Cavignac shrugged, "the valerian powders."

"I would like to search his chamber," Kathryn demanded.

"Impossible." Sanglier's head came up. "Delacroix was an accredited French envoy. His room contains documents—"

"I must search his chamber," Kathryn insisted. "Monsieur Vicomte, you simply can't sit at table here, banging your fist, demanding justice, truth, answers, and, when I try to help, impede my progress."

Sanglier opened his mouth to reply, then wiped his lips on the back of his hands, glancing sideways at his comrade.

"Let us compromise," Colum murmured. "Why don't Lord Henry and I search the chamber in the presence of both of you?"

After a slight hesitation, Sanglier accepted Colum's proposal and all four men left the hall. Once they were gone, Kathryn scraped back the chair and got to her feet. She walked over and examined the tapestry more carefully. She studied the different colours, dark reds, and blues, and marvelled at the way the artist had caught the sombre mood of Calvary, the hill with its three crosses, the tortured Christ taken down from the cross and laid in his Mother's lap. She turned her back on it and stared down at the polished wood floor. "What do we have here?" she murmured to herself. She walked back to the table and refilled her goblet of wine. The firelight was beginning to fade. Kathryn repressed a shiver. The solar no longer had that welcoming warmth, touched now by the chill of sudden death. She sat down and tried to marshal her thoughts.

"A Frenchman comes down for a goblet of wine," she remarked to herself, "he is prudent, careful, and cunning. He covers the goblet with his fingers and goes back to his chamber. He allows the guard outside to sip, he suffers no ill effects. Delacroix goes into his chamber, locks and bolts the door, adds a little valerian to the wine and falls asleep, which is, in fact, the eternal sleep. He cannot be roused, and we find him poisoned. No secret entrances." She recalled the window. "No one could have forced himself through that."

"Kathryn?" Colum stood in the doorway. He walked across plucking at a loose thread on his jerkin. He sat down in Lord Henry's chair at the top of the table, turning it round to stretch out his long legs, and gazed at Kathryn. "I've drunk too much, I'm tired."

"And the Frenchman's chamber?" Kathryn asked.

Colum shook his head. "Apart from the valerian powder, what do you expect to find in any clerk's chamber? Clothing, documents, but nothing suspicious. He was murdered, Kathryn, wasn't he?"

"That's what I've been talking about." She smiled. "At least to myself. How did someone get into a locked chamber, with a small window and no secret entrances, and poison the wine of a rather suspicious French clerk? You found no other wine cup in the chamber?"

Colum shook his head. "Apparently, Delacroix was most abstemious; he drank wine but very rarely by himself."

Kathryn closed her eyes. "There must be a way out of this, surely." She rose and absentmindedly tussled Colum's hair. "Come, my Irish vagabond. Time for bed." She poked and played with his shoulder. "And while you undress me, you can quote from Chaucer's "Book of the Duchess," loving lines about how my heart wishes to speak to yours and yours to mine."

Colum pushed back his chair, he drew Kathryn closer, and kissed her softly on the brow. She laid her head against his chest, putting her arms around his waist. Even as she glimpsed Delacroix's untouched place, the goblet still winking in the light, the chair pushed fast against the table, she quietly wondered what had happened in that chamber. Who had sent the Frenchman's soul to God?

Chapter 8

As hoot he was, and lecherous as a sparwe.
—Chaucer, General Prologue,
The Canterbury Tales

I n years to come the villagers of Walmer would call this the Killing Time when Death swept into their village and set up camp like some enemy host. It shattered their peace and tangled their community in a web of suspicion, deceit, and grisly murder. However, on that morning, the day after Mother Croul's cottage had been burnt to the ground, Simon the Sexton was not thinking about death but more about his own secret pleasures.

The morning had provided a fine one—a few white puffballs of cloud, the sun strong, and the sky so blue a man would think summer had returned. Even the earth felt warm, whilst the long grass, the holly cock, and the brambles sprouting so luxuriantly around the old yew tree, still provided him with sufficient cover. Simon had been down to the village. He filled his wineskin, bought a pie at a cookshop, and came into the cemetery to enjoy himself. He knew the lovers would soon arrive, Master Ralph and Alison. She was one of the most buxom and comely of the village wenches. Simon's hands stole down to his crotch, he caressed himself. He knew their habits. They wouldn't be able to resist a morning like this. Once their parents were busy, Ralph, who was an apprentice, would steal away from the stall to meet Alison here.

Morning Mass had been sung, the congregation dispersed,

and God's Acre, this cemetery, would fall quiet under the spell of the buzzing bee and the butterflies wafting like specks of colour above the wildflowers. Simon had carried out his usual survey. Father Clement was busy in the crypt. Benedict the Notary was waiting for a client so they could seal an indenture next to the baptismal font. Ursula was over at the priest's house with Amabilia in the sacristy. They would not come out here. Simon loved this place. He always knew what happened in the village, which young man was swiving which wench, and this was the place of discovery. Simon unstoppered the wineskin and took a mouthful. He swilled it around to allay the soreness of his gums and the tenderness of a rotting tooth at the back of his mouth, before swallowing. He bit gingerly into the pie.

"I have to be vigilant," Simon whispered to himself, "these murders." Simon sat up to eat the pie more carefully. Leaning back against the yew tree he half listened to the song of a thrush in the branches above. Simon was quiet, he always made sure he disturbed nothing or provoked no suspicion. He wished Ralph and Alison would come, but while he waited, he could think about what was happening in the village, who was behind those dreadful poisonings. Elias and Isabella reduced to cold slabs of meat! Adam the Apothecary, face all liverish, and now Mother Croul, her house reduced to ash, her corpse nothing more than a few burnt bones.

"Skin and bone," Walter the Constable had joked.

Father Clement had done his best, wrapping the remains in a white linen cloth, blessing and incensing them, but what did it matter? Mother Croul was gone, and Simon was quite relieved. The old crone had a sharp eye and a clacking tongue; she was one who might have learned about his secret pleasures.

Simon bit into the pie. The meat was tender, the juices strong and spicy. He chewed carefully, thinking, that's what everyone was saying in the Blue Boar and Silver Swan: *Watch what you eat, watch what you drink.* Simon bit again even as he heard the laughter. He froze, swallowed the pie, and went on all fours, sliding onto his belly like a lurking fox. He lifted his head and watched Ralph leading Alison by the hand. They had climbed the wall and were making their way to their usual love tryst. Ralph was carrying what looked like a wineskin and she a linen cloth, probably containing bread and cheese. Simon bit back his disappointment. That meant that they'd eat and drink first.

The lovers reached the place where the ground dipped yet provided Simon with such a good view. He watched breathlessly as they undid the linen cloth and began to eat and drink. Simon heard snatches of their conversation and lifted his head. Ralph was playing with the strings on Alison's bodice. She resisted but he became insistent. Simon's hand went to his crotch. Ralph was undressing her. Simon watched greedily as the girl's smock was pulled down over her shoulders to reveal generous breasts. Alison was laughing, head going back, golden curls falling even as Ralph seized her by the waist and pulled her close and then she went back. Simon moaned quietly with pleasure at her squeals of enjoyment. Glancing up, he saw the girl's legs high in the air, heard Ralph's grunting and moaning, her exclamations of delight. Perhaps he could edge a little closer.

Simon felt his face flush, a sweat broke out. He would watch and wait and, one day, when it so suited him, invite Alison here. He'd tell her about what he saw, and for his silence there must be a price. Simon licked his lips. He'd got to know a number of wenches through such meetings. They were always frightened of their parents being told, of being proclaimed in the church porch or the market cross as naughty, so they always complied; the only exception was that fey-witted bitch, Hawisa. Simon relished the thought that one day, very soon, Mistress Alison would be doing a similar dance for him. Simon had watched so many times, he knew exactly how close he could edge to this lovers' tryst. He watched the two make love, Ralph eagerly, Alison responding, and then it passed. Simon heard the murmur of their voices, whispered endearments, and edged back to his place.

For a while, the sexton waited. Lovers would always leave immediately: the same happened today. He caught glimpses of white as Alison dressed herself. Ralph stood up, pushing back his long hair and tying it at the back with a piece of cord, then they were gone. Simon hugged himself with excitement. He'd enjoyed that. He picked up the wineskin and sat with his back to the yew tree; closing his eyes, Simon recalled the scene, the pleasure he felt, and wondered when he should challenge Mistress Alison. He'd threaten her with Walter the Constable, and if Simon the Sexton was bad, the constable was no better.

Simon undid the stopper and lifted the wineskin to his lips. He'd taken two or three mouthfuls before he realised something was wrong, not with the taste of the wine but the wineskin. He'd not noticed it before—it was only a minor difference. He stared down in horror. This was not his wineskin. He felt a stab of pain in his belly, and jumped to his feet clutching the wineskin and hurried towards the priest's house.

Even as he walked Simon knew it was too late. The pain in his belly turned into fire as if he had drunk the coarsest apple wine; his face became sweaty, his hands rather cold, the more he hurried the worse it became. Eventually the pain was so intense he had to stop. Clutching his belly, Simon fell to his knees and tried to be sick, but his throat was closing up and the thudding in his temples was almost unbearable.

Simon looked up. He saw the door of the church, the tympanum above it, Christ in Judgement, His angels swooping downwards with swords of fire—were they coming for him? The sexton tried to recall what had happened that morning, the wine he bought at the Blue Boar. He'd watched his wineskin as it was being filled, but now, his thoughts trailed away. He tried to open his mouth to scream for help, yet no words came out. He felt his gorge rise, his stomach wanting to empty. He looked up again, and this time the church was moving, the sweat on his back was turning cold. Simon, unable to bear the pain any longer, collapsed to the ground, even as the church door opened and Benedict the Notary came out.

He saw the sexton stagger and fall to his knees. At first Benedict thought the man was drunk, but when he saw Simon collapse he ran towards him. The sexton was still alive, his body shaking as if in a fit. Benedict knelt down and tried to push him over, but Simon resisted, fighting back, clawing with his hands as if Benedict were an enemy rather than someone trying to help.

Benedict could do nothing. He stood up. The smell from the sexton was offensive, and the notary realised his bowels must have been loosened in his death throes, his coughing and retching, arching, legs flaring out.

Benedict remained rooted to the spot—he should hurry to get the priest but he stood both fascinated and repelled. At last, the sexton gave a groan. He tried to rise once more but collapsed and lay still, mouth open, one eye staring. Only then did Benedict finally realise what had happened. He picked up the wineskin, which had fallen from Simon's hand, and sniffed. Good claret, but something else, slight acrid. The notary dropped the wineskin, wiping his fingers feverishly on his garment before running back to the church to ring the alarm to proclaim to Walmer Village, once again, that another horrid death had occurred.

Kathryn and Colum were seated in Lord Henry's inner chamber. The manor lord was pacing up and down, stopping now and again to examine the tapestry from Bruges with its splendid reds, blues, and golds, which hung on the wall at the far end of the chamber.

"My lord," Kathryn repeated, "I have asked for this meeting in order to establish the truth."

"What is the truth?

"I appreciate that I am only your guest here," Kathryn replied, "yet last night, after I had retired, I sat and wondered about the truth."

"As did I," Lord Henry retorted, "with little satisfaction."

"Well, may I help you, Lord Henry?" Kathryn asked.

The manor lord sat down behind the great oaken desk, spreading his hands on either side of the bound ledger. He stretched out for a quill as if he wished to hold something, but then remembered himself, so he felt the silver collar round his neck bearing the insignia of the House of York. He watched Kathryn guardedly and quietly wondered about this dark-haired, clear-eyed young woman, who slightly unnerved him. Lord Henry knew he'd been leading them all a merry dance in pursuit of the truth. Now he was confused, slightly frightened. He regarded himself as the master of the game but the disappearance of the preacher deeply worried him.

"I think you'd best speak, Mistress Kathryn."

"A year ago, well, just over a year ago," Kathryn declared, "your wife, the Lady Mary, died of a fall from the cliffs near Gallows Point. Some people whisper suicide, others an accident, a few look through their fingers and murmur murder."

Lord Henry's hands fell away from his collar. Kathryn stared at an exquisite woodcut on either side of the Bruges tapestry. The wood was polished so the carving seemed to glow. It told the story of a knight lost in a magical forest being rescued by an elfin lady.

"I have been out, Lord Henry, to Gallows Point."

"And what do you think, Mistress Kathryn?"

"The Lady Mary did not commit suicide, nor was she murdered. Instead, I believe that she was so distraught, she missed her footing and fell."

Lord Henry stared unblinking back.

"I don't think you're a killer, Lord Henry." Kathryn ignored Colum's obvious agitation. The Irishman didn't know which path Kathryn was taking and was growing concerned. Lord Henry could act the calm, subtle courtier, but he had a ferocious temper. Colum would never forget the battle at Tewkesbury when the victorious Yorkists had pursued the Lancastrians into the abbey, its hallowed precincts shattered by the clash of steel and the screams of dying men. Lord Henry had been in the vanguard, visor up, sword and axe swinging.

"I'm waiting, Mistress Kathryn. I'm pleased to know I'm not a killer."

"Well, not in that sense," Kathryn replied, ignoring Colum's gasp of disapproval. "Yet, there are a hundred and one ways to kill another being. My first husband was guilty of that, a drunkard and a wife beater. Little by little he tried to kill the life within me. You married Lady Mary because it was a good match. She may have loved you, but you never really loved her."

"You presume too much, mistress, you do not know me."

"I didn't say I did; this is speculation." Kathryn's gaze returned to the woodcut.

"Lady Mary recognised that you didn't love her but something else happened. She saw or heard something." Kathryn searched for words. "You hurt her, I don't know why or how, so she rode out to Gallows Point to think, and then she fell. It would be so easy, a woman with tears in her eyes, to misjudge the ground. What concerns me is, why was she in such a state? You certainly feel guilty—you arranged for a special tomb to be built in the crypt of St. Swithun's Church for your wife, but your guilt becomes too much. You sit down and, pretending to be your wife and using her seal, write a letter of confession to His Eminence the Archbishop of Canterbury—"

"Kathryn!" Colum grasped her arm, but she shrugged it off, her gaze never leaving Lord Henry. He had paled, his agitation obvious.

"I've heard of other people doing the same." Kathryn's voice was hardly above a whisper. "They have to confess, they have to assuage their guilt. You may regret the letter later, but it had to be done."

"Why should I do that?" Lord Henry's voice was harsh. "It would lower me in the eyes of the Archbishop and the King."

"You feel guilty," Kathryn replied. "You saw that as just punishment. You may have regretted it afterwards, but it was done." Kathryn cleared her throat. "The letter was secretly despatched to Canterbury—in such a manner as to hide its true source. Naturally, the Archbishop would be concerned, especially as vicious tongues in Walmer were hinting at the same. Benedict the Notary would be one of these, an avaricious lawyer you use as your messenger boy. He'd be only too willing to sell such malicious gossip to the French—as he had other tittle-tattle, including the fact that you own many of the tenements in Walmer."

Colum would have objected but he could see from Lord Henry's face that Kathryn was telling the truth. Her earlier suspicions had now hardened into an indictment.

"But the letter." Colum had to say something in the manor lord's defence. "The letter was written in Lady Mary's hand."

"Lord Henry is a skilled clerk," Kathryn declared. "I wager he can copy any hand, whilst only he had access to Lady Mary's seal, which should have been broken after her death—but, of course, he kept it. In a way, Lord Henry, you must be relieved that the Archbishop showed the letter to the King, who took Master Murtagh into his confidence. You suspected that, didn't you? Any lowering in their eyes was just reparation. I have known men walk from London to Jerusalem and back to purge their guilt for some terrible crime. Your letter was your pilgrimage and atonement."

Lord Henry lowered his head. Colum, embarrassed, pushed back the chair and stared down at his boots as if he hadn't seen them before. Kathryn glanced at the woodcut.

"You're admiring it, Mistress Kathryn?" Lord Henry asked. "The Lady Mary loved wood, especially hornbeam."

"They say its gnarled branches," Kathryn remarked, "provide excellent shelter for robins."

"And murderers," Lord Henry added quietly. "Lady Mary kept a piece of hazelwood in her bedroom as protection against evil spirits. When the King was here on a royal progress through the eastern shires, he told her how Friar Bacon was the first to prove that hazelwood was an ingredient for gun powder. She died on August twenty-second. . . ."

"The Feast of St. Philibert," Kathryn finished the sentence for him. "It's the day you collect hazelnuts, isn't it? Lady Mary would know that."

"That's what she told the servant," Lord Henry agreed, "that she was going out to collect hazelnuts. If I'd known she was going to Gallows Point, I would have asked Marshall to escort her. She fell," he continued in a rush, "because of what she'd seen the previous day."

Kathryn remained silent.

"The blacksmith came to the manor house, his wife with him. I'd always found her attractive. I'd drunk too much claret, whilst her husband was busy in the stables. I took her into the garden," Lord Henry rubbed his eyes, "nothing stupid, just silly flirtation, a kiss, an embrace, but my wife came upon us." He shrugged.

"The rest you know. After her death I was full of guilt, seeing demons in every corner. I went to Father Clement to be shriven. He set me a penance that I should do something to atone for my stupidity." Lord Henry sighed. "Hence the letter. I regretted it, yet I felt my wife's ghost was dictating it. The French learnt about my guilt and, thanks to Benedict, I am sure they know more about my affairs than they should."

"The death of William Marshall?"

Lord Henry drew himself up. "Oh, that's a different matter."

"Did William Marshall know about the letter?" Colum interrupted.

"He knew I felt guilty. William simply advised that I build a splendid tomb, hire a priest to chant Masses, and go on a pilgrimage to the Virgin's shrine at Walsingham, the place where he was born."

"And his death?" Kathryn insisted.

"Marshall was a merry fellow." Lord Henry picked up a quill and balanced it between his fingers. "Sharp as a needle, a man for the ladies, Chaucer's squire to the very button. Lady Mary loved him, but as a son, whilst he treated her with every courtesy. William and I journeyed to Paris and took lodgings a short ride from the Gate of St. Denis. We were there to meet our spies and pay good silver to those who collected useful information.

"One night William came back to our lodgings very excited, he'd learnt something but wouldn't divulge what. He'd been out in the taverns along the Seine. William knew all the rogues, was a personal friend of the king of the beggars, Le Roi des Gueux.

"The following day, just before noon, he slipped from my lodgings. I saw him in the stableyard so I hurried down. William was very excited, he said he was going to meet someone, a lady, who'd made a hideous mistake. I walked with him through the street to the stairs of St. Pierre on the Seine. He climbed into a barge and that was the last time I ever saw him."

"And the Book of Ciphers?" Kathryn asked. "Marshall wasn't carrying it?"

Lord Henry shook his head. "Marshall's disappearance," he explained, "caused confusion and chaos. I didn't want the

French to know about him going to meet someone important, so I misled them, letting it be known that William was carrying such a valuable document."

"Is there such a book?" Colum asked.

"Of course." Lord Henry pushed back his chair, got to his feet, and offered them a cup of wine, which they both refused. He filled his to the brim. Kathryn noticed how his hand trembled as he raised the goblet to his lips.

"Did you think William betrayed you?" Kathryn asked.

"I feared that he was dead, mistress, though I feared more, and so did the King, that he had been taken prisoner and tortured."

"But he was an accredited envoy." Colum intervened. "The French would not do that!"

"That's what I came to believe." Lord Henry returned to his chair. "Eventually I concluded that he'd been murdered. I had no firm evidence yet I believed that Sanglier and those two precious clerks of his were involved. That's where the preacher comes in. Now, Irishman, as you know, I have spies and agents wandering every highway of France. The preacher is one of the best, a veritable greyhound of man, a great ferreter of secrets. He began to hear rumours amongst the river people along the Seine, how one of their boatmen had also gone missing on the same day as William. His corpse, covered in slime, was gathered from the river. I suspected this was the bargeman hired by William. I told the preacher to continue his hunt." He grinned at the look of astonishment on Kathryn's face. "You now realise, don't you, mistress?"

"Of course," Kathryn breathed, "you didn't invite Sanglier and his companions from France to discuss the Peace Treaty or a truce. You brought them here to discover what had happened to William and, if they were involved, to mete out justice to them."

Lord Henry was now hiding the lower part of his face behind the goblet.

"But they are official envoys," Colum insisted. "Their persons are sacred."

"But accidents can happen, can't they, Lord Henry?"

Kathryn gazed past the manor lord at the great mantelpiece. On each corner was a face of a gargoyle—a monkey with a human face, eyes narrowed, mouth opened as if roaring with laughter.

"Accidents can happen?" Kathryn repeated.

"Yes, mistress, accidents do happen. I wanted Sanglier and that precious pair to be here in England at the same time as the preacher returned with whatever information he'd found. I confess, I fooled them just as they tried to dupe me. They learnt about my wife, they knew about the disappearance of William. I made them think that my clerk was carrying the Book of Ciphers. I even hinted that my soul might be up for sale—Sanglier would never be able to resist that. What he didn't know"—the smile faded from Lord Henry's face—"is that I loved William as if he was my own brother. I have shown the people of Walmer what happens to those who hurt me or mine." Lord Henry swilled the wine round in his cup. "I even deceived His Grace the King. I wanted no one to know what I plotted. I realised, in time, the King would forget that letter, especially if I trapped the Spider King in a web of my own making." Lord Henry finished his wine. "I know what the King wants," he added enigmatically, "and I shall do my best to achieve it."

"And the preacher?" Colum asked.

"Well," Lord Henry answered, "you know the news he brought, how William's drenched body had been discovered with his throat cut?"

"But you don't trust the preacher fully, do you?" Kathryn asked.

"The preacher knew more than he told me. Before you ask, Kathryn, as God is my witness, he would not tell me why he was striding round the village involved in the mummery. He was absorbed in his own searches. True," Lord Henry conceded, "he may have held something back, and tried to sell that to Sanglier."

"And?" Colum asked.

Lord Henry cradled the empty goblet in his hands.

"Did the preacher meet the Vicomte, sell him secrets for a bag of gold, and then disappear? Or did Sanglier, or one of his men, cut the preacher's throat and hide his corpse?"

"What made you think Sanglier, Delacroix, or Cavignac were involved in William's death?" Kathryn asked. "You had no evidence."

"William was a clerk, mistress, a trained spy. He would never risk his life unless the price was very, very high, and what higher than some high-ranking clerk in the service of the Spider King?" He smiled thinly.

"Did you kill Delacroix?" Kathryn asked.

Lord Henry lifted his hand. "On the Gospel, mistress, no, though I was sorely tempted."

Kathryn splayed out her fingers and examined the beautiful betrothal ring. She believed she was approaching the truth. Logic dictated her explanation surrounding Lady Mary's death based on the obvious facts that only Lord Henry could have written such a letter out of remorse and a desire to make reparation. As for William Marshall, Kathryn found it difficult, but was forced to accept that the arrival of the French envoys had nothing to do with peace treaties or truces but personal vengeance. After all, this would fit with Lord Henry's character, the young Yorkist lord who had swept into Walmer years earlier to trap and hang that coven of wreckers. Kathryn breathed in, aware of a bee buzzing against a windowpane. Colum was sitting quietly next to her. She glanced up quickly. Lord Henry had opened the leather-bound ledger as if interested in some entry. He looked up quickly and caught her gaze.

"I know what you're thinking," he murmured. "I am a man who lives by the law of blood—an eye for an eye, tooth for tooth, life for life. True, if I knew Sanglier was responsible for William's death I'd gleefully take his head and fix it on a pike, but I know nothing, mistress, except the preacher went out in the dead of night and Sanglier followed."

"The guessing game?" Colum asked. "About the Book of Ciphers, if the French killed William surely they'd know that he wasn't carrying any book or manuscript?"

Lord Henry clicked his tongue.

"That's how you know, isn't it?" Kathryn asked. Colum's question had solved one problem.

"Know what?" Colum demanded.

"If William Marshall had been killed with the approval of the French King, he and his minions would know he wasn't carrying any such book. They would have rejected as a lie," Lord Henry whispered, "stories that William Marshall was carrying something precious, they would never have walked into such a trap."

"Which means," Colum agreed, "that Marshall was murdered by someone acting on his own, who dare not tell his royal master the truth?"

"Agreed," Lord Henry replied. "There are all sorts of possibilities." He pushed back his chair. "Did Cavignac and Delacroix, for reasons best known to themselves, lure William to his death, or was it Sanglier, or both his clerks, or one of them?"

"We should search all their rooms." Kathryn got up and walked to the window.

"I'm sure, Lord Henry, somewhere amongst their possessions, we would find some clue, though only the good Lord knows what."

"But you can't do that." Lord Henry came and stood beside her. "They are diplomats and envoys, they'd scream privilege, demand reparations."

"They are going to do that anyway." Colum laughed. "They are going to say Delacroix's death is our fault."

"Murder!" Kathryn declared. She watched a servant below come running up the garden path. "They will say we murdered him. Lord Henry, what will happen?"

"Delacroix's corpse will be taken to St. Swithun's. Father Clement has already been here to anoint the corpse. They can't take it to France. In a few days it will ripen and rot, so they will have him buried here and, when corruption is finished, the coffin will be transported back to France. Father Clement has agreed to sing a Requiem Mass this evening, even though canon law forbids it, so we should search their chambers then."

There was a knock on the door and a servant hurried in.

"My lord, a message from the village. Another poisoning! Simon the Sexton has been found dead in God's Acre."

The death house of St. Swithun's Church was one of the cleanest Kathryn had ever seen: a low beamed stone building, standing on its own patch of ground in the far corner of the cemetery opposite the corpse door. Its walls were lime washed, the floor of beaten earth. Lanterns slung on hooks provided welcoming pools of light, whilst the iron-barred windows high in the walls provided freshness. In the middle, in a narrow chest supported by trestles, lay the sexton's corpse. Some attempt had been made to straighten the body, to disguise the horrors of such a swift and terrible death. Nevertheless, in the poor light, his face was truly macabre, livid white with a purple hue on the cheeks, eyes popping, mouth gaping. Someone, probably Father Clement, had tried to place pennies on the eyelids but these had slipped and the sexton stared empty eyed, yet horror struck by something Kathryn could not see. Despite the incense burners, the charcoal burning, the fragrance strewed upon them, the odour in the death house was offensive. Kathryn held a bunch of wildflowers to her nose. She also detected the tang of burning, and realised it must be from Mother Croul's remains, which had lain here before being coffined and placed before the high altar. She put down the bunch of flowers and sniffed the corpse's mouth. The smell of almonds was strong. She crossed herself, left the death house, and walked across to join Colum and Father Clement. The priest stood, Ave beads in his hand, resting on the arm of Amabilia. Walter the Constable sat on the grass shredding the petals of a flower, murmuring to himself. Benedict and Ursula were talking in whispers. Roger the Physician had walked away to stare up at a gargoyle's face high on the church wall. The sun was strong, the smell of cut grass heavy, butterflies floated on the breeze, and the cemetery was full of the gentle song of the crickets and hunting bees.

"Who found him?" Kathryn asked.

Walter staggered to his feet, eyes blazing, face flushed. The constable pointed drunkenly at Benedict.

"Apparently," Colum anticipated Kathryn's question, "Father Clement was in the crypt working on Lady Mary's tomb. Ursula was over at the priest's house helping Amabilia, who was busy in the sacristy preparing for Mother Croul's Requiem Mass. Our noble constable was in the lane leading up to the church, whilst the physician claimed to be in town."

"I was in town," Roger snapped, cleaning his nose on the back of his hand.

"And why were you here, Master Benedict?"

"Business, mistress. I was to meet a client, a peasant farmer, who wished me to seal an indenture in the church porch. I brought my wife as a witness."

"I was helping Amabilia," Ursula declared heatedly. "She asked me to work on some tasks in the house as she was busy in the sacristy."

"So what happened here?"

Benedict described how the farmer had failed to keep his appointment. Later he decided to leave the church and sit a while in the sun. "I came out of the main door. There must have been lovers here. I heard a snatch of laughter, but that's not my business. Then I saw Simon staggering towards the main door of the church. He was in distress but, by the time I reached him, he'd collapsed. Within a few heartbeats he was beyond my help. I thought it was a fit, but it's poison, isn't it?"

Kathryn nodded.

"What was Simon doing in the grass?" Colum asked.

The Irishman's question provoked nothing but blank stares. Father Clement looked embarrassed whilst the constable smirked to himself.

"You find it amusing, Constable?" Kathryn snapped.

Walter's hand went down to his groin. He pulled up the leather jerkin, and scratched at his tight hose, a gesture Kathryn found offensive, but the way he was swaying on his feet showed his fat belly was full of cheap ale.

"You'd best sit down, Walter," Father Clement said gently. The constable needed no second bidding but nearly fell onto the grassy verge that surrounded the church.

"He liked to watch lovers. He thought nobody knew." Walter glared as the physician sniggered softly behind his hand.

"Simon," the physician declared, "lived for the good weather, when the sun warms and the grass grows long and lush. Lovers come here, mistress. They always have and always will, whatever warnings Father Clement thunders from his pulpit. Simon knew that. There were rumours that Simon used what he'd seen to coerce wenches in the village. It's an offence to be naughty in public, and no wench wants to stand on the pillory, do they, Walter?"

Kathryn stared across the cemetery. Here and there grew old yew trees, surrounded by long grass. In places the ground dipped and rose, an ideal place for a lovers' tryst as well as for snoopers like the sexton. She gazed up at the sun. It was now past noon. She guessed young lovers would slip away either midmorning, midafternoon, or as dusk fell. Simon would always be waiting like a fox in a covert for its prey.

"Did you know about this, Father?"

The priest disengaged himself from his sister's arm and walked across. "I suspected it," he replied. "I did have words with Simon, but he could not stop himself."

"I always knew when he was on the hunt," Walter slurred, "down to the Blue Boar or the Silver Swan to fill his wineskin. He did so this morning. I have already discovered that."

"He told me he was very careful." Amabilia's merry face was flushed, her eyes tearful. "I liked Simon, he had his kind ways, you know. He said he was going to be careful about what he ate or drank." She bent down, picked up the wineskin lying against the church wall, unstoppered it and handed it to Kathryn, who sniffed and drew away quickly.

"He was poisoned," Kathryn exclaimed, "with the same potion the blacksmith's wife drank. It works quickly, like an arrow speeding to the heart."

"Well, that's how he died!" Roger the Physician rubbed his hands together.

"Show me where," Kathryn urged.

They walked out across the front of the church following the path around the tombstones. Again, Kathryn noticed how these had been cleared of all moss and lichen. Here and there lay bouquets of flowers or posies, dried and wilted under the heat of the sun. They led her towards the wall where the ground became more uneven.

"Sometimes the grass is difficult to scythe," Father Clement explained. "Simon was responsible for that."

"And he always protected his hiding places?" Colum retorted.

Kathryn stopped at the bottom of the small dell. The grass here was flattened. She stooped and picked up a hairpin glittering in the sun. At the top of the bank sprouted holly and bramble bushes. A little beyond that, under the shade of a yew tree, she found where Simon the Sexton must have lurked. Here, too, the ground was disturbed, the grass trampled. In one place Kathryn found drops of red wine glistening on the black earth beneath the yew tree. Above her a bird sang, a sad haunting note as if it knew about the hideous events that had occurred below. She crouched down; she could see how sly Simon had been. The ground swept to a slight rise to provide a clear view through the tangled undergrowth where the lovers had met.

"Simon took his pleasure here," she said, getting to her feet. "He brought a wineskin but, while he lay here, someone must have come and poisoned what he drank."

"That's ridiculous!" Father Clement declared.

"He always prided himself on being sly," Benedict scoffed. "He thought no one knew about his snooping. If anyone ever approached he'd leave as fast as a whippet. This is a large cemetery and Simon knew every inch of the ground."

"If he was so sly," Kathryn mused loudly, "wouldn't he always be vigilant? The constable says Simon filled his wineskin this morning at the Blue Boar and came back here. Did anyone else talk to him?"

"I met him in the lane," the physician replied, "but he hurried by."

"As he did me in the church," Benedict added. "He was looking for Father Clement."

"I was in the crypt," the priest replied. "Simon didn't come down but shouted to me, asking if I needed him. I replied no, and the next I heard was Benedict pulling at the bell."

"We all gathered," Amabilia explained, "and helped carry the corpse to the death house." She fought back her tears.

"So, where and when was he given that poisoned wine?"

"He never came to the house," Amabilia whispered. The rest kept silent.

Kathryn glanced at Colum, who could only shrug and look away. Kathryn stretched out and gently pulled a branch down. From where she stood she could see the front of the church and the tympanum of Christ sitting in judgement. She was genuinely puzzled. The wineskin she'd handed back to Amabilia was half-full, definitely tainted. How had that happened to Simon, who had prided himself on his cunning and vigilance?

"I must go," Father Clement declared, "I have Mother Croul's Mass to say. There are no mourners."

"And we can't attend," Benedict spoke up, "I have already lost enough time." His words were echoed by the rest.

"I'll stay for the Mass," Kathryn offered.

"Kathryn," Colum said as he led her away from the rest, "we have this business at the manor. Lord Henry is concerned that Sanglier and Cavignac may leave."

"They won't leave," Kathryn replied. "Delacroix's corpse is still above ground. I suspect Father Clement will bury Mother Croul and the Frenchman together, just before Vespers. We have time enough. Someone has to mourn Mother Croul." She prised Colum's hand loose. "You go back to the manor. If you can, distract Sanglier." Colum made to protest, Kathryn pressed a finger against his lips and left.

"Father Clement," she called, "before you leave, may I see the Poor Man's Plot?" The priest agreed and, as Colum walked away, Kathryn crossed to the fenced-off corner of the cemetery. Father Clement opened the small gate into an area no bigger than a small paddock. In the centre grew a venerable yew tree, branches extended. All around it ranged neatly tended mounds of earth, each with a battered wooden cross above it. Father Clement, assisted by his Parish Council, explained how this part of God's Acre had been set aside by charter as the burial place for strangers, the poor, and those who had no kin.

"Usually beggars," Benedict explained. "People who travel through Walmer and are taken by God, a chapman who collapses in a tavern, or a beggar found dead in the lanes."

"You travel often, don't you?" Kathryn asked. "You act as Lord Henry's messenger to Canterbury, even to France?"

The notary's narrow face flushed, his eyes became more wary. "I'm a lawyer, mistress, and my profession often—"

"You go to Paris, I understand?"

"Two or three times a year." Benedict waved away a butterfly, as if to distract Kathryn. He gazed over his shoulder at Walter, who sat on the grass fast asleep.

"Look at him." Roger kicked the Constable's thigh. "Our noble constable. You know, mistress, a former scholar, he fought for Lancaster as a man-at-arms."

"And?" Kathryn asked.

"He was in the service of the Duke of Somerset, accused of cowardice though the allegation was never proved. So he came here to act as constable." Roger narrowed his eyes. "But don't judge a book by its cover. Walter can be a very dangerous man." Kathryn recalled how the constable had been close to the church when the sexton had died.

"What do you mean, dangerous?"

"He likes none of us."

"Tell me," Kathryn asked, "do any of you like each other?"

"Mistress, why are we here?" Father Clement moved impatiently from foot to foot. "I have a Mass to say, people to visit."

"The three fugitives," Kathryn looked round, "where are they buried?" She could tell by the reaction of her companions that this was a matter they did not wish to discuss. The notary hissed his disapproval, and Ursula snapped her fingers in annoyance and turned her back on Kathryn.

"Why are you interested in them?" Amabilia asked.

"Because I am," Kathryn replied. "I am interested in all murder victims."

"Murder?" Walter the Constable had now woken up. He sat

with his hands hanging between his legs. "Murder?" He repeated giving a loud belch.

"That's right, Master Constable, the law defines murder as the unlawful slaying of another."

"They were traitors." The constable wagged his fingers.

Kathryn noticed how they were dyed with paint.

"Didn't they offer to surrender," she retorted, "only to be cut down?"

"They're here," Father Clement interposed swiftly. He led them round the great yew tree to three mounds of earth, a wooden cross stood thrust into the earth at the head of each.

"They were wrapped in some old cloth," Father Clement murmured, "naked and bloodied from head to toe. That great oaf the blacksmith supervised the burial." He looked up, drawn faced. "You're correct, mistress, their blood is on our hands."

Benedict went to protest but Father Clement turned on his heel, muttering about Mass to be said, and, followed by Amabilia, went across to the church.

Kathryn made her farewells to the rest, and left them gossiping as she followed the priest into the church. The transepts were full of light pouring through the stained-glass windows, beautiful and clear like the sanctifying grace of God. Before the rood screen stood Mother Croul's coffin on high-legged trestles, covered with a black-and-gold drape and ringed by purple candles in sombre holders. Amabilia now lit these with a taper. Kathryn walked up the church; her hard-soled boots echoed like a beating drum. The priest's sister stopped her lighting and smiled across at her. In the poor light her face looked younger, more comely.

"You frighten the parishioners. We do not like to be reminded about our sins," said Amabilia.

Kathryn stared down at the coffin. In the centre of the funeral cloth lay the Franciscan cross of St. Damiano.

"So many burial Masses"—Amabilia finished lighting the candles—"so many deaths, and now Mother Croul goes into the earth, or what's left of her."

Kathryn glanced at the rood screen and the great cross that

hung above the sanctuary. The face of the crucified God looked angry. In the sanctuary itself candles glowed. Kathryn turned as Father Clement came out of the sacristy and into the chantry chapel, which stood in the transept leading up to the Lady Altar. He nodded at Kathryn, genuflected before the small altar, and began the Mass.

Kathryn and Amabilia knelt on cushions in the doorway of the chantry chapel, on either side the great wooden screen, which cordoned off the altar and the small place before it. Above the altar a stained-glass window depicting Anthony of Padua preaching to the birds showed that the chapel had been founded by someone devoted to the Franciscans. Kathryn half listened to the words of Father Clement, distracted by those three desolate graves in the Poor Man's Plot and the corpse stiffening in the death house.

She could not understand the sexton's death. How was he so brutally and swiftly murdered? Yet, the more she reflected on that and other grotesque happenings in Walmer, the more convinced she became that the death of those three strangers played a part in them.

Father Clement had now reached Thomas of Celano's hymn about the wrath of God.

"'Wondrous sound the trumpet flingeth,'" Father Clement described the Day of Judgement.

> "Through earth's sepulchres it ringeth,
> All before the throne bringeth
> What shall I frail man be pleading?
> Who for me be interceding
> When the just are mercy needing?"

Aye, Kathryn thought, what would happen on the Day of Fire, when the heavens are torn apart and the elements melt in flame, what would happen in Walmer when all these murdered souls rise to justice? She remained distracted during most of the Mass. Father Clement had left the chantry chapel when Amabilia tapped her gently on the shoulder.

"You seem perturbed."

"I keep thinking of those three strangers, cut down . . ."

"God rest them, mistress. Would you like something to eat or drink, perhaps a jug of buttermilk?"

Kathryn shook her head. The corpse door opened and Roger the Physician, followed by the constable, came into the church. They seemed not to notice her but walked down and stared at the wall near the baptismal font, just inside the main door. They stood whispering to each other.

"What is it?" Kathryn asked.

"Oh, didn't you know?" Amabilia pressed her face close, her breath smelt sweet. "Both our physician and our constable have a special talent, they are painters."

"What?" Kathryn got to her feet.

"Yes, I know it's strange." Amabilia laughed softly. "Yet both have a gift. They have done a number of wall paintings at my brother's request—that is, until they began to quarrel."

She led Kathryn down the nave. Roger and Walter turned and Kathryn heard their collective groan.

"I thought you were busy," she asked.

"We are," Roger retorted. He gestured at the half-finished painting on the wall, which depicted the young Christ separated from his parents, sitting with the doctors in the temple. Kathryn had seen similar paintings. This lacked some of the accuracy of a scene from an illuminated manuscript yet the painting boasted a peculiar vigour in its eye-catching colours. The temple was really a church, Jesus was dressed like any boy in a village, Joseph carried the tools of a carpenter, while Mary was a busy housewife.

"Where did you learn to paint?" Kathryn asked.

"We didn't," Walter and Roger replied in chorus like twins. The constable, embarrassed, shuffled his feet.

"I was an apprentice once. I worked in places like Ely and Norwich until the war came."

"In my days," the physician retorted, "I illuminated manuscripts but the great ones became more interested in killing each other than having their Book of Hours painted. I discovered

Walter's gift." The physician couldn't keep the sarcasm in his voice.

"You did not!" the constable declared. "I was drunk when I—"

"Anyway," Amabilia tactly interposed "when approached by Father Clement, they did a number of paintings until—"

"Until we couldn't agree." Walter sniffed. "It's the paint, you see, mistress. I think it should be mixed with oil. These deaths," he mumbled on, "they made us both think. Life is too short." He paused. The physician was eager to go, so they made their excuses and left.

"I must leave as well." Amabilia touched Kathryn on the hand. "Father Clement and I are to take provisions to one of the farms. Stay if you wish." She left, disappearing into the sacristy.

Kathryn recalled those graves and returned to the cemetery.

The afternoon sunlight was fading, making the wind from the sea feel a little colder, as it stripped the leaves from the trees and sent them whirling.

"Autumn will be here soon enough," Kathryn whispered. The sight of the green-gold leaves rolling in the air provoked a pang of homesickness. She wondered how Thomasina was coping with her patients, and although St. Swithun's Church was beautiful, the sky above a light blue, the sun shining and the remains of summer still apparent, she missed the narrow streets of Canterbury. She went across to the Poor Man's Plot and knelt beside the three unmarked graves.

"You died," Kathryn spoke aloud, "and within a year the killings began." Kathryn wondered why she'd reached such a conclusion. "Two reasons," she said to herself. "First, these heinous poisonings lack any motive. Secondly, why secondly? Oh yes." Kathryn buried her fingers into one of the mounds of earth. "Before you were killed, there were no murders, no poisons." She withdrew her hand and made the sign of the cross. Perhaps she was wrong.

And then she stumbled onto a third reason. The only people murdered were members of the Parish Council. Did the assassin, or assassins, hold them responsible for something? Was it the slaughter of these three strangers, or was it something else? She recalled Lord Henry sitting at his desk hiding his face behind his fingers. Were the poisonings connected to previous sins of the inhabitants of Walmer? The savage, bloody murders of the wreckers?

Chapter 9

To maken, vertu of necessitee.
—Chaucer, "The Knight's Tale,"
The Canterbury Tales

Kathryn chewed the corner of her lip and wondered if the ghosts of these murdered men haunted the cemetery. Was she to be God's vengeance? Yet how long could she stay in Walmer? She returned to the church. For a while she walked up and down the transepts admiring the different wall paintings. She had to concede that both the constable and his colleague possessed a talent for depicting harsh yet lifelike scenes from the Bible. The Prophet Samuel coming to anoint David, Abraham about to sacrifice Isaac, knife in hand, a firebrand in the other. Kathryn read some of the chilling scriptural verses beneath these paintings.

Rescue me, O God, from evil men. Protect me against violent ones! Day after day they harbour strife, their tongues are forked as the serpent's. Viper's venom stains their lips.

"True, true!" Kathryn murmured.

Amabilia came into the church to let Kathryn know she and Father Clement were leaving. Kathryn nodded absentmindedly and, a short while later, she heard the cart clatter across the cobbles. She went down the steps into the crypt, aware of the deathly silence, which chilled her as if a horde of ghosts watched from the darkness. In the crypt a cresset torch flared; the air was pungent with the smell of tar and resin. Two lanterns had been placed around the sarcophagus of Lady Mary. From the tools and chips lying about, Father Clement had obviously been busy carving the pure white limestone. She walked slowly around the crypt before examining the weepers carved in each of their niches either side of the sarcophagus. She noticed in amusement how in each of the panels there was always a tree. She could make out the broad oak, the spreading willow, the long elegant birch. Beneath each tree was a scene from the Bible: Mary and Joseph fleeing into Egypt, the presentation of Christ in the Temple. Some of these figures had still to be polished and smoothed but they showed Father Clement's undoubted skill.

Kathryn was aware how silent the church had fallen. She thought she heard footsteps but, when she called out, there was no reply. She sat on the stool Father Clement used to work on the stone, and stared down at a piece of parchment. She picked this up. It was a letter from Lord Henry giving Father Clement instructions on how the sarcophagus was to be carved. Kathryn sat with this in her lap and wondered what was happening in the manor. She was now certain that Lord Henry had brought the French envoys to England to exact vengeance for the death of William Marshall. So, was he responsible for Delacroix's death?

"Think, think," Kathryn whispered to herself. As she racked her memory, different images came and went. Sanglier and Cavignac in the hall. Delacroix locked in his chamber. He was a spy, a cunning fox of a man, who probably trusted no one, not even his own companions. In his chamber was that small pouch of valerian powder, a few grains of which Delacroix would mix with his wine whenever he wished to relax or sleep. It was possible, Kathryn reflected, that somehow the assassin had sneaked into his chamber with an identical pouch containing poison, changed it for the valerian, and then changed it back again. She thought of Lord Henry, then of Colum, and grinned. The Irishman seemed half-asleep most of the time.

"Except at night," Kathryn said aloud, her voice echoing around the crypt. Now, if Colum had such a pouch next to his goblet of wine it would be easy for her to change one for the other, but Colum was trusting, especially of her. Delacroix was different. A predator, always eager and watchful not to become the prey. He would be vigilant; for all Kathryn knew he may have hated his two companions. She already knew how careful he was with his wine. Wouldn't he be just as careful in his own chamber?

"Unless he was distracted," Kathryn whispered. She thought of the evening, the last time she saw the preacher alive. Another predator, a former soldier, as used to danger as a bird to flying. He definitely went out in the dark to meet someone. Sanglier? Kathryn recalled her sense of unease. Someone else was out there that night, deep in the shadows. Sanglier was undoubtedly a killer but the preacher would be wary, vigilant. If Sanglier had met him, if a fight had ensued, would the Frenchman have killed the preacher so easily? And what was the preacher doing out on the clifftop in the first place? Did he have information to sell?

"Kathryn!"

She jumped.

"Kathryn!"

She could not recognise the voice. A man, a woman? Someone was calling her from the church. Kathryn sprang to her feet. The stool fell over with a crash.

"Kathryn!" The voice echoed, disembodied, like that of a ghost. She was going to shout back but a deep unease, a cold flickering along her back, the way her hands became clammy, stopped her. Kathryn knew she was in danger. In the dim light, shadows danced around the crypt. She must get out of here! This was a trap! Picking up the hem of her skirt, Kathryn raced up the steps, paused at the top, and slipped into the church. She heard the squeak of a mouse, the slivery scamper as it jumped down from one of the purple candles that ringed Mother Croul's coffin, and fled into the shadows. Kathryn hid behind a pillar, her heartbeat quickened, her stomach clenched. She could see nobody. If they were looking for her, why didn't they show themselves?

"Kathryn!"

She glanced across the nave and, plucking up her courage,

hurried towards the corpse door. A bowstring twanged and an arrow whirred above her head to smack into one of the pillars. Kathryn reached the corpse door, pulled at the latch but, to her horror it was locked. Of course, it would only be open on a burial day. She gazed down the length of the church, where the main door was open. Using the transept pillar as protection, she slipped along the shadows. She managed to go once, before another arrow smashed against the stonework behind her. Despite her agitation, Kathryn crouched behind the pillar.

Since the corpse door was locked, the only way out was through the sacristy or the main door of the church. However, if she left the shadows and the protection of the pillars, the murderous archer would strike again. Kathryn recalled what Colum had told her about how he and others had been ambushed by Lancastrian archers in Hainult Forest.

"On the eve of Corpus Christi, it was," Colum had remarked. "We were looking for a tavern and became lost." Kathryn wrapped her arms across her chest as she tried to remember. "One thing I learnt, Kathryn, if a bowman is stalking you, hide, let him come to you. Run and you just become another beast in the forest, a target for his skill."

Kathryn drew a deep breath and fought the urge to run. A sound echoed from the far transept. She peered around the pillar, glimpsed a shadow crouching, and pulled back, just as another arrow sliced through the air. Kathryn gazed behind her but there was nothing to protect her. All she carried in her wallet was a small knife. She tried to wet her mouth, but her throat was dry. She screamed as loud as she could. Another sound—the archer was moving to her right—as more arrows were loosed. Soon she would have to move to the next pillar. Abruptly there was a rattling at the corpse door. Kathryn screamed again as loudly as her dry throat would allow. Farther down the opposite transept, the archer loosed another shaft. Kathryn screamed again but the rattling at the corpse door stopped. She knelt, sobbing for breath.

"What is the matter?"

Kathryn peered around the pillar. Amabilia had come through the main door of the church.

"What is the matter?" she called again. "Who is here, Mistress Swinbrooke?" The priest's sister screamed suddenly as an arrow flew above her head, digging deep into the wooden doorpost above her. She fled even as Kathryn heard footsteps racing up towards the sacristy. She waited for a while, rose to her feet, and came slowly round the pillar. She stared up towards the high altar and, gathering her courage, ran to the main door. She burst into the sunlight, stumbled down the steps and across the path, and threw herself down near a headstone.

Amabilia and a white-faced Father Clement came hurrying round the church. The priest carried a rusty sword; Amabilia had picked up an axe.

"Mistress Swinbrooke." They both crouched down beside her. Amabilia's face was red and sweaty. She loosened the collar of her gown, threw the axe down, and wiped her face with a damp cloth.

"What is it?"

Kathryn sat up and composed herself. Amabilia grasped one of her hands.

"Mistress, what was that?"

"I don't know." Kathryn made herself comfortable against the tombstone. "I was down in the crypt. A voice called my name. I came up into the church and there was an archer." Kathryn paused, and for a moment she thought she was going to vomit.

"Do you want some water?" Amabilia offered. Kathryn shook her head. "The archer must have shot perhaps seven or eight times."

"A man?" Father Clement queried.

"I don't know," Kathryn confessed, "I only glimpsed a shadow. Thank God you came. I thought you'd gone visiting."

"We had." Amabilia clambered to her feet, patting her brother on the shoulder. "Clement became ill. No, no, nothing serious, just something he ate. We came back. I thought I'd check on the church. Sometimes children play there, especially Hawisa."

"Hawisa?" Kathryn asked.

"Oh, you will meet her. They say she is fey. Anyway, I heard a scream," Amabilia continued. "The side door was locked so I ran through the main door of the church when that arrow whipped over my head. I thought I was in some nightmare. I ran out and roused Father Clement."

"Our attacker fled," Kathryn explained, "to the sacristy."

"Now, I thought I'd locked that," Amabilia confessed, "but when I returned with Clement I saw it flung open. That malignant must have ran across the cemetery and climbed over the wall. Come, mistress!" Kathryn grasped her hand and got to her feet. She felt light-headed, her body sweat drenched, as she followed Amabilia into the church. The priest's sister walked round picking up the shattered arrows, nine in all, each shaft a yard long with grey goose-feathered flights and cruel barbed points. Father Clement left them, quietly cursing the malefactor who had dared to violate God's holy place.

"I'd best get back to the manor," Kathryn declared.

Amabilia grasped her hand. "Do you want me to walk with you?"

Kathryn squeezed her fingers. "No, I'll be well." She pointed to a cluster of ash poles near the door. "If I could borrow one of those, I'm not too steady on my feet." They walked on to the steps of the church. Kathryn was about to make her farewells when a beautiful clear voice began to sing:

> *"Now the sun has turned,*
> *So has my heart.*
> *The day dies but not my love.*
> *The darkness falls made bright by you.*
> *The cold turns warm at the memory of you.*
> *The seasons change but never my love!"*

"I've heard those words before," Kathryn exclaimed, walking down the steps, "I know the style." She glanced back at Amabilia. "We have chanteurs who come to Canterbury, they recite poetry to a lilting tune. I understand it's all the fashion amongst the scholars in the halls of Oxford and Cambridge." Kathryn peered across the cemetery and saw a movement near the wall, a flash of a blue cloak and snow white hair.

"That's Hawisa," Amabilia explained. "You must meet her. Some claim she's witless. She lives with her mother on the far side of the village, a small house on a track leading down to the sea. The mother's the widow of a troubadour. They came here some years ago. He was stabbed to death in a tavern brawl. No one ever discovered who thrust the knife. Four months later Hawisa was born. They say the fairy did it."

"Did what?"

"You'll see, mistress. She stays away from here but, every so often, comes and sings her songs. Sometimes she'll take milk and honey, other times she just stares at me or asks where her father lies buried. She's not really a child, more a young woman. They say her father was killed by one of the wreckers." Amabilia went to go back up the steps; she paused halfway. "There's a badness in Walmer. My brother says it stinks of ancient sin, so you take care, mistress."

Grasping the ash pole, Kathryn walked down the winding path leading to the lych gate. She stopped just before it and glanced along the strip of grass that ran beneath the cemetery wall. Hawisa was sitting with her back to her, snow white hair falling down to a dress of dark blue, its patches neatly darned. Kathryn sat down against the wall, placing the pole beside her. Hawisa kept rocking backwards and forwards.

"Are you a healer?"

"I try to be," Kathryn replied.

"Did he hurt you? I saw a figure, black as night, climbing the cemetery wall. It had dark, gloved hands."

"You saw him?"

"I heard your screams as well, but this is a place of blood, mistress. You're not safe, even if you live in a manor. Death comes in many forms. Be ye man or woman, good or bad."

"Did you see my attacker?" Kathryn asked, trying to remain calm. "Were you not mistaken?"

"I saw what I saw." Hawisa turned and came on all fours

across the ground towards Kathryn, who did her best to hide her surprise. Hawisa was an albino, milky white skin with pink-rimmed blue eyes. She had her own strange beauty. Kathryn was tempted to touch her face, smooth and pale as mother-of-pearl, her hair white as freshly fallen snow. Despite her patched gown, the young woman looked spotlessly clean and smelt sweetly of mint and rose water.

"Are you shocked, mistress?"

"I'm surprised." Kathryn laughed. "You have a beautiful voice."

"My mother taught me." Hawisa knelt next to Kathryn, so close her knee pressed into Kathryn's thigh. She studied Kathryn's face as a child would, wondering what to make of her. "I saw you cross the marketplace. I heard what you said to that pig of a constable about releasing people from the stocks." One long-nailed finger pressed Kathryn's cheek, then she rubbed the sheen of sweat from Kathryn's forehead. "Kindness is what kindness does," she remarked, then stooped and kissed Kathryn fully on the lips. "The sexton tried that." She laughed, kneeling back. "They think I'm simple. He called me a frightened rabbit, so did the constable." She abruptly brought up her other hand, and grasped a wicked-looking knife, its blade long and thin. "I told them I'd slice their cocks off! You're not frightened, are you, Kathryn?"

"How do you know my name?"

"Everyone knows your name."

"And what do you know about the village, Hawisa?"

"Some good, some bad, and some indifferent. Adam the Apothecary was a dark soul; my mother said he poisoned people. He once tempted me, said he could sell me a powder to change the colour of my eyes!"

"And?" Kathryn asked.

She was aware that the day was dying, the sunlight fading, the sea breeze strengthening, yet this enigmatic creature fascinated her. Kathryn had met the likes of her before. Men and women, because of their reputation or their looks, being pushed to the edge of life, excluded from the everyday small things, treated like outcasts. Such people were wary, vigilant, and often glimpsed things other people didn't.

"The priest is a good man," Hawisa chatted on, "and so is his sister. They are kind. Mother Croul was good, that's why I came to sing a song. I would have gone into church but, yes, I saw that dark shadow, racing under the sun, fast and slinky like a rat."

"Who could it be?" Kathryn asked.

"Anyone from Walmer, even the great lord, they have all got secrets. I found her body, you know, Lady Mary's. I find lots of things on the beach." She turned and pulled the leather bag alongside her.

"I call these my treasures. Do you want to see them?" Hawisa was gazing intently at the brooch Kathryn had pinned to her cloak, a gift from a patient who'd visited the shrine of Thomas à Becket. Her hand went out and stroked the silver. Muttering to herself, Hawisa undid the sack and emptied the contents onto the ground. She sifted amongst the polished seashells and trinkets. Something caught Kathryn's eye, a beautiful silver button. She picked this up and recognised the coat of arms.

"The Bastard of Faucomberg!"

"The who?" Hawisa asked.

Kathryn turned the button over. "Where did you find this?" Hawisa pressed her lips tight and tapped the side of her nose. "I'll give you the brooch in exchange." Hawisa smiled and nodded. Kathryn unclipped the brooch and handed it over. "Now, where did you find it? When those men were killed here?" Hawisa shook her hand.

"Can I have the ash pole? I like a good walking stick."

Kathryn handed it over. Hawisa got to her feet and, leading Kathryn by the hand, took her back up the cemetery path and pointed at the steps of the church.

"I found it there." Hawisa crouched down and shook the weeds growing between the slabs. "Before they were buried, I saw it there, so I took it. I thought it belonged to them. I was in the village the day they entered. I saw their coat of arms. They shouldn't have come here. You don't expect help from demons. I must see Mother Croul now and make my farewell." She went up the steps banging the ash pole against the paving stones.

"Oh, Mistress Kathryn." Hawisa turned back and grinned. "I told you I find things. I found a corpse this morning. I told Lord Henry." She patted the small purse around her waist. "He gave me a silver piece."

"Whose corpse?" Kathryn stepped forward.

"The fiery-eyed preacher. He was amongst the rocks. The sea had spat him back, his throat was cut"—she gestured with her finger—"from one ear to the other. All drained of blood, he was, like a pig on a butcher's stall. Farewell, physician. He's beyond your help."

Kathryn was already hurrying down the path into the village, keen to reach the manor. Once she slipped on the cobbles but managed to steady herself. People stepped aside, wary of this guest of their powerful lord, hurrying along the High Street, white faced and anxious.

She climbed the trackway to the gate and found Lord Henry and Colum in the courtyard. The preacher's corpse was already sheeted, wrapped in canvas, the sandaled feet, soaked with sea water, poking out.

"Kathryn." Colum came and grasped her hands. "You look pale. There is grass on your cloak." Kathryn just stared at those water-soaked sandals.

"A strange young woman found him," Colum murmured.

"I know," Kathryn replied, "I met her in the cemetery."

"You were longer than I thought." Lord Henry came over, dressed elegantly in a dark blue gown with a high collar, the velvet sleeves pulled back to reveal snow white cuffs. He played with a silver chain around his chest, as someone else would their prayer beads. He looked calm and composed.

"Murdered!" Lord Henry gestured with his head towards the corpse. "His throat cut and tossed like a sack from the cliff. The sea has brought him back." He shouted an order to the waiting retainers. They hurried across, picked up the canvas-bound corpse, and took it to an outbuilding.

"We'd best go." Lord Henry nodded. "I told my ostlers to prepare a cart. Sanglier is taking his dead down to St. Swithun's."

Lord Henry escorted them into the manor house, along the corridor to the library. Servants brought jugs of cool ale. Lord Henry asked Kathryn about her visit to the church, had she discovered anything about the identity of the poisoner. Kathryn replied evasively. Colum was glaring at her furiously but she did not want to tell him about the assault in church. Lord Henry sensed her mood. He put down the jug of ale and sat opposite.

"Do you suspect me, Kathryn?"

"I suspect everyone except Colum."

Lord Henry laughed.

"You're a strange man, Lord Henry." Kathryn gestured around. "You act the scholar, the collector of books, the builder of a fine house, with well laid-out gardens, but the truth is you are also a man of blood. You live in the shadows, and if necessary, mete out sudden death."

Lord Henry was not taken aback. He shrugged and played with the ring on his little finger. "You make me sound like Tiptoft."

"I'm sure she doesn't," Colum intervened.

"John Tiptoft, Earl of Worcester, a scholar, and a great traveller," Lord Henry explained. "He visited Wallachia and met Vlad the Impaler. When he came back to England he brought impalement with him until he was caught and lost his head on Tower Hill." Lord Henry sipped at his ale. "Are you saying I'm a Tiptoft?"

"You want revenge for William Marshall."

"Oh, it's more than that." Lord Henry cocked his head. "Ah, our French guests are leaving." Kathryn heard the faint creaking of cartwheels, the crack of a whip, the neigh of horses as Lord Henry's retainers escorted the coffin down to the church.

"Father Clement has been busy," Lord Henry remarked, putting the tankard down, "and so shall we."

Once he was assured that the French had left, Lord Henry took the two of them upstairs. His steward was already waiting with a bunch of keys. Lord Henry took these and slipped one into the lock. The door opened with a crack as the French had placed wax seals at the top and bottom, which now hung in shreds. Inside, the room was neat, saddlebags and chests already packed.

"They are set to leave at dawn," Lord Henry murmured.

Two of the small coffers were locked. Lord Henry however, helped by Kathryn and Colum, went through the leather saddle-bags, pulling back the lids of chests and emptying the contents onto the floor, yet there were nothing more than clothing, trinkets, a Book of Hours, and some personal items. Lord Henry groaned when they'd finished. He ordered his steward to do a thorough search of the room. The old man did so, grumbling under his breath, but nothing was hidden away. They visited Cavignac's chamber, and again the door had been sealed. They broke these only to find the same as in Sanglier's—one small locked coffer, panniers already packed, and two chests, one of which hadn't been closed. Their search proved to be equally futile.

"They've probably taken important documents with them," Colum asked.

"But what about these locked coffers?"

"They are too small," Kathryn enigmatically replied.

"For what?" Lord Henry asked. Kathryn sat down on a stool and cupped her chin in her hands.

"Sanglier will love this," Lord Henry commented bitterly, "he'll come back to fluster and bluster, how one of his men had been slain and the belongings of the other two French envoys ransacked and pillaged."

"Strange," Kathryn took her hands away, "Sanglier has not protested much, has he, about the death of Delacroix?"

"Oh, he'll do that soon enough," Lord Henry remarked, "won't he, Colum, once he reaches London? But the real storm will break in Paris. The Spider will demand huge reparation."

"Kathryn," Colum asked, "what are you looking for?"

"Where are Delacroix's possessions?"

"But we've searched his room."

"Let's search again."

They went back to the chamber. The steward explained how Sanglier himself had insisted on packing the dead man's possessions. Once again they opened chests and saddlebags.

"What on earth!"

Kathryn looked up. Colum had tipped the largest chest over, spilling out items of clothing, doublets, hose, boots, a belt. Amongst these were two dresses and a wooden box with a lady's face painted on it. Kathryn picked this up, opened it, and burst into fits of giggles.

"Face paints!" she explained.

They continued their search. Other items were found, a choker that was too long for Kathryn's neck, a phial of perfume, a pair of stockings. Lord Henry also began to laugh.

"I have heard stories. Mistress Kathryn, how did you guess? Did Delacroix like to dress as a woman? In London there are certain taverns, meeting houses, where men can dress as women and act the harlot in the hall." He paused, closed his eyes, then clapped his hands in glee. "Marshall!" This is the lady he was going to meet. He discovered Delacroix's secret and was murdered."

"Perhaps," Kathryn replied evasively.

"What do you mean?"

"There's more to it than this," Kathryn replied. "Let's put everything back as it was except these items. Lord Henry, have your steward bring a travelling casket, fill it with these and bring it down to the library. Let's wait for the Frenchmen to return."

"Kathryn," Colum warned, "you should tell us the truth."

"Colum, my heart, I don't really know it myself. I am going to trap the murderer with a lie. I've done it before. If I speak falsely"—she winked—"Lord Henry can blame me. But, for now, I would like something to eat."

She walked away before Colum could continue his questioning, and went down to the hall where the servants were preparing the evening meal. Lord Henry and Colum joined her. Both tried to question her but Kathryn pointed at the servants. Lord Henry and Colum gave up and let Kathryn eat her food.

Afterwards, she returned to her own chamber and lay on the bed for a while marshalling her thoughts. She drifted into a light sleep and was woken by sounds of shouting. The Frenchmen had returned! There was a knock on the door, which Kathryn answered. Lord Henry's steward, all agitated, hands beating in the air, begged her to come down to the library.

"The Frenchmen," he wailed, "are in a furious temper. I am frightened for my master." Kathryn hurriedly made herself presentable. By the time she reached the library, Lord Henry and Sanglier were almost at blows. They stood a few inches apart, shouting and screaming at each other, raising old grievances, alternating in their fury from English to French. Lord Henry grasped the hilt of his dagger: Cavignac, standing behind Sanglier, had already drawn his sword whilst Colum stood the blade of his weapon flat against his shoulder. Kathryn went and sat on a chair. She picked up a beer jug and threw it to the floor.

"My lords!" she shouted. "I have a story to tell!"

Sanglier replied with a stream of obscenities. Cavignac laughed. Colum would have sprung forward but now Lord Henry intervened, raising his arms, blocking Colum's passage.

"My lord." Kathryn smiled sweetly at Sanglier. "You are noble born; whatever grievance you nurse, can you not spare me, a lady, a little of your time?"

Sanglier breathed noisily, pretending to be in a rage. Kathryn could see he was thoroughly enjoying himself.

"Sit down, my lord." She tapped the edge of the table.

Sanglier obeyed, Cavignac beside him. They sat opposite Kathryn, whilst Lord Henry and Colum took seats farther down the table.

"I am sorry, *madame*." Sanglier clasped Kathryn's hand and, before she could resist, kissed the tips of her fingers.

"I apologise profusely for my hot words but an envoy of the French King, his Most Christian Majesty, has been most foully murdered. Our seals violated, our belongings ransacked—"

"And you, my Lord Vicomte," Kathryn replied softly, "have violated our King's peace. You and Monsieur Cavignac are guilty of murder! The death of Monsieur Delacroix, not to mention the man known as the preacher, are laid at your door."

Sanglier was so shocked he gaped. Cavignac would have lunged across the table but remembered where he was.

"You could be arrested," she continued. "You could claim immunity, but I do not think you will."

"I protest!" Sanglier rose to his feet. Cavignac followed.

Kathryn saw the fearful look in the Frenchman's eyes.

"You'll be arrested at Dover," Kathryn insisted. "We will send back your belongings, including the women's dresses, the jewellery, the perfume, and the face paints. Our noble King Edward will ask, in an open letter to your King, why his French envoys were carrying such items? Why not sit down, my lords? You're not set to leave till dawn."

Sanglier glanced at Cavignac, who nodded. They both retook their seats.

"We are not responsible," Cavignac answered, "for anything you found in Delacroix's chests and coffers."

"Who told you we found them there?"

"Tell your tale," Sanglier snapped.

"William Marshall was a merry fellow," Kathryn began, "I say that, though I never met him. He was a squire, body servant to Lord Henry here, and I wager to his lady. A man who would slip in and out of taverns, perform a merry jig, write a ballad of love, or sing a sweet carol. He came to know the haunts of Paris, where all the twilight creatures live, those mysterious meeting houses where men with bizarre dreams can act out those dreams. A man of charm, young William was a personal friend of the king of the beggars, who knows all the lairs and hiding places of your great city."

Cavignac's face was no longer so olive skinned. *A worried man*, Kathryn reflected, *he knows that I speak the truth*. And Sanglier? The Vicomte's foxlike face was flushed, his light blue eyes furtive. *He'll wait until I tell my tale*, Kathryn thought, *and, if he can, pounce on me*.

Cavignac, unnerved by Kathryn's stare, shifted uneasily.

"Are you saying he met Delacroix?"

"No, *monsieur*, he either met you or, more probably, learnt your secret."

Cavignac would have leapt to his feet.

"Oh, don't act," Kathryn snapped, "none of that mummery. You know I speak the truth, you dress like a woman, Cavignac. I can tell that, it takes one woman to know another—"

Cavignac sprang to his feet, hand on his dagger. Sanglier stood up and pushed him back.

"You've proof of this, mistress," the Vicomte rasped.

"Cavignac's nails," Kathryn replied. "Look at them, all polished and clean. He removes the paint. I noticed a dash of red on the corner of his mouth. Yet, my Lord Vicomte, you know all this. You and Cavignac are lovers."

"You have proof?" Sanglier asked softly, gesturing at Cavignac to keep quiet and remain seated.

Kathryn glanced down the table at Colum and Lord Henry, stealing herself for the lie.

"Marshall discovered your secret and laid that information in a sworn document before a notary in the rue Saint Antoine: the document was signed by witnesses." Kathryn decided to place all on one throw. "A priest who haunted the same place. The preacher brought this document back—it is written in cipher— not even he knew its worth."

"A dangerous pastime," Sanglier murmured, "for royal servants and officials."

"Is it?" Kathryn smiled. "Aren't there others in the French Court? Such tastes are shared in Paris as they are in London. Men who wish to be women: men who take their pleasure from the bodies of other men?" She stared at the ceiling and noticed how the sculptor had carved white and red roses, the rim of the petals lightly gilded. "Holy Mother Church has terms for such practices: buggery and sodomy, both are condemned by canon law as well as the ordinances of your own King. They burn such men at the stake—that's when they capture them. But, of course, who would dare give information against the powerful Vicomte Sanglier? You are lovers. God knows, perhaps the love between the two of you is as deep as that between Master Murtagh and myself. I've seen you touch each other."

"And Marshall?" Cavignac asked.

Kathryn glanced quickly at Lord Henry and Colum, who tried their best to hide their shock and surprise.

"Marshall hoped to blackmail you," Kathryn continued. "I don't know if he discovered the secret of one of you or both. I suspect the former; that's why he agreed to meet you." She pointed at Cavignac. "Marshall was a roaring boy, a man used to the street brawl, the clutch of a sword, the thrust of a dagger, he wouldn't fear one man. He made a terrifying mistake which cost him his life: there was not one waiting to meet him but two. You both cut his throat and tossed him into the Seine. Lord Henry gave out that his principal spy was missing; he embellished the story, talking about a Book of Ciphers. In truth, he was baiting you. You knew, he knew, there was no Book of Ciphers. Yet, what could you do? You couldn't refute what he said without admitting that you were responsible for the murder of one of England's accredited envoys." Kathryn pointed to the arrow chest. "It contains women's clothing—your clothing, Cavignac. You should have destroyed the clothing, the paints, the trinkets, but of course, you couldn't, so you tried to hide them amongst Delacroix's."

"And who murdered him?" Sanglier asked guardedly.

"Why, my lord, both of you did." She lifted her hand. "Please, don't protest. This is not some mystery play and I am sick and tired of empty oaths and hollow threats. The preacher arrived at the manor. He not only brought news about the discovery of Marshall's corpse but, I think, he suspected the truth. He played the same game as Marshall, only God knows what he really knew. But he met the same fate as Marshall because he made the same mistake. He went out on the cliffs expecting"—she pointed at Sanglier—"to meet you. The preacher feared nothing. He was a fighting man, he wanted to sell you information about Cavignac which he'd withheld from his own master. Instead he met both of you, his throat was cut, and his corpse tipped over the cliffs for the sea to wash out and back again."

"I was not—" Cavignac was breathing noisily.

"What, *monsieur*, you were not seen outside the manor that night? I saw you," Kathryn declared, "I felt your presence. You are an accomplished spy and assassin. To steal in and out of a manor such as this is not beyond your capabilities!"

"And Delacroix?" Sanglier's voice betrayed his fear.

"Oh, Delacroix was ambitious and he was no fool. Perhaps, from the start, he knew something was wrong, and what a prize! To creep back to his King in France and whisper his suspicions into the Spider's ear: Delacroix was dangerous, an archrival, so he had to be silenced. You, however, planned to put the blame on Lord Henry and trot back to Paris—pleased at the way the game went. No one could blame you for Marshall's death. Your royal master probably suspects there is no Book of Ciphers, whatever he hints at. You'd dismiss the rumours swirling about for what they were, lies, the imaginings of Lord Henry's fertile brain."

"Delacroix!" Cavignac shouted the name as if it was a curse.

"Sharp as a sword blade," Kathryn replied. "He had his suspicions about both of you, though I know nothing of these. The preacher may well have approached him but, again, I have no evidence of that, I can only tell you what I know. Perhaps Delacroix suspected your relationship long before he left France. He must have seen something, entertained suspicions, but he would never move against the great Vicomte unless he had proof."

Kathryn played with the ring on her finger. "Perhaps you decided his death before you left Paris. You see, sirs, I truly believe William Marshall, the preacher, and Delacroix made the same mistake. They suspected one of you, but not both. Marshall and the preacher died violent deaths. However, here in Walmer, you learnt about the poisonings and that provided you with both the means and the opportunity; it's a matter of logic. Monsieur Delacroix, as both of you are aware, was very careful about what he ate and drank. He would cover his cup with his hand, would be wary of who poured his wine. In his chamber he felt safe. No one entered that chamber except you two. Only the good Lord knows which one he suspected. He felt secure when both of you

visited him. I suspect you, sir"—she pointed at Cavignac—
"were probably the suspect. Earlier in the day Delacroix died,
you both came to his chamber to chat about the doings at
Walmer, and Sanglier used the opportunity to change one identical pouch for another.

You then left, knowing it was only a matter of time before
Delacroix opened that pouch, poured what he thought was valerian into his wine, and drank his own death. Now, remember the
events as we entered Delacroix's chamber? At night, the poor
light, people pressing forward all concerned, in the first instance,
about Delacroix? In such confusion it would be so easy to
change one small pouch for another, done in the twinkling of an
eye. Once back in Paris, the Vicomte would cheerfully report
how Delacroix's murder was the work of the perfidious English,
the treacherous Lord Henry."

"And you expect our master to believe this?"

Lord Henry pulled back his chair and got to his feet. He came
and sat between Sanglier and Cavignac. Kathryn glimpsed the
pure pleasure in his eyes, so gleeful he could hardly contain himself. Like an opponent in some game of hazard when he has
thrown the dice three times and won.

"Gentlemen"—Lord Henry stretched out his hand to empha-
size his points—"we all play chess." He smiled. "And, mes-
sieurs, the game is nearly over. I know your King. Louis the
Suspicious, who trusts no one, doesn't he have his own orchard?"

Kathryn noticed Sanglier swallow hard. Cavignac slouched
like a man sentenced to death.

"Does he have an orchard where he hangs his own fruit?"
Lord Henry chuckled. "Those servants who fail him? We have
Marshall's death, the murder of an accredited English envoy. We
will announce that he carried no Book of Ciphers, we will produce what we have found in the chest and coffers here. We will
describe the preacher's death. After all, my Lord Vicomte, you
did go out in the night to meet him. Now we have Delacroix's
murder and, above all, William Marshall's deposition locked secure in my strongest coffer.

"We wish to see this!" Sanglier rasped.

"Nonsense," Lord Henry retorted, "and betray the names of trusted agents in Paris! Is that your best defence, Vicomte—to challenge us to produce a document? Think," he urged, "how that sounds. You are almost conceding you are guilty and regard that deposition as the proof, a poor defence in law! What would the great Spider think?" Lord Henry shrugged. "As for black-mailing me?" He clicked his tongue. "Oh, I know all about Benedict the Notary's treachery. He sold you the stories about my wife's mysterious death and what other tittle-tattle he could collect from the village. Now it's my turn. True, the evidence is not overwhelming, but we will plant the seed in Louis's suspicious mind and the tangled weed will grow. How long, my Lord Vicomte, do you think he would continue to trust you—a month, a season? If I laid a wager, I would say by Easter you'd be in disgrace, dead by midsummer, probably hanged at Montfaucon." Lord Henry sat back in his chair. "Of course, that is, if we allow you to leave Walmer. You are under suspicion of the murder of my squire." He smiled faintly. "Marshall I loved as dearly as you love Cavignac. Of course, there is also my good servant the preacher, sent to God before his time."

Cavignac lifted his head, face all fearful. Sanglier spoke quickly to him in French. Kathryn could tell by his gesture that he was ordering him to remain silent.

"An interesting story. What do you want?" Sanglier lifted his hand from the table and Kathryn glimpsed the sweaty imprint on the polished wood.

"I could ask for your agents in London, their names, identities, the places they live."

"Impossible!" Cavignac shouted. "We'd be signing our own death warrants!"

"I thought as much." Lord Henry rubbed his hands together. "My price is quite simple. Henry Tudor!" He smiled at the astonishment in Kathryn's face. "The Tudor," Lord Henry continued, "the last Lancastrian claimant to the English throne. Your master shelters and sustains him."

"He will not hand the Tudor over," Sanglier declared.

"We're not asking that. We want him banished from France. We want guarantees that the Tudor will no longer be welcomed by your Seigneur or any of his subjects. You can advise him so, my lord, that is the price!"

Kathryn lowered her head. That's what all this was about, she concluded. Lord Henry may have wanted justice for his murdered squire, but he'd brought Sanglier to England to trap him. The Tudor's expulsion from France was the real aim of this subtle game. Kathryn glanced down the table at Colum; he sat head in hands. When he looked at her, Kathryn could only wink at his astonished look. On any other occasion she would have risen, gone down, and stroked his honest face. She would have kissed that forehead and laid her hand on his chest to comfort him. She would have reassured him that his surprise was not due to a lack of wit but more the result of an honest heart, unused to such subtle treacheries. Sanglier sat, eyes closed, fingers gripping the edge of the table.

"If I agree?" He spoke slowly.

Lord Henry looked at Kathryn. Kathryn pulled a face but Lord Henry remained silent, pleading with his eyes for her to offer some sort of solution.

"You could go back to Paris," Kathryn replied, "you could report that these negotiations were successful, that your master should consider a lasting peace between England and France, that Marshall's death was an aberration and the story of the Book of Ciphers a mere fancy. Finally, you would advise that Henry Tudor be expelled and not allowed to seek sanctuary on French soil."

"And Delacroix's death?"

"An unfortunate accident; you are satisfied there was no foul play. In return for which," Kathryn continued quickly, "no mention will be made of your three victims, whilst your relationship with Cavignac remains secret."

"How do we know," Cavignac snapped, "that you will keep your word in days to come?"

"I will take an oath." Lord Henry rose and walked to the far corner of the library. He placed his hand on the Bible chained to its high wooden lectern.

"I swear now on the word of God, on my wife's soul, on my judgement after death that these matters will be forgotten." Lord Henry tried to keep the amusement out of his voice. "It will be forgotten, as if it never existed in the first place." He let his hand fall away. "But you don't trust me, do you Sanglier? So, I wouldn't be surprised that, perhaps in a year's time, both you and Cavignac retire from the royal service. However, Tudor must be gone by Christmas. You'll be given safe passage to Dover. Delacroix's death is recompense enough for that of poor Marshall."

Sanglier stared at Cavignac, who nodded.

"In which case," Sanglier replied as he rose to his feet, "I will not shake your hand, Lord Henry, but I will be gone from this place before nightfall." He turned and sketched a bow to Kathryn.

"Madame, as soon as you arrived here, I began to wonder. You remind me of a peregrine falcon I once owned. You sit and you watch. That's a very powerful gift, though at times a dangerous one." He smiled faintly and gestured at the arrow chest. "We will not be taking them. After all, they shouldn't have been brought in the first place." And, spinning on his heel, Sanglier left the library, followed by Cavignac.

Chapter 10

This noble ensample to his sheep he yaf,
That first he wroghte, and afterward he taughte.
—Chaucer, General Prologue,
The Canterbury Tales

O nce the door was closed, Lord Henry gave full rein to his delight, laughing and clapping. He shook Colum's hand and kissed Kathryn on each cheek, promising her any gift she wanted.

"What made you suspect?" He stood back and grasped her hands. "Look at you, with the calm face of a nun, yet eyes and wit as sharp as any sword. You should be careful, Colum." He squeezed her fingers, then let go, escorting Kathryn back to the head of the table. Once seated, he served them wine.

"Tell me, Kathryn, how did you suspect?"

"A conjecture, I suppose." Kathryn felt embarrassed and wished her face wasn't so flushed. Colum was grinning at her. Lord Henry sat down opposite, beaming as if he still couldn't accept his good fortune.

"I'll explain." Kathryn sipped her white wine, sweet and cool to the taste. "I realised that your wife's letter could only have come from you, I have already explained that. I also wondered why William Marshall should be carrying such a valuable document around Paris. I could see that his mysterious disappearance seriously disturbed you. Marshall must have gone to see someone of importance. He told you it was a woman but that was his own private joke. When I met Cavignac, I noticed the smudge on his lips, how carefully he tended his nails, but I was fascinated by how he stared at me—not as you do, my lord. He seemed more intrigued by what I was wearing. One morning, in my own chamber, I had this uneasy feeling that someone had gone through my own possessions, yet nothing was missing. I believe it was Cavignac, unable to control his curiosity; a servant would have stolen something. I also glimpsed Cavignac and Sanglier in the hall, the afternoon before the banquet. It was the way they touched each other, like Colum would do to me, a lover's gesture, that opened my eyes."

She cradled her wine cup. "I reflected on the three deaths—Marshall, the preacher, and Delacroix. These victims were not country bumpkins but wary killers in their own right, as accustomed to treachery as fish to swimming." She put her cup down. "Yet all three seemingly died in the blink of an eye. I concluded that, when each of them was slain, particularly Delacroix, two assassins must be involved. This meant either you, my lord, with someone else, or Sanglier and Cavignac. They made one mistake. Cavignac lives a secret life, and he brought that life with him, like a man who cannot live without the taste of wine in his mouth. It's his one weakness, which forces him to take terrible risks, be it bringing those clothes or entering my chamber. Such risks lead to mistakes, which is probably how Marshall found out. In the end . . ."

"What, Kathryn?" Colum asked.

"Perhaps Monsieur Cavignac is like everybody else," Kathryn replied wearily. "We all wear different masks. We can put these on and off without too much trouble. For Cavignac it's harder, he assumes a more alien role. He wears his mask more openly than anyone else." Kathryn pressed the wine cup against her cheek. "Solving this riddle was like fitting keys into locks," she murmured. "You wrote your letter to Cardinal Bourchier, Lord Henry. At the time it was a way of purging your guilt, but later, you were not above using it to bait the trap, as you did with Marshall's death. That snake, Benedict the Notary, would ensure that the French would know all about your discomfiture." She pushed her wine cup away. "A matter you would exaggerate along with other morsels of information such as the Book of Ciphers. When the French didn't reject it outright, your suspicions deepened. The Spider King might wonder about the truth of the story, but Sanglier was not in a position to comment, and the least said about Marshall's disappearance the better. You also realised your spy was not going fishing—not in the literal sense—but engaged in the great game. He made the mistake of not informing you, but"—Kathryn shrugged—"he wanted to be sure. Marshall was impetuous, young, he wished to impress his masters. He thought Cavignac, deeply embarrassed, would be by himself. . . ."

"Marshall did not know about Cavignac's illicit relationship with Sanglier?" Colum remarked.

"No, he didn't and they both murdered him to maintain their secrecy," Kathryn continued. "Now, Delacroix may have entertained suspicions about his colleagues, but nothing more. Sanglier and Cavignac were only too eager to dismiss Marshall's death and prove their worth in the eyes of the royal Spider by depicting Lord Henry as vulnerable. They came strutting here like cocks in a barnyard, eager to seize any advantage. The arrival of the preacher on their trail changed all that. A wily fox, the preacher brings you startling information about Marshall being murdered. He strides around the village putting the fear of God into people."

"Why?" Lord Henry demanded. "I asked him that myself. He replied that he enjoyed his role—"

"Nonsense!" Kathryn sipped at her wine. "The preacher was treacherous, playing both sides against the middle. He, too, knew all the stories about Lady Mary's death, but he was also intrigued by the poisonings. He wanted to know if there was any connection between the arrival of the French and the poisonings; there was not, as he discovered."

"And then he resorts to blackmailing Cavignac?" Colum asked.

"Oh yes," Kathryn agreed. "I am not too sure exactly what did happen. I suspect the preacher had been very busy spying both for you and for his own ends in Paris, and stumbled on the same damaging discovery Marshall had made about Cavignac. Remember, Lord Henry, you had secretly instructed him on all the details about Marshall's death. The preacher thus makes his own discovery and returns to England delighted: Lord Henry will reward him for his information about Marshall's murder, but, at the same time, he will have to reveal the preacher's true identity, so there'll be no more journeys to Paris for him.

"Like the unjust steward in the Gospel, the preacher has to plan for the future. He approaches the Vicomte with certain knowledge. Of course, the preacher does not realise the full truth: Sanglier is both furious and frightened, not only of the preacher but of the ever-inquisitive Delacroix, whom the preacher might also approach, so both men must die."

"That's why Sanglier did not protest too much or question the evidence," Colum observed. "Your story, Kathryn, possesses a logic all of its own. Louis XI would be intrigued and never forget it."

"They're not only fellow murderers, they're also lovers," Lord Henry added, "eager to protect each other."

"And therefore very fearful," Kathryn murmured.

"Of being arrested in England?" Lord Henry asked.

"Sanglier will be back in France," Kathryn replied, "before he realises that his arrest in this country, even execution, would be of little profit to the English Crown: Sanglier and Cavignac would simply be replaced by creatures of the same kind." Kathryn stood up. She felt tired and wanted to be alone. "I suspect the Vicomte will retire from the royal service." She patted Colum's shoulder. "But, for as long as he lives, he will never forget Walmer."

Lord Henry stayed to celebrate. Colum, inordinately proud at what Kathryn had achieved, followed her out to the courtyard, where he embraced and kissed her, begging her to join in the celebrations. Kathryn, however, pleaded tiredness and returned to her own chamber.

She rested there for a while, watching the shadows lengthen as the sun set. A servant brought up food and a goblet of wine. Kathryn nibbled at the slices of venison, then pushed her platter away. She recalled Hawisa sitting by the wall of the cemetery, that silver button amongst her treasures.

"Why?" Kathryn whispered. "Why was such a precious treasure missed?"

She recalled how those three strangers had been slaughtered, been stripped of all their clothes and weapons, which the villagers had shared out amongst themselves. So where did that button come from? Kathryn crossed to the desk, lit the candles and, opening her writing satchel, took out two sheets of parchment. She laid them out on the table, uncapped the inkpot, and sharpened the quill. She ignored the noise from below as she reflected on what she had learnt about the poisonings.

It was growing dark when Kathryn went to the window and looked down. Three servants squatted beside the fountain in the courtyard below. One of them had brought a flute and played a bittersweet tune that provoked memories of half-forgotten dreams. Kathryn recalled her first husband, Alexander Wyville. He could play the most lilting tunes on a flute. She thought of her last memories of him, face full of blood, belly full of ale, and heart full of anger, standing over her, fists clenched, before leaving to join the Lancastrian forces outside Canterbury. He, too, had become a fugitive after the great Yorkist victories.

"It all began there." Kathryn leaned against the wall by the window. The men who had been killed in Walmer were fugitives, two archers led by a squire. Ostensibly they had come to Walmer to secure a boat for swift and sure passage abroad. Or was it for something else? Why had Hawisa found that button so close to the church? Kathryn crossed to her desk, sat down, dipped the quill into the ink and began to write.

Item: *Three men are slaughtered in the graveyard at St. Swithun's in the early summer of 1471, no one knows who they were or why they came to Walmer.*

Item: *Lady Mary falls to her death from the cliff at Gallows Point in August of 1471.*

Item: *William Marshall disappears in Paris in the late spring of 1472.*

217

Item: In September 1472 someone scrawls on the floor of
St. Swithun's Church that phrase from the Book of
Daniel. Father Clement is also threatened. By the
preacher? No!

Item: On the eve of Michaelmas, the blacksmith and his
wife are poisoned. The man dies because someone
has put poison into a water butt which only he
drinks from. Who did this? How and when? His distraught wife goes to the kitchen and broaches that
mysterious cask of claret, but where did that come
from? How did the assassin arrange for the wife to
die the same time as her husband? Why was he, or
she, so certain that, on that particular evening, the
blacksmith and his wife were marked down for
death?

Kathryn chewed the edge of her quill. She found the blacksmith's death most puzzling. Kathryn continued her writing.

Item: Adam the Apothecary, a mysterious man with a
nasty soul. Yet how did the assassin enter his house?
He or she could have only done so by coming up the
outside stairs and crossing the bedchamber of
Adam's mother. The assassin would then have to go
downstairs and place poison in that blackjack. But
how did he or she get in and out without being noticed? And why choose that particular blackjack?
How did the assassin know Adam would drink from
it?

Kathryn closed her eyes. She'd seen something wrong in that
house, but what was it? She opened her eyes and grasped the
quill.

Item: Mother Croul? Who left the funeral ceremony, has-
tened to that lonely cottage, killed the old woman,
then returned without being noticed? And why mur-

der her? She was a member of the Parish Council but, apparently, didn't approve of many of her colleagues.

Item: Simon the Sexton, sneaking through the grass like a viper: the peeping Tom, the bully boy who liked to spy on young lovers! He'd been very careful of what he ate or drank. He'd filled his wineskin at a tavern, so how did the assassin manage to offer the tainted wine?

Item: Who followed me into that church, armed with bow and arrow? Hawisa had seen the murderer, apparently it looked like a man, fleeing the church and climbing the cemetery wall.

Kathryn stopped and reflected on what she had written. Colum came up full of wine, merry and eager to congratulate Kathryn again. She absentmindedly listened to him but refused his invitation to join Lord Henry below.

He left again, and Kathryn returned to her ponderings. She concentrated on the murder of Adam the Apothecary and, the more she reflected, the more certain she became that Adam's mother was lying. So impatient was she for the truth, Kathryn kicked off her slippers and put on a pair of walking boots. She snatched her cloak from a peg and went down to the solar, where Lord Henry and Colum sat, heads together like two boys, surrounded by a group of retainers playing hazard. They stopped and looked up when Kathryn entered.

"Oh no!" Colum put his face in his hands.

"I need to go to Walmer." Kathryn tapped the toe of her boot. "I must go now!"

"Kathryn, you'll soon be . . ." The words died on Colum's lips. Kathryn's face was stern, her gaze resolute.

"I could think of nothing better," he moaned, "than a walk."

Lord Henry also offered to come but Kathryn kindly declined his offer.

A short while later she and Colum left the manor and took the path down to the village.

"You are supposed to help me," Kathryn hissed, steadying Colum, who, full of wine, stumbled and swayed. He stopped, grabbed her, pulling her close and stared up at the sky.

"Feel the cool breeze, Kathryn," he whispered. "Look, the sky is clear, we could lie in the long grass."

"I prefer my bed," Kathryn retorted.

Colum sighed and let her go. She set a vigorous pace. By the time they entered the village, Colum was clearer, the sounds of the night and the growing coldness sobering him up. The High Street was empty, apart from one or two villagers hurrying home, or a door swinging open to let out a dog or for a lantern to be hung on the doorpost.

They reached the apothecary's house. Kathryn could see a glow of light through the window and, followed by Colum, went up the outside stairs. She knocked on the door.

"Come in!" Mistress Mathilda screeched.

Kathryn pushed the door open. A young woman, a villager, was clearing pots from the bedside table.

"You can go now." The old woman glared at her. "Tell your mother next time the stew should be hotter."

The girl glanced at Kathryn, raised her eyes heavenwards, and went down to the kitchen.

The chamber had been cleaned and smelt sweet, clothes hung on pegs, chests and coffers closed. The bed linen was crisp though marked here and there by fresh spots of stew. On the far side of the bed a thick tallow candle glowed under its pewter cap. A lantern had been placed on the chest at the foot of the bed, another one just near the door leading to the apothecary's chamber.

"Well, sit down, sit down." Mathilda gestured at the stool next to her bed. "Have you brought me some sweetmeats?" She screwed up her little black eyes and pulled her shawl about her. "All of Walmer is talking about you." She pointed at Colum. "And watch where you put your big boots. There's a chamber pot beneath the bed." Colum crossed his arms and glowered at her. "I don't care what my son did," Mathilda snapped. "You could have brought me something sweet."

Kathryn opened her purse. Mathilda moved quickly, her claw-like fingers whipped out and snatched the coin from Kathryn's hand.

"You can use it to buy something nice," Kathryn declared sweetly, trying to control her anger. "And I will give you another one if you tell the truth." Her smile faded. "And if you don't, I'll have you taken up to the manor for questioning."

Mathilda's head went down. "I have told the truth," she whined, "I'm only an old woman."

"You're a liar," Kathryn replied harshly, "the bane of your late son's life."

"What do you mean?"

"He couldn't tolerate your nagging, that's why he gave you a drink every night. What was it? Buttermilk or ale? With a sleeping draught! You never woke early in the morning, you slept late, long, and hard, so your son could have some peace. The King and his army could have marched through here and you wouldn't have noticed!"

"I wouldn't take any of his powders. Oh, by the way, your Irishman has fallen asleep." Colum started awake. "Perhaps you have given him powders, mistress?" Kathryn made to go. "In truth, in truth," Mathilda continued hastily, "my son gave me powders. At first I objected, but they also gave me peace. I could sleep, dream."

"And you know what happened?" Kathryn pressed the point. "On the morning your son was murdered, someone came up the outside stairs, through your bedchamber, and down into the kitchen, where they placed the poison in that blackjack." Kathryn pulled another coin from her purse. "Now, Mistress Mathilda, you are going to tell me how the assassin knew which blackjack to choose." The old woman began to sob, face in hands, shoulders shaking; Kathryn could see she was crying through her fingers. "You're not sorry your son died." Kathryn stretched across and pulled one hand away. "You now have this house and whatever wealth he made. You can hire people to come and look after you like some lady in a manor. You don't really grieve for your son; he regarded you as a nuisance, whilst you considered him not much better."

"He was a murderer and a thief," Mathilda screeched righteously. "He acted all grieving but he killed that scold of a wife."

"And the blackjack?" Colum asked. At first he had been angry at Kathryn's request to accompany her, but now he was intrigued. Colum drew his dagger and placed it on the bed. "The blackjack?" he repeated.

"That tankard is not like the others," Mathilda confessed hurriedly, wary of that wicked-looking dagger. "His uncle, my brother-in-law, was one of the wreckers."

"Ah!" Kathryn closed her eyes and scratched her forehead. "I know what you are going to say, mistress. The morning I came here, I noticed that blackjack weighed very heavy in my hand."

"It's really a silver tankard," Mathilda simpered, "hidden in a leather casing. His uncle took it from one of the ships. Lord Henry demanded all such treasures be handed back, on forfeit of life and limb, but Adam wouldn't give it up."

"So he concealed it in a casing of leather." Kathryn finished the sentence. "Yes, your son would like that, he'd relish drinking from such a tankard. But the murderer also knew. Tell me, how many people know about that blackjack?"

The old woman was about to shake her head, but Colum's hand covered hers and pressed down gently.

"Adam used to boast about it. A number of people knew. I suppose he told some and I told others—one of those village secrets. There's plunder from the ships still hidden away in many houses in Walmer."

Kathryn rose and crossed to the inside door. She went down the ill-lit stairs. Nothing seemed to have changed since her last visit. The place smelt sweeter, the kitchen had been swept and scrubbed, whilst the blackjacks still hung from their hooks. Kathryn soon discovered that the precious one had gone, either stolen by the assassin, she concluded, or by some villager who knew Adam's secret. She returned to the bedchamber.

"I don't think I'd ever have an Irishman in my bedchamber," Mathilda snapped.

"If I had my way," Colum muttered, "I'd be the last!"

"What was that? What was that?"

Kathryn tactfully intervened; she gave the old woman a second coin, made her farewells, and almost pushed Colum through the door.

"You should have questioned her more closely," Colum said crossly when they reached the bottom of the steps. Kathryn stared down the alleyway, distracted by the cats fighting over a midden. Somewhere a child cried, a man shouted, and the melodious plucking of a harp carried through the night air. Darkness had fallen, the only light was the glow of a candle or the dancing flame of a lantern in a window.

"Well?" Colum asked.

"That old woman couldn't tell us any more. How can she? On the morning when her son was murdered, she was fast asleep. The assassin knew this, crossed her bedchamber, went down, poisoned the blackjack and returned. Oh, by the way, the blackjack has gone just now, but from the little I know about these villagers, I am sure Mistress Mathilda has had a river of visitors, with greedy eyes and itchy fingers. Come, my glorious Irishman."

She looped an arm through his and went back along the High Street. As they passed the lights of the Blue Boar the constable came stumbling up to them. He lifted his lantern, gazed bleary-eyed, and staggered off, mumbling under his breath, to the welcoming light of the tavern.

Kathryn and Colum arrived back at the manor. The journey from the village had been cold, the sea breeze biting. Colum went looking for Lord Henry while Kathryn returned to her own chamber. What she'd learnt from Mathilda had been important. Kathryn listed the members of the Parish Council and began to tease at the threads that bound them together. She felt one of the buttons on her dress and remembered what she'd taken from Hawisa. She threw the quill down.

"They weren't killed in the cemetery!" she exclaimed. Kathryn closed her eyes. She recalled the warning scrawled just inside the church. The cemetery outside, the grey headstones, and the Poor Man's Plot with those forlorn crosses. In her mind's eye, she went down into the crypt. Colum entered with some food, slices of pork roasted in a sauce until they were crisp, with bread and cheese, and a tankard of ale. He stared over Kathryn's shoulder at the list of names she'd written in a circle and, in the centre, three crosses.

"Forget it." He leaned down and kissed her hair. "Eat, rest, and come to bed, sweetheart."

"Shortly," Kathryn murmured.

Colum kicked off his boots and lay on the bed. He propped himself up on his elbow. Kathryn had not touched her food but sat motionless, shoulders slightly hunched, as if praying. Colum groaned loudly and lay back on the bed. Kathryn was now in her own world, lost in some problem, treating it as she would a maze, determined to thread her way through and resolve the mystery. He stared up into the darkness. She was pale and distracted. Colum wondered what had happened down at the Church. Should he ask her now or wait?

He woke cold. The hour candle had burnt through the twelfth ring and almost reached the next. Kathryn still sat at the desk but, from the tankard on the floor next to her, she had obviously eaten and drunk. He rolled himself up in the counterpane and, before he knew it, was back asleep. Kathryn shook him awake.

"What hour is it?" He peered up at her.

"The hour of judgement, Irishman!" she mocked. "Are you going to keep the counterpane all to yourself?" Colum unrolled it, and Kathryn lay down next to him and cradled her head in his arm.

"What is it?" he whispered.

"I'm tired," she replied sleepily. "It's still dark, let's wait for the light."

When Colum woke the next morning Kathryn had already washed and changed. She looked a little pale, but was otherwise ready for the day. She sat at her desk studying the strange cipher she always used. Colum rolled off the bed and went out to the garde-robe. When he returned Kathryn was seated on the bed.

"Come on, Irishman." He slouched down next to her and nuzzled her neck, but Kathryn pulled away, gripping his hand.

"Look." She dug her nails in. "I want Lord Henry and the Parish Council to meet me in his solar. The girl Hawisa, also. No, Lord Henry will know who she is—she has to be there."

"You're going to confront the assassin?"

"I don't know," Kathryn replied. "But before this day is much older, we will, at least, confront the truth."

It was midday before Lord Henry was able to gather everyone in the solar. Father Clement and Amabilia were first, the priest still looked pale faced, he carried the Parish Blood Book in a leather satchel strapped over his shoulder. He was wearing a dark brown gown and reminded Kathryn of a Franciscan priest. Amabilia was dressed in black with a white wimple because, as she quietly confessed to Kathryn when she took her seat, "So many deaths demand mourning!"

Benedict and Ursula, his wife, also arrived, both in their best attire, the notary even wore a black skullcap. His lined face looked most anxious. He kept licking his lips and fiddling with the silver chain around his neck, whilst Ursula couldn't get any closer to him. They sat at the table like two malefactors at the bar of judgement.

Hawisa arrived dressed in a dark green gown, her white hair combed neatly down to her shoulders. She'd put a wreath of wildflowers on her head and the basket she carried was half-full of wild herbs she'd been picking. Kathryn noticed these and asked where she had been gathering them. Hawisa, who sat separate from the rest, whispered her reply, and Kathryn smiled. She patted the young woman on the shoulder.

"Do you feel comfortable here?"

"If you remain here, yes. What a beautiful chamber!" Hawisa glanced dreamily about. She asked Kathryn to explain a red-and-green tapestry showing the Fall of Troy.

Roger the Physician and the constable bustled in. Both had hurriedly prepared themselves but their hands were stained as they'd been busy painting in the church.

Colum closed the door and leaned against it. Lord Henry sat down at one end of the table, Kathryn at the other. A servant knocked and came in. He served tankards of ale and small silver bowls of fruit and cheese for each of Lord Henry's guests. The servant had no sooner left when two of Lord Henry's armed retainers entered and stood behind their master, who now acted very much the lord of the manor. Lord Henry was still joyful at the discomfiture of the French and had revelled until late the previous evening. Nevertheless, he'd washed and shaved, then dressed in a red-and-gold livery, the silver chain of a justice round his neck.

"Why are we here?" the physician asked, rapping his thin fingers on the tabletop.

"Because I ordered you!" Lord Henry replied. "I am the King's justice in these parts."

"Is this a court?" Benedict the Notary asked.

"If I wish it to be," Lord Henry replied. "I am the justice and Mistress Kathryn will present the case."

The constable, more sober than Kathryn had ever seen him, glared down the table at Hawisa. She was busy eating, but now and again, she'd break off and hum beneath her breath.

"She's my guest," Kathryn warned.

The constable made a rude sound with his lips. He picked up the tankard and thrust his face into it, gulping like a dog.

"Most of you," Kathryn began quietly, "most of you are guilty of murder." Kathryn deliberately timed her words to make the constable splutter on his ale.

The physician half rose from his chair. Lord Henry drew his dagger and banged its pommel on the table for silence.

"In the early summer of 1471," Kathryn continued, "the King fought two battles, one at Barnet, north of London, and the other at Tewkesbury in the west country. The Lancastrians were utterly defeated and the highways and byways were full of men fleeing for their lives. Many had nothing to fear, as the Crown only named the leaders as worthy of arrest. Now, three Lancastrians fled to Walmer, a young squire and two yeoman archers—"

"Rebels and traitors," the notary interrupted.

"I shall talk to you later about traitors," Lord Henry retorted.

The notary, discomfited, sat back in his chair. Ursula, trembling with fear, clung to her husband. This woman knew what Kathryn was about to say.

"They were Englishmen," Kathryn declared. "They didn't flee to Walmer for a boat, they came to seek sanctuary in St. Swithun's Church. Now, it is the ancient law of this kingdom that any man or woman, whatever their crime, may claim the sanctuary and protection of Holy Mother Church. How many of you were present when those poor three died?"

Apart from the priest, Amabilia, and Hawisa, the rest reluctantly raised their hands. "You told everybody," Kathryn continued, "they were caught in the cemetery and killed, but that's a lie! They reached the church. They may have even entered the sanctuary. You, Master Constable, and the rest dragged them out." She opened the pouch and placed on the table the small silver button that Hawisa had given her. "This button was found on the steps of the church, wasn't it, Hawisa?" The young woman smiled and nodded.

"But you told us—" Father Clement sprang to his feet, his face mottled with fury. He shook his fist at the constable. "You told us they were killed just before the lych gate."

"Their killers committed sacrilege as well as murder," Kathryn continued. "Everyone who was there is guilty of a hideous crime. You dragged that young squire out and, in the struggle, one of his buttons came off and lodged in the church step. You then hustled them into the cemetery—"

"They were unarmed!" Amabilia, face white as a sheet of linen, spread her hands and gazed beseechingly around. "They must have been unarmed!"

"They were," Kathryn agreed. "Men who seek sanctuary must leave their weapons at the church door."

Both the priest and his sister sat, horror-struck. Amabilia began to cry, a truly soul-wrenching sight, tears streaming down her face though no sound came from her mouth.

"Is this true?" Lord Henry asked.

"You dragged them out," Kathryn repeated, "you hacked all three to death, unarmed men who sought the protection of Holy Mother Church."

The constable made to protest but Kathryn lifted the silver button.

"You stripped their corpses. You stole their possessions and divided them amongst you like soldiers do the spoils of war. You wouldn't have missed something like this deliberately. Father Clement and his sister were absent on that day. By the time they'd returned, your murderous rage had cooled. You'd cleaned the church and the accepted story became the truth; three traitors, Lancastrians fleeing royal justice, had refused to surrender, so they had been killed. You exhibited their corpses at the market cross until Lord Henry ordered a decent burial. By the time you, Father Clement, and Amabilia returned, the three unfortunates were sheeted and in the ground. Your Parish Council told their farrago of lies, leaving you nothing to do but bless the graves. You must have been shocked, distraught, but you hid it well."

"No, he didn't!" The constable wagged a finger. "Remember?" He gazed around, eyes popping in his red face. "He and Amabilia fell ill of a strange sickness. They were locked in their house for at least a week."

"True," the physician added. "There was sickness in the village, so I never gave it a second thought."

"Who was that squire, Father?" Kathryn asked softly. "A brother—or a son?"

The priest gazed back sad-eyed, oblivious to the consternation Kathryn's question had caused. Amabilia kept her head down.

"Shall we go to God's Acre?" Kathryn insisted. "Shall I ask Lord Henry's servants to dig up those graves? Will you explain how we shall only find the remains of two men wrapped in their canvas shrouds?"

Lord Henry sat gaping at Kathryn. Even the retainers behind him had forgotten why they were there, looking mystified at the priest.

"Well, shall we?" Kathryn insisted. "And then shall we go down to the crypt and open the sarcophagus of Lady Mary? If we do, we shall find two corpses, one of a young woman who died before her time, and a beautiful casket of yew or walnut containing the remains of that hapless young squire."

"Is this true?" Lord Henry pointed his dagger. "Does my wife's tomb contain two coffins?" Father Clement, however, appeared lost in his own thought, half smiling to himself as if relishing a joke, although every so often he would glare at the constable. Beside him Amabilia acted like a nun, hands clasped, head bowed.

"Are you happy, Father, that you carried out justice on behalf of your son?" Kathryn confirmed, "Yes, I will call him your son until you correct me. Father, we have all the proof we need. The Poor Man's Plot would surely prove what I have said. It would be so easy for you and Amabilia to move the corpse at night, to fashion a coffin, prise open the paving stones in the crypt and lower the coffin down. You would have your own funeral service, a Requiem Mass chanted in the dead of night with candles burning. You'd recite the Mass for the dead and Amabilia would act as your server. No one would ever know. You loved that young man. Your church is full of paintings and carvings of Joseph and Mary with Jesus as a child or young boy. You took similar themes about youth from the Old Testament. You knew of Lady Mary's love of fine woods. Along the side of her sarcophagus you carved different trees, but beneath them is always a mother and child similar to the paintings in the rest of the church. They are a secret, silent tribute to the son and wife you loved."

"But the priest has no knowledge of poisons," the physician declared.

"He made you think that. Father Clement and his so-called sister are rivers which run deep. Read your Chaucer, Physician: 'The cowl doesn't make the monk.' In this case the robe doesn't make the priest. Father Clement and Amabilia are very skilled people. Their church and its cemetery are surrounded by fields where every herb can be plucked. Somewhere in the cellars of that priest house, we will find dried herbs, poison ivy, crushed rowanberries, poisonous mushroom, hemlock, and perhaps jars of deadly powders, red and white arsenic, not to mention the powder which kills within a few heartbeats and smells pungently of bittersweet almonds."

"What do you say?" Lord Henry asked the priest.

"Stretch out your hands, Father," Kathryn demanded.

Clement pulled a face but stretched both hands across the table.

"You work with stone, Father. I've seen mason's hands, chapped and cut. Many times wounds heal badly, but look at the scars on your hands. Master physician?"

Roger leaned over the table to look. "Almost nothing," he murmured. "I never thought of that."

"Or your teeth," Kathryn continued, "or the skin of your face. Your breath, and that of Amabilia, is sweet, because you know how important it is to chew on fennel and mint. You'd have made a good leech. I noticed the gravestones in your cemetery. The moss and lichen had been scraped off, whilst near an outhouse door I found a bucket of very stale milk."

"Of course!" the physician intervened. "I've heard of that remedy for wounds. Milk which has stood for a long time leaves a powder on the side of the jar. Yes, yes," he continued in excitement, "mix that with dry moss, they say it can even cure roughness of the throat, clear lungs of an excess of phlegm; dirty wounds become clean and the skin heals easily."

"You claim to have pained joints," Kathryn declared. "I don't think so, an excuse for not visiting Mathilda. You certainly did not visit her son, Adam, yet you claimed you did. However, his ledger contained no entry for you or your so-called sister. You had no reason to, for you leeched yourselves."

"I wish I'd killed you," the priest remarked abruptly. He joined his hands as if in prayer. "I'd wished I had killed you all, the Parish Council and others in the village. Look at me and despair; I am the anger of God."

" 'I have numbered, I have weighed in the balance and I have found wanting,' " Kathryn murmured.

"I did that," the priest replied evenly, as if talking to himself. "I have served this coven of malefactors for years. I have baptised their children; I have gone out in the dead of night to anoint their dying with holy oils. I have sung Mass for them. I have preached; I have sat in the shriving pew; I have listened to their filthy sins. I served them, but they killed my son."

The shock of the priest's abrupt, pointed confession seemed to have knocked the very breath out of his parishioners.

"I see you brought the parish Blood Book as I asked," Kathryn remarked. She left her chair, walked down the table, picked up the leather satchel and brought it back. Neither Father Clement or Amabilia moved. Kathryn took out the leather-bound ledger with its thick leaves and opened it.

"You scrawled those words on the floor of the church, didn't you? It was a warning of things to come. The letter pinned to your door was just a distraction. You wrote it to divert suspicion."

Father Clement interrupted. "I came like a thief in the night, they knew neither the day or the hour! The vengeance of God fell on them."

"The blacksmith and his wife were first?" Kathryn asked.

"Killers!" Father Clement scoffed. "Elias was always a killer, I knew he would have led the pack." He gazed down the table at Lord Henry. "Elias and his hot-eyed wife with her full mouth and juicy breasts, eh, Lord Henry?" The manor lord did not reply.

"You sent them a cask of wine," Kathryn accused. "You knew it was their wedding anniversary on the twenty-eighth September. You knew they'd celebrate. So you bought a cask of wine, poisoned it, and left it as an anonymous gift on the doorstep. Elias and his wife were greedy, they'd see it as a gift not to be questioned or talked about. After all, smuggling is frowned on in these parts. They broached that cask to celebrate, which is why they did not attend your council meeting. You're a priest, Father Clement, you know all the dates, times, and the seasons, the daily routine of the village, the personal habits of each of your parishioners. It wouldn't be difficult for Amabilia to slip across the smithy yard and pour the poisoned powder into Elias's famous water butt. People came and went—who'd notice, who'd remember? How long does it take, as the day grows dark and the blacksmith's yard is full of people milling about, for a woman to slip powder into a water butt?"

"But the council meeting?" The physician spoke up. "Father Clement was there all the time."

"Amabilia wasn't," the notary declared, now wishing to be part of the hunt. "Don't you remember, she kept coming and going, bringing in food to the priest, or food and wine for us?"

"Adam the Apothecary was next," Kathryn remarked, "an evil man who sold powders and philtres well away from the light of day. He enjoyed the power and wealth it brought him—a man who undoubtedly killed his own wife."

Kathryn tapped the Blood Book. "Father Clement knew the anniversary of the death of the apothecary's wife. You thought it fitting justice that he die the same day as his victim. On that morning you managed to secure his services in bringing those two corpses to the manor house. They were then taken back."

Kathryn paused. "You and your sister had learnt how the apothecary was treating his own mother so that she slept long and late. I'm a physician, and I know sleeping draughts work most effectively, especially with the old. Once you'd returned to the manor, Amabilia slipped through the early light, up the outside stairs, through the bedchamber and down into the kitchen. You knew all about Adam's favourite blackjack, or tankard, the one looted from a cog, concealed in its black leather casing. As I've said, all the gossip of an enclosed village like Walmer eventually reaches the priest. Adam always used that tankard and did so that morning. After his death, either you or Amabilia returned to his house and stole that tankard. Rest assured when we search the priest's house at St. Swithun's we will find it."

"This is true," Ursula, pale with fright, whispered. "We all drink ale in the morning, Adam was no different. But"—she pointed at Amabilia—"she could have been seen."

"Cloaked and cowled?" Kathryn replied. "Little Amabilia, sweet-natured Amabilia, in the poor light of dawn or the dusk of eveningtide. Oh yes, Amabilia, whom no one ever really notices. How long does it take to go up some stairs or across a smithy's yard? A few heartbeats? You parishioners dislike each other, so why think of sweet Amabilia as the vengeance of God? And, of course, there are others to point the finger at, like the preacher. That's why Father Clement allowed the preacher to sleep in the

232

cemetery whilst he knew all about the preacher's visit to the apothecary. He decided to use all that to divert suspicion from himself."

"Poor Adam!" Ursula wailed.

"He was an assassin!" the priest exclaimed. "He should have hanged. I was simply carrying out judgement!"

"And Mother Croul?" Kathryn asked. "Father, that was a wicked act! She was innocent of any crime except, of course, she knew all the gossip of the village. Perhaps she was collecting information about your former life, the true relationship between you and Amabilia. She made some reference to this when I met her at Gallows Point. Did you, or Amabilia, see us talking, and decide she had to die? She had no time for other members of the Parish Council, and she was no hypocrite. You must have known she wouldn't have attended these funerals. Imagine that day, Lord Henry: the corpses had been taken out for burial, and the assassins struck again, not the priest but his common-law wife, now sitting here like some pious nun, hands clasped, head bowed."

Amabilia looked up and smiled through her tears, as if proud to acknowledge her true status.

"Busy, busy Amabilia." Kathryn held her gaze. "In and out the sacristy, in and out of the church, but this time scurrying as fast as a dog across the fields to Mother Croul's cottage. You murdered that old woman but arranged for the fire to break out sometime after you'd left. How did you do it? A taper, or a candle, burning down to a pool of oil, or a piece of rope hanging from the table, the flame flickering down to the waiting oil?" Kathryn paused. "By the time the conflagration started, you were back with the funeral party in the cemetery. No one would miss you. People see what they are accustomed to, docile Amabilia scurrying about like a little mouse, looking after her brother. Who would think a saintly, pious faced woman would commit such a murder just to ensure an old lady remained silent?"

"And Simon the Sexton?" the constable barked.

"Oh, Simon's pleasures were probably better known than he thought. Isn't that true, Father? Did you see him hiding in the grass, or did he confess to you?"

"I used to watch him from the bell tower," Father Clement murmured. "A snake, an evil man who took his pleasure from others. He used to think he was so cunning. I decided he should die in his sins."

"On that morning," Kathryn continued, "Simon was very careful. Of course, like all God's creatures he had his habits, he wanted to know where everybody was. In truth, he was a fool. Simon didn't realise his own behaviour signalled what he intended. On a beautiful morning he'd gone off to Walmer Village with his wineskin. He was obviously planning to go snooping and so you plotted to kill him. Benedict the Notary was in the porch, his wife sent off to do petty tasks in the priest's house, Amabilia was in the sacristy, and Father Clement working in the crypt. He went down to visit you, didn't he, Father, as he always did? He just didn't shout, he wanted to make sure. Of course he didn't want you to see the wineskin, so he left that at the top of the steps. Amabilia was hiding in the shadows, she exchanged one almost identical wineskin for another. Simon thought he was safe. He hurried up from the crypt, picked up the wineskin, only a matter of a few seconds, then he was out in the cemetery to drink his own death."

"I used to see the sexton," Hawisa remarked abruptly. "He would spy on me and thought I didn't know, but I spied on him!"

"Just like you did me," Kathryn declared, "the day I was attacked in the church."

"What!" Colum sprung to his feet. Kathryn put a restraining hand on his arm.

"You didn't tell me," he shouted.

"I am telling you now," Kathryn replied, "but no harm was done." She turned to the young woman. "Hawisa, you saw the assassin leave, didn't you?" Hawisa nodded. "He used both hands to climb the wall; that's because the assassin had hidden the bow and arrows amongst the tombstones which he and his accomplice could collect later. Bow and arrows are difficult to carry if you have to run or scale a wall. It was you, Father," Kathryn accused. "You used arrow after arrow, but you knew Hawisa was in the cemetery. The game had gone on too long. You'd planned it all. You pretended to leave, you locked the corpse door. Afterwards you pretended to be ill. No wonder you were pallid faced, hurrying about that darkened church. Amabilia, acting the innocent, came through the main door, and it was time for you to flee."

"We didn't mean to kill you," Amabilia replied, face all trusting. "We just meant to frighten you. You were in no more danger from an arrow than I was."

"I'll see you hang." Colum leaned across the table.

Amabilia's hand grasped that of her lover. "If we had intended to kill her," she continued sweetly, "we would have done so. Clement is a fine archer. You are very kind, mistress." She spoke evenly. Kathryn wondered if this woman had lost her wits, not realising the real danger she was in. "We wouldn't kill you," Amabilia repeated, "you're in love, you were kind and gentle with us, but with your sharp questions and prying eyes." Amabilia's smile faded. "We thought you'd be frightened and leave."

"Why?" Kathryn pleaded. "Tell me how it all happened?"

"I'll make my confession," Father Clement's lip curled, "here, in the presence of my enemies. Once I was a stonemason, the very best in Dover, but I also had a vocation to become a priest. I was accepted by the Church, trained and ordained. I thought I'd found my life's work until I met Amabilia. She was a young widow, her husband, a leech, had been killed by the French, or died at sea when they sank the cog on which he served." He put his arm around Amabilia. Kathryn was astonished to see how these two were lost in each other, seemingly unaware of the mayhem they had caused. "Amabilia was penniless, but the Bastard of Faucomberg owned tenements in that town. I had done him good service and so I entreated him to give one of these to Amabilia. She helped in the parish where I had been appointed. We fell in love." He joined his hands together. "She became pregnant, a lovely baby boy."

"I didn't want him to be a defrocked priest," Amabilia pleaded, "I didn't know then how much he loved me. I went to Faucomberg"—Amabilia blinked away the tears—"a cruel man but a just one. He protected me during my pregnancy, took me into his own household. The boy was born, we baptised him James. Afterwards, when Clement was moved, I went with him, acting as his sister housekeeper. James was reared by Faucomberg, he became his page and squire. When he came of age he was told who his true parents were. He never visited us at Walmer, we always met in some other place, well away from prying eyes and clacking tongues. He was a lovely boy." She sighed. "A fine warrior. He said he would fight with Faucomberg to the death. We loved him and he loved us."

"He came to us," Father Clement intervened, "when all was lost. He just wasn't seeking sanctuary, he wanted to visit me and his mother before fleeing beyond the seas. But you"—Father Clement sat straight in the chair—"you miscreants, whom I've served over the years, whose filthy sins I've absolved. You, with your murderous hearts and narrow evil souls, you butchered him, you dragged him out of sanctuary, slaughtered him and his companions, then abused their corpses." He rocked himself backwards and forwards. "On that day, I was absent. I used to think I was your shepherd but, on my return, when we heard what had happened, we hid our grief behind our rage. You're not sheep," he spat out, "you're ravening wolves."

"So you plotted their deaths?" Colum asked.

"No, Irishman, I plotted God's vengeance. That message scrawled on the church's floor was a warning that I was coming." He waved a hand at Kathryn. "I realised you were hunting us. I was resolved on as many deaths as possible. I regret Mother Croul's, but she was dangerous; that grey-lined face concealed cunning wits and a love for gossip. It was only a matter of time before she began to pry." He shrugged. "But the rest, the filthy ones, as I called them, they had to answer to God for their sins."

"And you, sir," Lord Henry barked, "will answer to the King."

The priest sprang to his feet, knocking back his chair. Colum rose as Lord Henry's retainers drew their swords.

"Put away your swords," the priest scoffed. "I have better protection than that. I will plead benefit of clergy. I can only be judged by a Church court."

"Your lover will hang or burn," Lord Henry replied.

Father Clement clicked his tongue, shaking his head, one hand resting on Amabilia's shoulder.

"Lord Henry." He made no attempt to hide his sarcasm. "Whatever Mistress Kathryn says, Amabilia is innocent. I will confess to all these murders. I will say she had no hand in them."

"But in God's eyes, she is a murderess," Colum declared.

"Is she, Irishman? And you?" The priest turned to face Colum. "How many men have you killed in battle? Which one of my so-called victims was innocent? Even Mother Croul, she knew what had happened. Did she protest? Elias and the rest, they committed blasphemy, sacrilege, they dragged innocent men—"

"They were traitors," the constable shouted.

"Innocent men," the priest repeated, glaring malevolently. "Innocent men dragged from sanctuary, and you butchered them.

"Oh, by the way"—the priest gestured at the constable—"you should get on your knees and thank God, because you, pig, were marked for slaughter next!"

"Arrest them!" Lord Henry turned to his retainers.

"I'm glad to be gone." Father Clement extended his hand to Amabilia, who rose and clasped it as if they were two lovers going to their betrothal ceremony.

"Take them to the cellars!" Lord Henry shouted. He turned to the rest. "You'd best leave too," he declared quietly, "although there are matters, Master Constable, I wish to discuss with you. As for you, sir"—he pointed to Benedict—"you will be out of Walmer and beyond my reach by the Feast of All Souls."

The rest of the Parish Council quickly and furtively left. Hawisa still sat quietly, playing with a string of Ave beads she'd taken from her purse. Kathryn wondered how much she'd understood about what had happened. Lord Henry whispered in Hawisa's ear. She looked up, smiled, and kissed him full on the lips, so quickly that Lord Henry couldn't prevent her, then she was gone.

"They should hang." Colum sat, hands on the table. "They should both hang. They plotted to kill you."

Kathryn shook her head. "I don't think so. They were skilled in dealing out death, they meant to frighten me, they wanted me to go away so that they could continue their bloody work."

"And will they hang, Lord Henry?" Colum asked.

The manor lord was pouring wine. Kathryn refused a cup. Lord Henry served Colum and raised a goblet towards Kathryn. He sat down and stared over his shoulder at the door.

"In a sense, they are innocent, except for Mother Croul's death, because they brought justice to malefactors." He sighed deeply. "Father Clement will plead benefit of clergy. He'll assert that Amabilia is totally innocent even though the evidence shows otherwise."

"And?" Kathryn asked.

"He'll be immured in some lonely monastery. Amabilia will be freed, but, I suspect, wherever he goes she'll follow."

"And their son?" Colum asked.

"I noticed how they never really mentioned that," Lord Henry replied. "Though it's the evidence which forced them to confess. If I bothered to dig, we will only find two corpses in the Poor Man's Lot. Their poor son now lies in the same grave as my wife. Leave the dead to bury the dead." He smiled briefly at the quotation. "I'll let them both rest there. Mistress Kathryn, I am grateful. What reward can I offer?"

Kathryn was staring through the window. The sky was clouding over, the sunlight fading.

"Hawisa?" she asked.

"I'll look after her—I mean honourably," Lord Henry added quickly. "But you, mistress, you will be pleased to leave this place of murder?"

Kathryn watched the shadow move as the sun became hidden. "We will return to Canterbury, Lord Henry, but, I assure you"— she glanced over at Colum—"wherever we go, murder will follow!"

Historical Note

A Feast of Poisons gathers together certain strands of late fifteenth-century English history. The Wars of the Roses were, for a time, brought to a brutal and swift end by the outstanding Yorkist victories at Barnet and Tewkesbury. Lancastrians fled to every corner of the kingdom and political allegiances changed very swiftly. The murder of the three refugees at St. Swithun's churchyard is a fair reflection of the massacre of Lancastrian captains in Tewkesbury Abbey. Of course, poison was always an effective way of removing an enemy with the great advantage, in many cases, of not being traceable. (Wholesale poisonings occurred in medieval England as they have in our day.) Not until the late nineteenth-century did proper post mortems establish the effects of arsenic and other deadly potions.

Louis XI of France was both wily and ruthless. He wished to unite his kingdom and remove any internal challenges to the French Crown. He constantly negotiated to keep Edward IV of England and his victorious armies out of France, and managed to achieve this by the Treaty of Picquigny in 1475. Louis agreed to pay Edward an annual pension but never handed over to him Henry Tudor, who slipped backwards and forwards over the border between Brittany and France despite the best efforts of Edward's agents. Of course, it was the French who, in 1485, backed Henry Tudor in his successful bid to topple the last York-ist King, Richard III.

Espionage and the activities of secret agents were just as intense in the fifteenth century as they are today. Often the work of these men and women was cleverly hidden, and only known to us when it achieved success, for example the subtle negotiations of Lady Margaret Beaufort and Christopher Urswick to bring Henry Tudor to the throne in 1485.

Finally, customs may change but sexual mores do not, the only difference being that in certain times in history, specific modes of conduct were frowned upon. However, David Cressy's excellent book, *Travesties and Transgressions in Tudor and Stuart England* (Oxford University Press, 2000), demonstrates that cross-dressing and transvestism were more common during this period than was previously thought.

TELL THE WORLD THIS BOOK WAS		
GOOD	BAD	SO-SO
✓